VAMPYRE
THEORY

Elizabeth Ramsey, MD
Series Book 2

Tammy Battaglia

ISBN: 979-8-9925641-2-9 - hardcover

ISBN: 979-8-9925641-1-2 - paperback

ISBN: 979-8-9925641-0-5 - ebook

CONTENTS

BEFORE YOU BEGIN...

I would like to thank you for joining me on this journey by offering a free eBook copy of *The Master Rises*, a novelette prequel to the Elizabeth Ramsey, MD Series. Just follow the QR code link and tell me where to send it.

Chapter 1

Beth

Beth tasted the blood on her lips, cold and thick like syrup. She gulped at it, ravenous, nearly tearing through the bag that held it. She didn't pause to wipe the dark crimson rivulets that dripped down her chin. Though the blood was cold on her lips, when it hit her tongue, it turned to liquid fire, warming her from within. The heat spread down her neck, to her chest, and then out to her limbs. She moaned at the sheer pleasure of it.

Having drained the entire unit, she reached for a second and downed it nearly as quickly, oblivious to anything else around her. She closed her eyes, beginning to feel the hunger subside.

Beth awakened from her dream to Luc's arm slipping around her and pulling her backward against him. He snuggled his cheek into her hair, and she felt the tickle of the stubble on his chin on the back of her neck. He had awakened her this way most nights since they had come to New Orleans and his French Quarter shotgun house.

Beth smiled. "Good evening." Working the night shift all those years had been perfect preparation for this new life. She could feel the sun setting outside but didn't want to move from Luc's embrace.

He trailed kisses down her neck. She stretched her head back to give him more access then slowly rolled over to find his mouth with hers. The arm that had been wrapped around her waist was now at her back, pressing her chest to his. She felt the kiss deepening and caught her fingers in his wavy hair. She raised a leg and wrapped it over his thigh, pulling him even closer. Her breasts beneath her thin nightshirt rubbed against his bare chest, and her nipples hardened. But then her fangs began to press her lip and she reluctantly pulled away.

Luc trailed his fingers along her side and over her shoulder to her chin, which he rubbed gently with his thumb.

"I'm sorry," Beth said.

"It's okay, I understand how you feel. It's weird at first."

"It's more than that, Luc," Beth said, wanting him to understand, even though the conversation was difficult. "I feel the pull from the blood and it's potent. I know I fell in love with you before you turned me, but I can't help wondering just how much of your longing is for blood and not me. When we are fully together, I want it to be as two humans who love and want each other only for the person they are."

"I will wait for you as long as I have to. But you will see when I am cured that my feelings will be unchanged. I love you, Beth. Vampire or human, I love you."

Beth looked into his eyes, riveted on hers. She didn't question if he believed his words. It was clear he did. But how much was bloodlust and how much was love? And no, she wasn't used to the fangs yet. She imagined them protruding when she became aroused must be something like young teenage boys getting erections in the middle of English class. As someone who wasn't used to sharing a lot of emotion, it was a bit embarrassing for Beth, even with Luc who would understand more than anyone. It made the desire to do the research for a cure even more urgent.

She dropped her eyes and buried her face in his chest, feeling her fangs retracting slowly.

While she knew Luc wanted to be free of the bloodlust, she also knew he was satisfied, for now, just having her with him. And she, too, loved every minute. They had been in New Orleans for two months since the night she'd been turned. But after just those few short weeks, she had to admit, she really did miss her old life. Not the life exactly, but her career. She loved medicine and felt like a fish out of water not working. She tried to fill the gap by reading every *Forensic Pathology* journal and article she could get her hands on as well as brushing up on her virology. It helped, but it wasn't the same.

Going back to her old life would be nearly impossible. It could only happen if she was able to find a cure and expose the Master, an ancient vampire who had been hunting her and Luc since his attempts to kill them had failed. The Master didn't want the vampire world exposed for what it was, but that was exactly what they had to do. Even then, she wasn't sure the Master would stop hunting them. His hatred for both of them wouldn't fade when they revealed a cure. If anything, it would be worse. But at least with proof backing up her story, she may be able to return to the profession she loved. So much depended on her success. It was a lot of pressure to carry.

For just this moment though, she would push it aside and enjoy the comfort of Luc's arms.

CHAPTER 2

LUC

"So basically you need to grow the virus from my blood and then make a map of all the genetic material it contains so you can change it to keep the things we want and get rid of the things we don't," he said.

They walked hand in hand down Decatur Street toward Jackson Square. Luc could smell the Cajun seafood from Acme Oyster as they passed Iberville, and from where they stood he could see a long line of customers waiting in the street outside. He could smell the sweet chocolaty aroma of fudge from The Fudgery and the earthy scent of the mules waiting to take tourists on the carriage rides from Jackson Square around the French Quarter; familiar and comforting smells.

"Yes, essentially. We need to map your DNA to determine where the things we want to change are located in your genome. When the Vampyre made the virus, they either added some genetic material they didn't intend to or put it in places it didn't belong. Even good genes put in the wrong order can cause problems. And after we figure out what the vital genes are and where they go, we have to figure out how to package it up to put it back in a virus so we can be infected with it," Beth said, both of them whispering at a level low enough that only vampire ears would hear it.

"So how long would something like that take?"

"I have no idea. Until we get into it and see what genes the virus contains, we don't know what we're dealing with."

"And why do you need the other scientist if you are reading all of the virology books?" Beth was brilliant. While Luc knew little about science, it was hard to imagine her not being able to add to that knowledge until she knew all she needed.

"Well, for one thing, the equipment required is expensive. It's not something I could just buy outright without getting on the Master's radar. Tracking those purchases would be an easy way to find us. Plus, understanding the process and actually doing it are very different. I'm like a baby learning to speak. I can understand the words and follow the commands, but actually making the sounds on my own and putting sentences together takes time and practice. Working with a virologist and geneticist would quickly improve my learning curve."

Beth's analogy did make sense. But knowing why she felt she needed another scientist to work with didn't make him less uneasy about the risk.

"But the moment you engage with one of the scientists, you make us vulnerable. We can't be sure they will keep our secrets if they know we are still alive. If they breathe a word to the scientific community, the Master will be on our heels. Right now, we are safe," Luc said. They crossed Decatur to circle Jackson Square with the Saint Louis Cathedral, the bronze statue of Andrew Jackson, and carefully groomed lawn; a tall iron fence separating the sidewalk from the grass inside.

"I know it puts us at risk. But we've been watching Dr. Giffard for months now. She works alone and hasn't shared a single detail of her research since she picked up the specimens from the tissue bank. I think we can trust her. And we have to trust someone." Beth's eyes pleaded with Luc to see it from her side. "Besides, she's beginning animal research. These animals are going to be strong and a single nip could infect her. We're immune. I'm one of the few people on the planet who could do this research with no personal risk. I owe it to her to help."

He had remained silent as they finished their circle around Jackson Square, thinking and listening to the jazz music of the masters playing in Preservation Hall.

Luc knew Beth was right about the research. It was dangerous for the human scientists, but revealing themselves, and putting Beth at risk, was what bothered him the most. He had hoped she would be content watching their progress on the video cameras they'd had installed in the labs of all eight of the scientists Beth had sent copies of her research and Luc's tissue samples to. It had not been an easy process in the New Orleans and Chicago labs, but there was always someone willing to provide a service, no matter how shady, for the right price.

The overseas cameras had been far more difficult. For a time, Luc thought they may need to make a trip to Italy or Australia. When he'd been turned, traveling by boat, with all the challenges of remaining hidden and still being able to feed, had been the only option. The twenty-first century provided many other choices. Privately chartered planes were available for the right price and the eccentric clientele that used the service made certain those providing it were used to unusual requests, like blacking out all the windows and boarding and disembarking only at night. Travel in multi-layered, light-proof crates was also an option on aircraft transporting other questionably legal goods. But Luc had been relieved when they were able to accomplish the task without the travel.

"Let's take a ride and enjoy the night," Luc said.

They stopped at one of the mule-drawn carriages. The mule was nervous at first, dancing around as Luc and Beth held out their hands submissively in front of his muzzle. Luc wasn't sure the mule would settle since animals were often nervous around vampires, but it slowly accepted them and they asked the driver for a ride.

They traveled the streets of the French Quarter slowly, reveling in the night spent together. Beth was completely lost in the stories the driver shared about the history of the area, the origin of the shotgun houses, and the French-style cottages with elaborate courtyards. They drove by Lafitte's Blacksmith Shop Bar, Beth giggling at the wobbling tourists sipping on hurricane cocktails from the bar. They rode past the Central Grocery, an Italian grocery and deli, on their way back toward the square, and finally by Cafe du Monde. The smell of the world-famous beignets was heavenly. Although he had never tasted one, he assumed that to a human, the taste would match the smell.

Luc knew their discussion wasn't over, that Beth would not be satisfied until they moved forward. Resisting her was like holding back a tsunami with an umbrella. But they had agreed to enjoy the evening together, and he was going to cherish every moment.

Luc watched Beth as she consumed yet another virology book. She sat with her legs curled under her in the oversized leather chair. She wore her favorite pair of worn denim jeans and a light blue cotton t-shirt. Her running shoes were tossed on the floor beneath the chair. She seemed at home here in his shotgun house, and that pleased him.

New Orleans was the perfect place to blend in. Nightlife in the French Quarter was vibrant and full of interesting characters. Street performers crooned over guitars playing jazz, their open instrument cases littered with small bills. A man entirely covered in gold paint and little else posed like a statue on a ladder leaned against the side of a building on Royal Street while another man, dressed in just enough denim to be called cut-off jean shorts, a pink sequined bra and full makeup, flirted with passersby, striking ridiculous poses as they tucked dollar bills into his waistband. Luc and Beth, walking quietly hand in hand down the darkened streets as they had last night, didn't even make the radar.

The little shotgun house was one of Luc's holdings under the name Hank Green. Something he had purchased back in the 1940s. The shotgun houses were named for their layout. All rooms opened one to the next from the front to the back. Most, like Luc's, had a front door near the street with a small porch. The brightly painted houses, his a vibrant sky blue, had a front door that opened into a living room, then a bedroom, followed by another bedroom with the kitchen and bathroom at the back of the house. There was no hallway, so one had to walk through the bedrooms to reach the back. It was said that with the doors to each room open, one could shoot a bullet all the way through the house from front to back without hitting anything.

The fronts of the houses on his block faced the street on all four sides of the city block, sides touching, but all opened into a center shared courtyard, lush with green plants and fragrant flowers and filled with the sound of running water from the many fountains and water features within. The courtyard was more of a French style, hinting at the mash-up of building styles and influences in the Quarter.

Luc's house had been remodeled along the way with the living room in front, kitchen next, and two bedrooms now in the back of the house with a shared bath in between. You still walked through each room to the next, but it did allow for the bedrooms to have relatively more privacy. The home was lavishly decorated, New Orleans style, with richly textured fabrics, gold hardware and deep jewel tones, the windows hung with heavy brocade drapes to keep the daylight at bay. It was quite a contrast from the simplicity of Beth's home in Kansas City, but she seemed to have fallen in love with it just the same.

The guest bedroom was furnished as such but served as a music room, having a small seating area to the side of the bed with three saxophones and some other instruments he had collected through the years. Beth had seemed surprised when he played for her the first time. She didn't play any instruments but seemed keenly interested in his talents, asking questions between pieces. Perhaps one day, when Beth's research was complete, he could teach her and they could play together. For now, he would help her where he could and protect her from the Master.

He flipped through the pages of a novel, but ended up staring blankly, alone with his thoughts. He had picked up their new IDs just after sunset. He had contacts with lawyers who had a few vampire clients and had requested new identification records for both of them. They were now Janice Gates and Brian Hoffman. She a paramedic by schooling and he a history teacher. If asked about their professions, both would be able to reasonably imagine plausible answers. Luc had considered making them a married couple but wasn't sure what Beth would think of that. She was fiercely independent, and they hadn't been together that long. He feared it would be overstepping and opted for single identities.

Being married again wasn't something he had thought possible—if his first and only night of marriage, which ended in tragedy at the hands of the Master, actually counted as a first marriage. Luc had assumed he would never fall in love again, but here he was, some three hundred years later, having found love once more with Beth. Perhaps one day he would ask for her hand, but now was not the time.

He glanced at Beth. As she read, she twisted a lock of brown hair around her index finger. Over the two months since escaping the Master's grasp, Beth had read hundreds of virology books. Luc had read a basic book in an attempt to understand a little of what she was up to, but without a medical background, it was very superficial.

While he was certain she had been a fast reader before she was turned, she read at vampire speed now, turning page after page within seconds. Beth's eyes narrowed from time to time as she paused on a page, her expression intense. Luc supposed those were the pages with information most useful to their purpose.

He knew it was a matter of time before she pushed again to proceed with her research. She was tenacious and completely convinced she could figure out a way to make them both human again, or at least closer to human than they were now. And he had to admit, being able to tell Beth he loved her free of the bloodlust was a powerful motivator and would remove another barrier to moving forward in their relationship. A chance to see the sun, to feel it on his skin, and to be free of the dependence on human blood and the guilt that went along with it were also tempting. But now that he had Beth, the latter things seemed so much more tolerable. The loneliness he had lived with for so long was gone. His heart was full, and he would do whatever it took to keep them both safe to enjoy it.

CHAPTER 3

Dr. Kathryn Giffard (Kate)

THE SHRIEKING OF ANIMALS met her as she approached the door to her lab, and she quickened her pace. Fumbling in her bag for her ID badge, she found it, scanned it, squeezed through the door, not opening it any further than she had to, and closed it quickly behind her.

"Damn it!" Kate mumbled, seeing her most recent test subject's cage door open and askew, the lock broken and bent. Her body became rigid. Crouching slightly, she dropped her bag to the floor, hands out as if to ward off an attack.

Her eyes trailed across the darkened room looking for any signs of movement. The lab was filled with rows of bench tops covered in instruments and microscopes of varying sizes, and a line of cages was on the wall furthest from the door housing the lab animals needed for her experiments. She could see several of the cage doors had been ripped off their hinges. The carcasses of the smaller animals, rats mostly, were visible inside them or draped haphazardly across the openings, covered in blood that had dripped to the floor.

The chair nearest her desk had been knocked over, and papers had been strewn on the floor, which was spotted with bloody footprints. She saw the UV light on the examination table beside it and grabbed for it. A loud bang, followed by shattering glass, made her jump and spin in the direction of the main lab door. A desk lamp with its metal lampshade rolled back and forth, creaking on the cement floor.

Kate, UV light in hand, slowly started for the door.

Her heart pounded in her chest, and she held her breath. She knew the rhesus macaque would be strong but never imagined it could break free from its cage. It had torn through the cage door like it was paper. She had seen the creature just after it had turned and had kept blood at the ready to feed it as soon as it awakened. She never imagined he would wake and escape before she returned.

She heard the monkey making low grunting noises and continued toward the sound.

"It's okay, little one. I don't want to hurt you," she said aloud. And it was true. She didn't want to harm an animal if she could avoid it. But he was also the first turned and she needed him so she could observe the effects of the virus in order to counteract the changes it induced and to replicate more virus for testing. She had only chosen to inject him after attempts with smaller animals had failed. She assumed it was because the virus was intended to infect humans and that all but primate DNA was just too different to take the change.

She saw movement beneath the lab bench just to the right of the door and crept toward it, stopping at the medication refrigerator. Placing the UV light on the table beside her, she watched the lab bench closely while using a syringe to draw up a sizeable dose of tranquilizer. If she could just get close enough to inject him, she could find a more appropriate cage to hold him.

She leaned over slowly to peer under the bench and saw a small mound of gray fur.

"There you are," she cooed, trying to keep the animal calm. She reached forward slowly with the needle extended. Almost there...

With a loud shriek the monkey jumped toward her, sinking its teeth deeply into the heel of her hand. The pain caused her to drop the needle and attempt to shake free. The monkey would not release her. She could feel blood beginning to trickle down her arm and shook wildly, but the monkey grabbed onto her arm and dug in his claws. She swung him through the air, clearing the surfaces of the lab tables around her and knocking the UV light to the floor. Tripping over it, she fell backward, landing hard on her hip. She groped wildly for the UV light, screaming as the monkey tugged again at her flesh, thrashing and tearing at her skin, the pain unbearable as she tried and failed to get free.

Switching the light on with her left hand, she trained it on the monkey. His fur burst into flames. Screeching, he released her hand and bulleted toward the door, a ball of flame leaving a trail of light, like a sparkler in the night that was moving too fast for her eyes to follow. Crawling forward, Kate followed, keeping the UV light on the monkey until it collapsed into a pile of ash, the last few embers popping and drifting on the air to the floor.

Kate dropped the light and grabbed for her hand, struggling to her feet. She ran to the sink and turned on the water, flushing the wound and watching the red-tinged water as it coursed down the drain. Not bothering to shut off the faucet, she turned and pressed handfuls of paper towels beneath her hand. She walked to the storage cabinet and grabbed a large container of 95% isopropyl alcohol, returned to the sink, and poured the alcohol over her wound. The burning made her wince, but she continued, hoping the water and alcohol would wash away any traces of the virus.

After using the entire liter of alcohol, she dried her hand to examine it.

Two main punctures extended deep into the muscle of her palm near the base of the thumb. The flesh was torn around them from her trying to shake free of the animal, and blood still oozed from the wounds. She would certainly need a course of antibiotics for any normal creature's bite, but that was the least of her worries now.

She wrapped her hand in paper towels and returned to the medicine storage cabinet. A vial of antibiotics and another containing an antiviral she had kept on hand just in case an exposure occurred were on the second shelf. She had never imagined she would actually need it. But now she drew both into separate syringes and jabbed one into each hip in turn, depressing the stopper to deliver its contents.

How could this have happened? And with the first animal she had inoculated that survived. Not only did she know the risk of her being infected, her experiment had been lost.

She walked to the far side of the lab, past the rows of bench tops, and pulled the first aid kit from the wall. Smearing the wounds with antibiotics and covering them with gauze 4 x 4s, she then wrapped the majority of her hand with rolled gauze and secured the ends with tape. The files Dr. Ramsey had provided said nothing about the infectivity of the virus or the percentage of those exposed who converted, likely because she was too early in the process to have knowledge of those things.

Her notes had mentioned that her patient had turned overnight, but that patient had been drained of blood and then had been fed blood from an infected host. It was likely a sizeable viral load to a severely weakened host. Given how different her circumstances were, she had no idea how quickly the virus would begin to take effect if she did turn. And with no one to confide in about her research, she would have to monitor her own vitals and symptoms closely for signs of transformation.

She returned to her desk and sat, the enormity of what just happened beginning to sink in. She had been rash and careless by not being there when the monkey awakened to properly sate his hunger with blood. She had also not taken appropriate measures to ensure his cage was strong enough to hold him.

She silently scolded herself. Her mistakes may cost her life.

CHAPTER 4

LUC

BETH ENTERED THE LIVING room and walked to Luc, who was sitting at the computer, and handed him a bag of blood. "Hungry?" she said, kissing him on the cheek. He wrapped his arm around her as he took the blood bag and kissed her deeply.

When they finally separated, Beth said, "What are you working on?"

Luc was at the computer, finishing an email. "I'm just touching base with a friend of mine. His name is Jon Wilks."

"You've never mentioned him before. Are you close?" Beth asked.

Luc nodded. "Yeah, I suppose we are. We've been friends since 1963. When I get a new number, I contact him by email and make sure he has it."

"So, he's a vampire?" Beth asked, sitting on the desk beside the computer.

"He is. Since the night after we met."

"So Jon Wilks as in John Wilkes Booth?" Beth asked.

Luc chuckled before answering, the memory taking him back.

"Would you like another drink, sir?" the waitress asked. Luc had been pretending to nurse the same glass of bourbon for the last hour and ordered another to keep up the facade. He liked to spend time in a pub from time to time. It made him think of his own in Venice so long ago. The usual din of laughter and music were muted tonight. It was 1963 in Dallas, Texas, the weekend after Thanksgiving. Kennedy had just been assassinated days before, and the nation was reeling.

Jon was in Dallas on leave with a buddy of his who had family in town. They sat at the bar, a couple of tables between them and Luc. They were drinking heavily, occasionally buying rounds for the bar. As the night grew on and the drinks flowed, they became louder and more boisterous, but the men in the bar seemed to welcome the relief from the melancholy and sang along with one of their renditions of the *Marines' Hymn*.

Jon yelled, "Another round on me," which was answered by cheers from the bar. A large and rather drunk fellow ambled up to the bar next to them.

"Thank you for the drink, name's Tim Stewart," the man said and reached out his beefy hand.

Jon took it, shaking it firmly, "Jon Wilks, damned pleased to meet you."

The man recoiled like he had touched something nasty. "Did you say John Wilkes? Like John Wilkes Booth?"

"Of course not. No relation to that traitor," Jon said, anger coloring his cheeks.

"You should be ashamed to share his name," the man spat at him, followed by a string of curse words and more insults, the last of which was, "*You* are anti-American."

For Jon and his buddy, active duty US Marines, it was apparently the last straw. They stood up to defend themselves. The local man, though, had many friends in the bar who backed him up, shouting things like *traitor* and *murderer* and then the first punch was thrown. Jon and his buddy clearly had no intentions of backing down and gave it right back.

In a few short moments, the whole bar was involved and all came after the two of them. The fight spilled out into the street, and Luc followed, keeping to the shadows. It lasted for several minutes as the locals all ganged up on them.

At first Luc thought they might actually have a chance. He could smell the blood from the fight as drops flew through the air and dripped from broken noses, hearing more than a few bones crunch as Jon's punches hit their marks.

The two held their own until one of the locals pulled out a knife and started slashing at them. The man cut Jon's buddy up badly then started on Jon. He fought to protect his friend until, under a pile of locals, the man with the knife stabbed him in the chest, burying the knife up to the hilt. His buddy had already bled out on the street beside him, and the call of that large amount of blood was difficult for Luc to resist.

As Jon lay on the ground, also bleeding profusely, the knife-wielding man spat on him and said, "You deserve to die for the traitor you are, John Wilkes Booth."

With the two down, the crowd quickly dispersed. Sirens rang in the distance. Jon lay there in the street, breaths becoming ragged and wet with the knife buried in his chest. As Luc began to take a step forward, a man's figure appeared and loomed over Jon, the street lights behind him casting a shadow over Jon's face and his.

"I have never seen a man fight like that," the man said. "You of all people deserve a second chance." Luc watched as the vampire who would become his maker opened his vein and fed Jon his blood before he disappeared into the night.

Luc, remembering what it was like to be turned and left to fend for himself, paused, wanting to leave but feeling compelled to help. Reluctantly, he walked forward and slung Jon over his shoulder, hauling him home to make the change.

"He awakened the following night, and I taught him what I knew. We've been friends ever since. Jon is as patriotic a man as I have ever met, an incredible fighter and fiercely loyal, but he has never gotten over the incident. Whenever someone even mentions the name John Wilkes Booth in his presence, let alone asks him about it in reference to his name, he goes a little crazy, no matter who mentions it."

"I suppose I can understand why. That was horrible," Beth said.

"The country was a mess then. Their fear got the best of them, but it was no excuse. Jon will protect his friends with his life. He might be a little... off... but he has a heart of gold. Anyway, I'm finished. The computer is all yours," he said as he pushed back from the desk and stood, taking a sip of blood and pushing the chair in for Beth.

Beth had been at the desk for no more than a few minutes when she yelled, "Luc, get over here!" Her eyes were wide, hand over her mouth.

Luc was immediately at her side, following her eyes, which were riveted to the screen in front of her. The motion-triggered cameras in Dr. Kathryn Giffard's lab had chimed, alerting them they had been activated. Beth had pulled up the live feed to check in on her.

The lab was in disarray. Beth could see cage doors askew or missing and papers scattered on the floor from Dr. Giffard's desk. Dr. Giffard had entered the lab and was moving slowly toward the examination table next to her desk. Beth saw the UV light she kept in the lab there and knew that the monkey she had recently infected with the Vampyre virus must be loose in the lab.

"Luc, we have to go and help her. If she's bitten—"

"Beth, it's broad daylight and even if it wasn't, it is too dangerous. If she knows we are alive it will only put her at greater risk. We've talked about this."

"But this is my fault!" Beth shouted back, turning to glare at Luc as Dr. Giffard opened a cabinet and drew up something into a syringe. "Oh, God, she cannot think she will be able to inject it with something. It'll be too fast. It will kill her, or at the least infect her with the virus. We have to think of a way to get there."

Beth rose from her chair and paced back and forth from the desk to the door, moving too fast for human eyes.

"Beth, wait, it's too late," Luc said as he watched the scientist lean forward, needle extended beneath one of the lab benches.

Beth ran back to his side just in time to see the scientist fall backward, mouth open in a scream, flailing with a small monkey clinging by its teeth to her hand.

"Oh, God, no!" Beth rasped.

They both watched as Dr. Giffard struggled, grabbing the UV light and training it on the monkey, which burst into flames as it fled across the lab.

Beth fell heavily into the desk chair and watched silently, open-mouthed, as Dr. Giffard cleaned her hand, bandaged it, and injected herself with what Beth could only assume was an antiviral.

"This is all my fault. I've killed her," Beth said, closing her eyes and lowering her head.

"We don't know that she will turn, Beth. You know not everyone who is bitten does. And she knew the risks. Your notes and letter clearly spelled out the danger. She *chose* to continue with the research," Luc said.

"It's not enough. I didn't do enough. I should never have let her continue alone. Whether she turns or not, it's time we met." Beth's tone was definitive, arms crossed in front of her chest, jaw set.

There was no more use in arguing. They had been over this conversation multiple times before, but now that another life was at risk, Luc could see the determination on her face. Not only was the infection a danger to Dr. Giffard's life, but if she turned with no one to guide her, she could be a danger to others as well. A rogue vampire, especially a scientist, would certainly draw unwanted attention, potentially alerting the Master to their location. Just like Jon, Dr. Giffard shouldn't be left alone.

It was time to turn his focus to how he could protect them from discovery for as long as possible and plan their next move, even if it included training another new vampire.

CHAPTER 5

BETH

BETH AND LUC HAD been waiting outside the building that contained Dr. Giffard's lab since dusk. It was nearly identical to all the other buildings on this part of campus—stark, institutional, and made of molded cement. Three low steps led up to a single entrance with two tall glass doors. A fluorescent light flickered, humming and popping, illuminating a badge-scanning panel just to the right of the entrance. Through the doors was a small lobby with an elevator, accessed by another badge-scanning panel. The lobby contained no furniture but did feature a large corkboard littered with various fliers and announcements. Even though it was a good twenty feet away, with her new and improved vision, Beth could read every line.

After waiting nearly an hour, they finally saw Dr. Giffard exiting the elevator and heading toward the main entrance. They met her just as the glass exterior doors closed behind her.

"Dr. Giffard?" Beth began.

"Yes, do I know you?" she said, looking from Beth to Luc and back again. She paused for a moment and pulled her keys from her leather messenger bag. Beth noticed a small can of mace dangled from the ring, which Dr. Giffard now caught in her bandaged hand.

"Dr. Giffard, my name is Dr. Elizabeth Ramsey."

With this, Dr. Giffard raised the can of mace ahead of her and aimed it back and forth at each of them. Beth couldn't help but wonder if mace would even hurt them but didn't wish to find out.

"That's impossible, Dr. Ramsey is dead. Who *are* you? I won't ask again."

"Please, Dr. Giffard, just hear me out." Beth raised her open hands, fingers splayed, and took a half step back. "When I sent you the information about the virus and the tissue samples, my life was in danger." She paused briefly, considering her words. "It still is, but I assure you that I am very much alive. I am happy to answer any questions you have to prove it to you."

Biting her lip and blinking rapidly, Dr. Giffard pondered her next words. "What abnormalities were present on chromosome 10 of your test subject?"

"There were no abnormalities of chromosome 10. It was the only chromosome not altered."

Dr. Giffard lowered the can of mace but still held it tightly. "And who is he?" She jutted her chin toward Luc.

"I am Luciano Verde. I suppose you would refer to me as the 'test subject.'"

Dr. Giffard's mace-wielding hand once again took aim on Luc, although now it trembled. Her eyes were so wide they looked as though they were seconds from engulfing her head.

"Please, let us explain. We're here to help you, not harm you. I know your research of late has been... difficult. I thought I—well, we—could assist you," Beth said.

Dr. Giffard slowly lowered her wavering arm to her side. "So he is a... a vampire? Are we in danger?"

"Yes, I am a vampire. But you are in no danger from me," Luc said, remaining completely still and being careful to keep his voice soft and low. Beth wondered if he was attempting to calm Dr. Giffard with hypnosis, but if he was, it didn't seem to be helping.

"We escaped those who were after us for now, but not unscathed. We were dying, and I had to be turned for us to survive." Beth was surprised at how matter-of-factly she could say those words now, as if being turned had not completely flipped her world on its ear. She was still trying to adjust to the changes, but clearly Dr. Giffard was in no shape to hear that now, especially after having just recently been bitten by her infected lab animal.

"You... you're a vampire too?" Dr. Giffard rasped as though she hadn't had a drink in a week. "Oh my God." She leaned back onto the railing surrounding the building's entryway, clinging to it as if it were a life raft in the middle of the ocean. Beth could understand how she felt. Discovering Luc in the morgue months ago had shaken her as well.

"Is there a place we can sit and talk for a while?" Beth asked.

"Perhaps in your lab?" Luc suggested.

Beth shot him a warning glance. She knew he wanted to keep them all under the radar, but she wanted Dr. Giffard to feel safe, to trust them, so she could assist with the research and begin work toward the cure they needed. Being alone with two vampires in a lab was likely not that place.

"Or maybe there's a coffee shop nearby where you would feel more comfortable?" Beth offered. She saw Luc's jaw clench.

"I'm not sure," Dr. Giffard said. "It has been a very... rough day. Maybe another time." She took a step backward.

"Please, Dr. Giffard. We know about your accident. I'm here to help," Beth said.

Dr. Giffard stared at her bandaged hand for a moment, forehead creased in thought. "How can you know?"

"It's one of many things we need to discuss, and the sooner the better."

Beth watched as Dr. Giffard considered her response and hoped she would be concerned enough about the outcome of the bite to hear them out.

After a long pause, Dr. Giffard spoke. "There is a coffee bar around the corner. I suppose I could drive us." She dropped her keys and nearly fell over bending to retrieve them on wobbling legs.

"Perhaps we should walk instead. I think some cool night air might do us all some good," Beth replied.

Dr. Giffard nodded in agreement. "It's this way," she said. She began to make her way to the sidewalk, knees seeming none too steady and shooting glances over her shoulder at them as she went.

Beth glanced at Luc, widening her eyes and exhaling softly before turning to follow Dr. Giffard. All things considered, Dr. Giffard had taken a casual meeting with two vampires pretty well... so far.

They walked in silence for a few moments, Beth trying her best to remain quiet to give Dr. Giffard time to process her thoughts about meeting two vampires, one of which she had believed was dead. Dr. Giffard, clearly lost in thought, caught her toe on a raised corner of the cement walk and lurched forward. Beth easily caught her before she could fall, moving much too quickly in public. She glanced around them. Luckily, there were no streetlights above them and, at this time of night, no one else on the sidewalk to have seen her mistake.

Dr. Giffard gasped, righted herself, and quickly withdrew from Beth's grasp, a mixture of fear and disbelief in her eyes. "How did you do that?"

"Enhanced strength and speed, remember?"

Dr. Giffard nodded with her mouth still hanging open before once again continuing down the sidewalk to the coffee shop entrance.

Beth avoided looking at Luc. She could feel his mix of fear and anger. Whether the anger was at her for her mistake or at himself for allowing the meeting to happen she wasn't sure. She decided she didn't want to know. But as he walked in front of Dr. Giffard and her to open the coffee shop door for them, he gave her a small but forced smile.

Beth returned it, thankful for his silence.

Chapter 6

Kate

"Please take a seat, Dr. Giffard. What would you like to drink?" Mr. Verde asked, pulling out a chair.

"Thank you," Kate replied. Having Mr. Verde so close to her was unnerving, but her legs were still wobbly and she needed to sit and regain her composure. She half sat, half fell into the white vinyl-covered chair, setting her messenger bag in the seat next to her. "I would like a black coffee, please, and two sugars."

"Beth?" Mr. Verde asked, offering a polite grin.

"A hot chai latte, please," she replied.

Mr. Verde nodded and strode toward the counter.

The coffee bar was familiar, and Kate loved its vintage feel. The tables were mismatched but all with a similar vibe. Most had glass tops and arched metal legs that made Kate think of the Jetsons. The bar was surrounded on both ends by glass pastry display cabinets full mostly of muffins and scones, all with a heavenly smell that usually called to Kate, but tonight the thought of food made her nauseous. Her thoughts were racing and jumbled, wondering in one second what the pastries must smell like to heightened vampire senses and in the next if she would be finding out for herself soon if she turned from the monkey bite.

She rubbed her hand, the motion painful but helping her to focus.

She saw Mr. Verde at the counter. The back wall facing him contained several blenders, grinders, and espresso machines with a menu, handwritten in chalk, above them. As she sat, the smell of coffee began to register, and Kate breathed it in deeply. The familiar smell was comforting, calming, and she needed both right now to get through this.

She looked at Dr. Ramsey, who quickly averted her gaze to Mr. Verde, clasping her hands together on the table. After another centering breath, Kate broke the silence.

"He isn't what I expected."

Dr. Ramsey smiled back at her, blue eyes piercing, making Kate wonder if they had always been so striking or if it was enhanced now that she was a vampire.

"How so?" Dr. Ramsey answered.

"I suppose I imagined the worst, that he would be more predatory, less... less..." *What's the word? Normal? Average? Human? No, he is definitely not normal or average or human...*

"Civilized?" Dr. Ramsey suggested.

"Yes." Kate nodded slowly, grateful. "I expected him to be far more animal than human, to better fit the blood-sucking vampire lore, considering he must kill to survive." Kate couldn't believe the words had escaped her lips. She was just so nervous and out of sorts. She felt the blood drain from her face and dropped her gaze. If she became infected from the monkey bite, she could be forced to live on blood as well. "I'm so sorry, I suppose you too must survive on blood now. I didn't mean to offend you."

"You haven't," Dr. Ramsey replied, a smile in her eyes. "Before Luc recovered from his injuries and woke up, I didn't know what to expect either. But as for the blood, we both survive on rejected blood units from various research facilities. We are resistant to all infections I've encountered so far. So the infected units are perfect for us without taking away from the healthy human blood supply."

Kate's shoulders relaxed a bit with this bit of information. While the thought of drinking blood did not help with the nausea, it was comforting in an odd sort of way to know that they had chosen to live in a manner that didn't require harming humans. Her mind raced again, question after question about their lives and physiology bombarding her.

Mr. Verde returned with their orders, having brought a second black coffee for himself.

"I thought you couldn't eat or drink regular food," Kate said, bringing her coffee to her lips and taking a sip, forgetting in her nervousness that it was hot and wincing at the burn. Here they were, both vampires with cups in hand, vampires blending in inside a coffee shop. She wondered if she had been around vampires before and never known.

Are there others here now? Oh, God, am I surrounded by vampires?

Her heart began to race yet again as her eyes darted around the room. She saw a woman one table over take a bite of her scone, chew briefly, and swallow. A man next to her was tilting his cup of iced coffee back to drain the last few swallows. Humans. She was not alone. Kate's head snapped back toward Dr. Ramsey as she spoke.

"We can't tolerate food, but it might look odd if we sat here having nothing. I've never been one for coffee, but I do miss the taste of a good chai." Dr. Ramsey raised her cup to her nose and inhaled deeply. She brought the cup to her lips and pretended to drink.

"Dr. Giffard—" Mr. Verde began, shaking Kate from her thoughts and bringing her focus back to him.

"Kate, please," she responded, trying to still her shaking hands while attempting another sip of coffee.

"Kate... Beth and I have been keeping track of your research. I know Beth's letter suggested the danger it would place you in, but you must understand that others... like me... like us"—he looked at Dr. Ramsey—"will take your life for even knowing us, let alone continuing Beth's research. As strongly as Beth feels about a cure, I must ask you to stop for your own safety."

Dr. Ramsey looked at Mr. Verde with a gentle smile and placed her hand on his forearm.

Kate glanced at her hand and then back to Mr. Verde's face. There was more between them than a doctor and her patient. The look on Dr. Ramsey's face was soft, tender, loving even. They could be characters in one of the romance novels she loved to read. Kate had been so taken aback by meeting them, so overwhelmed, she had failed to remember they had once been human. And Dr. Ramsey had been human very recently. She had immediate, first-hand knowledge of what it was like to be infected and turned. Perhaps they both had information on how likely Kate's bite was to result in her becoming a vampire as well, even if Mr. Verde did seem reluctant.

She had never considered meeting an actual vampire, let alone working with one, although while studying the virus and its effects she certainly should have. She had decided to move forward with the research after reading Dr. Ramsey's notes and considering the possibilities for using the genetic alterations caused by the virus for human good. She had been idealistic, believing in her altruistic endeavors, believing she really could make a difference.

Intellectually, she knew there were risks, but having worked with so many other viruses, she never seriously considered that she would be exposed. And the warnings on paper of other vampires threatening her life had seemed like fantasy at the time. She was a scientist, working in near isolation most days, barely a blip on anyone's radar. Why would they ever suspect her? And even if things went awry, she told herself her life was worth the potential benefits the research would bring to humankind. Now the reality of what it all meant began to hit home.

If she turned from the bite, she, too, would need a cure to become human again. Perhaps working with Dr. Ramsey could speed the process. But she didn't know her, didn't know if she could even trust her. But the experiments she had run had depleted her supply of virus. If she turned, she could culture more from her own blood, but did she really want to wait and see when she had two vampires here that could help move her research forward right now?

And what if she did turn all alone? She hadn't even known if vampires could drink coffee or if they drained a human every night for a snack. She had no idea how to survive as a vampire. She needed help.

Kate realized she had been silent for a long while as she processed her thoughts. Dr. Ramsey and Mr. Verde sat patiently, but both studied her with looks of concern.

"I'm sorry, what did you say?" Kate asked, shaking her head to clear it.

After Mr. Verde repeated his request for her to stop her research, she answered, "I'm sure I don't fully understand the risks, although given recent experiences I have begun to imagine. But like Dr. Ramsey, I saw the possible benefits of continuing this research. While I never truly considered that it would come to this, I believe one life, my life, would be worth this risk." Saying the words aloud, they sounded as idealistic to Kate as they must to Mr. Verde. But deep down, she knew she meant them. She was afraid, uncertain, and overwhelmed, but she was sitting

across a table from two creatures she didn't believe existed until a few
months ago. Changing the world through her research was what she
had always dreamed about. This was the opportunity of a lifetime.

It was clearly not the answer Mr. Verde had hoped for. He breathed
in and exhaled loudly, looking down at his coffee. Kate wondered for a
moment if he had ever actually tasted coffee. Dr. Ramsey had written
that he was over 300 years old. Was it a drink common to Italy before
he was turned? She would have to remember to ask him later.

"There is a very old and powerful vampire, the Master, who will stop
at nothing to protect this secret. He has nearly unlimited resources
combined with all the same abilities I possess and the cunning
developed over more than a thousand years of existence. He sees no
value in human life and would not hesitate for a moment to take yours
or those of the people you know or care about to further his cause.
You cannot fathom the havoc and destruction he could cause and then
cover it all up like a bad accident."

"I am a loner, Mr. Verde."

"Luciano, please," he responded.

"And please call me Beth," Dr. Ramsey offered.

Kate nodded and continued, "I have no living family, which is, I'm
sure, part of the reason Dr., er... Beth chose to contact me," Kate
said, turning to Dr. Ramsey for confirmation. She gave a small nod
in return. Kate knew she was a borderline hermit. It was part of what
made the decision to continue easier. She didn't have to worry about
harming others she loved. "I have a handful of colleagues that I interact
with on occasion, but none that I would consider close friends. If
anyone would be a good choice for this kind of... project, it would be
me."

"I would like to continue the work with you," Dr. Ramsey said.

"I believe we could move forward more quickly together. And with us here, you will also have ready access to additional viral and tissue samples which will keep us at least a little more under the radar. And..." Dr. Ramsey paused. "Luc and I can help if your... wound... causes you further issues."

Kate released her coffee cup and rubbed her bandaged hand. "How did you know?"

Dr. Ramsey looked at her from beneath her lashes, her eyes darting to Mr. Verde's and back before speaking. "We installed cameras in the lab to monitor your progress and to see if we could be of help."

"You've been watching me?" Kate asked, leaning forward, eyes wide and insistent. *What have they seen?* Her mind searched for anything she had done that she would be embarrassed about. She couldn't believe they had installed the cameras without anyone knowing. *Oh my God, are they at my house too?*

"Do you have cameras at my house?" Kate was outraged at the thought. Her lab was an invasion of privacy, but her home would be downright creepy.

"No, no, of course not," Dr. Ramsey answered, holding her hands in front of her, fingers splayed. "We only installed them to monitor your research and *only* because meeting is risky for all of us. We had hoped to watch for signs that you were in danger as well, but when you were bitten, it was still daylight. We couldn't help." Dr. Ramsey's guilt was obvious on her face.

"I see," Kate said, closing her eyes and breathing shallowly. Her brows furrowed as she processed the information and considered her next question. She was still unnerved about the cameras, but the bite was more important than her privacy right now. Perhaps it was best to let it go in hopes of getting more information.

"What are my chances of turning given my exposure?" Kate asked.

Mr. Verde and Dr. Ramsey exchanged a glance before Dr. Ramsey spoke. "We don't really know. From what Luc has seen in the past, the risk seems to increase with repeated exposure. Those that turn most quickly are drained and fed the blood of an infected host."

Kate shook her head slowly, taking it all in. That wasn't the answer she was hoping for. But at least they were being honest and not giving her false assurances. Dr. Ramsey had survived the infection and turned. If they couldn't predict whether or not Kate would turn, maybe she could get more information about the change.

"Is that what happened to you?" she said, looking up at Dr. Ramsey.

Dr. Ramsey nodded and Kate saw Mr. Verde's lips quiver. "We were in an impossible situation. It was my choice and I would make it again."

Kate looked back and forth between Mr. Verde and Dr. Ramsey, knowing there was more to the story and their relationship, but decided not to pry. With this Master vampire searching for them, allowing her to know they were alive and in town was a risk to them. Yet here they were.

The cure Dr. Ramsey sought for herself and for Mr. Verde could also be Kate's only hope if she turned. Dr. Ramsey's notes had been thorough and insightful given her limited knowledge of virology. As much as she would hate to admit it, Kate was frightened and in over her head. She needed their help as much as Dr. Ramsey needed hers.

She took a deep breath and exhaled. "So, where do we begin?"

CHAPTER 7

BETH

BETH AND DR. GIFFARD sat opposite one another at one of the empty lab benches. Luc, never away from Beth for long, sat at a corner bench. He had his feet up and crossed at the ankle and was reading another one of the historical fiction novels he was so fond of, this one with bowl-helmeted soldiers standing with rifles at the ready on the front. He read them slowly, seeming to linger page to page, enjoying each.

He looked delectable in his navy round-neck tee and faded blue jeans, a favorite of his now that she'd introduced him to them. Her eyes lingered on his lips, full and inviting. Though he seemed engrossed in his book, his lips curled upward ever so slightly, and she wondered if he had heard her thoughts. Beth wasn't sure what he saw in historical fiction, with monsters, fantasy and horror being far more to her liking, but he seemed content nonetheless as she and Dr. Giffard discussed how to continue.

Beth turned to see Dr. Giffard glance at Luc and back to her, a curious smile on her lips.

"I'm not sure how he can read those," Dr. Giffard commented.

"I know. Me either."

"To me, there's nothing like curling up with a good romance novel. It's my guilty pleasure," Kate said.

Beth smiled. She had never picked up a romance novel. She

would be embarrassed to have someone see her holding one with the salacious covers emblazoned with bare-chested men and women wearing low-cut dresses, hair flowing.

"I've spent so many years consuming everything I could get my hands on about forensic pathology, I can't remember the last time I just curled up with a novel. I favor fantasy and horror, though. When we finish our research, I might just have to pick one up and treat myself. But for now, back to the research."

Dr. Giffard sighed. "Right. As you discovered, the virus has to be maintained in blood or it degrades as quickly as vampire tissues do away from the host. I have had some limited success culturing the virus in this manner. From what I've observed from examining the genes in the virus, it's composed of RNA. That along with both my own studies and the electron microscope pictures you sent makes me certain it's a retrovirus, similar in many ways to HIV."

"That fits perfectly with what I saw and with the vampire lore Luc shared with me," Beth said.

"Vampire lore?" Dr. Giffard asked, one eyebrow rising just above the other in curiosity.

"Yes, Luc told me the vampires believe there was a race of advanced humans or human-like creatures called the Vampyre that had considerable strength, speed, and perfect health..." Beth shared the whole story about the primitive human tribe that had assisted the Vampyre, with Luc filling in the details she missed.

"It would be difficult to believe that level of sophistication existed back then, but there are still things we can't explain from many parts of the world. With the regenerative abilities that you've described, there would be far fewer generations when compared to humans from the time of that event and present day. You would think this would make the passing down of their history more accurate with fewer retellings in between to mess it up," Dr. Giffard answered. "Right or wrong, we are dealing with a retrovirus."

Beth nodded in agreement. "Have you had any luck yet with sequencing and mapping the virus's genetic material?"

"No, I had limited sample so I decided to use it to infect lab animals so I could obtain more virus for cultures to study. I started with mice, then rats, then guineas, but the animals just died, none turned. With the last of my samples, I injected the rhesus macaque hoping that his DNA, being so much closer to human DNA, might mean he would be a more suitable host."

"And it worked. So the virus must be too complex or different to combine with the smaller mammals' genome," Beth added.

"Yes, but as you saw, I underestimated his strength. I had intended to sustain him with blood and study the effects of the virus while gathering additional samples for further attempts on smaller mammals as well as for culturing. But as you know, it didn't go as expected."

Beth remembered watching the incident all too well and couldn't suppress a shudder.

"I was devastated since I believed you were dead and that I had destroyed all that remained of my study material," Dr. Giffard said.

"Well, now you have the two of us and as many viral samples as you need to move forward," Beth said.

"I would like to draw blood from Luciano as he is the source for your original study. We know so little about the virus right now, and it's possible it could mutate from host to host, so sticking with a single strain will be best as we begin. We can compare it to yours later when we know what we're dealing with. And not to be selfish, but it would be nice to have something to use as a target for screening my own blood for infection. Up until now, I haven't been able to culture the virus effectively to get anywhere close to enough information to formulate a test. And I don't have access to an electron microscope as you did."

"With you having no symptoms of infection, we would have to assume your viral load is very low. Even if we had an electron microscope, it would be like searching for a needle in a haystack."

Dr. Giffard nodded in agreement.

"I saw your instruments," Beth began, "so I know you have the ability to run a complete blood count and basic chemistries. Let's start there. We can look for changes in your white count and differential as well as your chemistry studies. If they and your vitals remain stable, it would be a good sign you aren't infected."

"You're right, thank you. I've been so overwhelmed that I didn't think to run them yesterday for a baseline. Let me draw Luciano's blood and get it started processing, then you can draw mine."

Instantly, Luc was at her side. Dr. Giffard startled, clearly not yet accustomed to the speed of vampire movement and having underestimated his hearing from across the lab.

"If you have both chosen to move forward and giving my blood can make the process faster, I am happy to donate. Let's find a cure before the Master finds us," Luc said. He rolled his sleeve, purposefully moving slowly enough that Dr. Giffard could follow his actions.

"Okay then, let me grab my supplies," Dr. Giffard said as she stood and headed toward the storage cabinet beside her desk. She returned with an IV set up but with a blood collection bag at the end. When she had nearly reached Luc's side, she tripped, dropping the set and falling to one knee. Beth jumped up to help, but Dr. Giffard scrambled to her feet and scooped up the collection kit.

"Bugger!" she mumbled under her breath. She glanced back up at

Beth and Luc and said, "I'm okay."

That was two episodes of tripping in two days. Beth wasn't sure if she was just clumsy or if it was the effects of her nervousness but wasn't about to ask.

Dr. Giffard continued on like nothing had happened. "Will this be too much? I have no understanding of your physiology."

"It should be fine," Beth said. "From what I've been able to ascertain, we maintain a relatively normal blood volume compared to humans. But I believe the blood we ingest is lysed." She turned toward Luc. "Broken down, by the virus in our bodies." She returned her gaze to Dr. Giffard. "I hypothesize that the blood we ingest directly enters our bloodstream and is broken down to supply our metabolic needs. It's a perfect system with no remaining waste from the process. But it does mean we need blood regularly."

"I see," said Dr. Giffard, looking at Luc's arm for a vein. "Luciano, would you like to have a seat? I wouldn't want you passing out and falling."

A broad grin spread across Luc's lips. "Now that would be something, a vampire afraid of needles or blood." But he took a seat anyway and offered his arm.

Dr. Giffard cleaned the site with alcohol before inserting the needle into his vein. Beth knew Dr. Giffard was aware of their immunity to infection, but old habits were hard to break. Reminding her would only make her feel awkward, and Beth had no desire to strain their newly found partnership.

"Now, gently squeeze and then release your fist every few seconds until the bag is full, but let me know if you feel lightheaded," Dr. Giffard instructed.

As the bag neared half full, the needle extruded itself from Luc's vein and dropped, splattering blood onto the bench top.

"Oh, goodness!" Dr. Giffard exclaimed, grabbing for Luc's arm with a cotton ball, ready to put pressure to stop the bleeding. But the puncture site was already gone. Her eyes were wide as she cleaned the site with another alcohol wipe and looked closer. "You're already healed," she said, shaking her head.

"Sorry, I should have thought of that. I had to use several needles to infuse a unit of blood when Luc was healing from his burns. He wasn't even at full power then," Beth said. "Our bodies seem to extrude anything foreign and heal the wound rapidly."

"Just use another and finish your sample, Kate. It's not painful," Luc said.

He managed to fill the remainder of the bag with the second needle still in place. Dr. Giffard removed the needle from his arm while thanking him and placed a cotton ball over the site to dab away any blood. While still visible, the puncture was already sealed.

"That's amazing. Reading your notes about the regenerative abilities is one thing, but seeing a wound completely heal before your own eyes is quite another. To think of what this would mean for so many in the world, the healing, the improvement in quality of life..."

"I agree. If we can just separate it from the pesky little things like catching fire in the sun and surviving only on human blood." Beth gave Dr. Giffard a crooked grin.

"Yes, yes, I suppose the devil is in the details," Dr. Giffard said, returning the smile.

"Okay, your turn," Beth said and used the supplies on the tray to fill two tubes with Dr. Giffard's blood. "I'll put this on the machines and we'll look over the results together."

"Okay, when you're done, I'll show you how to set up the cultures using some donated blood and we'll get this show on the road."

Giddy at a chance to use her new skills, Beth was gone and back at her side nearly immediately. *This is going to be fun.*

Chapter 8

LUC

Luc had been kicked out of the lab for an hour or two each night for the last week. While he preferred to stay at Beth's side, apparently he was a distraction, even from just outside the lab. Beth was getting better at shielding her thoughts and emotions when she wanted to, as well as communicating directly, but was still struggling with keeping his emotions and thoughts at bay. She had very politely asked if he would step out to give her a couple of hours a night where she could focus completely on the task at hand.

He didn't like it but understood. Being around other vampires had been difficult for him at times in the past. He needed to give her time but wanted to be close should she need him, and with his vampire speed, it was only five minutes from the Quarter to the lab.

So in his blocks of forced free time, he'd been practicing his saxophone. He had played it for so many years now he hardly needed the practice, but auditioning for the Preservation Hall Legacy Jazz band was something to take seriously. He was auditioning to play with the masters of their craft. It had been just over seventy years since Luc had played in New Orleans alongside famous jazz players like Sweet Emma Barrett and Kid Thomas Valentine. It had been both a pleasure and an honor to be in the presence of such great musicians and to play at memorable venues inside and outside of the Quarter.

Though segregation was still in place, he played wherever he could, even the supposedly all-black Dew Drop Inn. The only people having a problem with it were the police, who periodically raided the place and arrested them for "mixing." He had played with many bands in the area for nearly twenty years, but the time to move on had come as the others aged and he did not. He had spent time playing with the Bennie Moten Orchestra in Kansas City and with Muggsy Spanier in Chicago in the late '20s before that, but none of them had touched his soul like the musicians in New Orleans.

The notes flowed out of his instrument like a song from a bird, smoothly and seemingly effortlessly. His vampire speed allowed him to easily navigate through runs that would make others break a sweat. He supposed it was cheating a bit, but he was a vampire and might as well use those skills for something beautiful. And making the music that had stolen his heart so many years ago seemed like a wonderful purpose. For as long as they might be in town working with Dr. Giffard, it seemed like a small way to give back for what he had taken.

Beth was tenacious, and what he had seen of Kate so far told him she was equally determined to find a cure. If they were successful, would it mean all of his vampire abilities would be gone? He didn't know if they would be able to remove the bloodlust and sun sensitivity without also taking the speed and regeneration. If he lost it all, it was possible he would lose some of his skill on the saxophone. Perhaps this was his last chance to really play before becoming human. The change, being with Beth with no more questions between them, would be worth it, but he would be lying to himself if he said he wouldn't miss it.

He also wanted a chance to play for Beth with a great band, rather than just solo. She seemed to enjoy listening to his music. He had to admit, the way she marveled at what he could do, having no musical experience of her own, made him feel special. He hadn't told her he was going to try out, and decided that if he was invited to join the band, he would surprise her with his first performance.

"Mr. Green, you're up." It was the receptionist for the Orpheum Theater calling him in from the practice room. Tall and lean, she smiled at him broadly, her white teeth nearly glowing in contrast to her blood-red lipstick. She wore a tight-fitting equally red dress and matching heels. Her black hair was cropped short, making her large gold hoops even more pronounced as they swayed back and forth from her earlobes.

He pulled his narrow-brimmed hat down over his forehead. He had considered a disguise, but he hadn't been to New Orleans for over seventy years. The humans he had known should be dead.

The receptionist led him to the auditorium and, just before opening the door, said, "I'd wish you luck, but I heard you warming up. You won't be needing it."

"I hope you're right," Luc responded. He received a wink back as she opened the door.

Chapter 9

MASTER

THE GLASS DOORS TO the Master's veranda were open wide, and he stood looking out at the green fields behind his home. The land here, close to the Missouri state line, had gently rolling hills, but was still flat enough to see for miles. The earthy smells of the vegetation filled his nostrils, reminding him of Emmer wheat fields near his home long ago. His round wire-rimmed glasses reflected the nearly full moon which provided more than enough light for his vampire eyes. He stood completely still with his hands clasped behind his back, as was his habit. He was dressed all in white with a long-sleeved linen V-neck shirt and white linen pants, loose-fitting but perfectly tailored. Brown leather sandals poked out from beneath the fabric.

The Master had been watching Luciano's burned home, his plasma center, and Beth's tiny bungalow for a couple of months now, but there had been no sign of either of them. The investigation had become tedious. He knew through Peter that Beth had not returned to work and had notified no one to explain her absence. Her partners assumed she'd been kidnapped or that she was dead. They could think of no other explanation for her vacating her duties. They had notified the police immediately when they couldn't contact her. An investigation was underway.

Dr. Ramsey was too smart for her own good, and now, because

of his failure, she was also a vampire. It would make her even more difficult to capture. He had never expected Luciano to have enough control to feed on her and stop before killing her when so starved. It seemed he had underestimated him again in his desire for vengeance. He would not repeat that mistake. If they should meet, he would kill him immediately. No more games.

He had tasked Peter with monitoring all of Beth's fellow forensic pathologists in case she attempted to contact them, but there was nothing. He had a private detective, a repulsive but effective overweight slob of a man who always smelled of sweat and cigarettes, pull her financial and phone records. The phone records were a dead end with no calls to or from her cell since the night his humans had chased her from her home. The financial records, however, were more promising.

The day after their escape, Beth had made several large debit and credit card withdrawals, emptying and maxing out her accounts by way of multiple banks around the St. Louis, Missouri area. The Master was certain this meant they had just passed through the city. They wouldn't be stupid enough to leave a trail and stay. He supposed the police would have this information now as well and focus their efforts in that area.

He was certain they would find nothing. Luciano had evaded him for nearly three hundred years. He would cover his and Beth's tracks well enough to elude the police.

The most promising lead, though, came from a wire transfer Beth made the morning of the day she had come to him to attempt to negotiate Luciano's freedom. It had been for $5,687.00 to the law firm of Williamson, White and Martin in Kansas City, Missouri. Beth had threatened to release her research to the world, and knowing both she and Luciano were soon to be captured, the Master had to assume she'd reached out to them to accomplish this task.

Beth was smart, he had to give her that. But it would not be enough. He would track down anyone she had contacted and have them killed, starting with the lawyers. Handler, the detective, was already on his way to acquire the second of the three.

The Master would make certain he talked.

"But I don't know anything," Henry Williamson, the second lawyer the Master had interrogated this evening, screamed, droplets of blood spraying from his lips into the air. His voice echoed from the exposed brick walls of the Master's sub-basement. The blood spray made black polka dots on the dirt-covered floor.

"I already told you, Dr. Ramsey paid us to send the letters she'd written on the given date and then shred everything related to her case." His head lolled. A rivulet of saliva and blood slid down his chin, elongated, and dripped onto his blood-splattered dress shirt, once white, now pink-red and drenched with sweat. His shoulders slumped forward slightly, pulling against his wrists, which were tied behind his back and to the chair he sat in with yellow nylon cord.

Detective Handler put his foot up on another rickety wooden chair and dug a packet of cigarettes and a lighter from his pocket. Placing the cigarette in his mouth, he flicked the lighter twice to get a flame and lit his cigarette, drawing deeply, tip glowing red.

The Master strode slowly around the lawyer, fingers interlaced patiently behind his back, dressed in an immaculately pressed white dress shirt and fitted tan pants. His polished dress shoes glinted in the light from the single bare bulb that illuminated the room. His small round glasses encircled his cold dark eyes.

"Mr. Martin said you handled the account," the Master said, gesturing toward the blood-soaked body of Michael Martin, slumped forward from his bindings in the chair opposite Williamson. He watched as Williamson glanced quickly at Martin's body, eyes wide, taking in the torn clothing and clotted blood surrounding bits of missing flesh. "Surely you can remember where you sent the letters."

"No." Williamson slowly shook his head.

From his predatory circle around him, the Master was immediately at his side, fangs bared as the man screamed in horror. The Master sunk his fangs into the man's shoulder, taking a few deep draws before tearing out a hunk of flesh and fabric and spitting it aside. The man's screams became raspy sobbing.

"Jesus!" Detective Handler exclaimed, nearly losing his cigarette while dropping his foot back onto the floor. He instinctively backed away, arms spread to his sides until he bumped against the wall and froze, staring at the scene before him.

The Master dabbed delicately at his chin with a white handkerchief. He then looked down at his shoe, frowned, and bent forward to wipe away a small drop of blood. He folded the handkerchief and replaced it in his pocket before continuing his circular path around the man.

"Tell me what you know, and I will kill you quickly."

The man continued to sob but did not speak.

"Very well, then, piece by piece it is," the Master said, again at his side.

"Wait! Wait!" Williamson screamed, bouncing in the chair despite his bound hands and feet. "I don't remember the names of the scientists. I just remember the cities. But I will only tell you if you release me."

"Get on with it," the Master said.

"And you promise you will release me if I tell you?"

"Of course. I promise to release you. And I am a man of my word." The Master stopped in front of Williamson, meeting his gaze.

Williamson shuddered and dropped his eyes, avoiding the Master's face. "New Orleans and Chicago in the US; Rome, Italy; and Victoria, Australia," Williamson said, shoulders slumping in relief.

The Master could hear the detective exhale deeply from the shadows.

"And how many letters in all?"

"Eight, two to each city."

"And did Dr. Ramsey say where she was headed or when she might contact you again?"

"No, no, she said she wouldn't require additional services and left only her address in Kansas City," Williamson said, not raising his gaze. "I've answered your questions and told you everything I know. Please, please, release me."

"Thank you, Mr. Williamson," the Master said, grabbing him by the hair and lifting his face, forcing the man to look him in the eye. "You have been very helpful. I will now release you as promised. I release you from your suffering and your pitiful human life."

The Master sunk his fangs deeply into the man's neck and drank. Williamson screamed, straining with every muscle to break free, but to no avail. His jerking slowed with the draining of his blood until he slumped in the chair, lifeless.

The Master turned to Detective Handler, blood still on his chin, and said, "Well done. Now bring me the final lawyer from the group and your work here will be finished."

Detective Handler, cigarette dangling loosely from his lower lip, stared at Williamson, eyes wide, and nodded.

The Master knew from Williamson and Martin that the third partner had not been involved in the transaction. But he was a part of the firm. It was possible he could discover the link between Dr. Ramsey and their deaths. But more importantly, the interrogation had been exhilarating, and he was still hungry.

CHAPTER 10

KATE

WITH THE TWO DOCTORS working side by side, the work had flown by. The slowest steps were waiting for growth of the virus and for the computer to slog through the results. They recruited Luciano to help with any tasks they could. His and Dr. Ramsey's vampire speed allowed them to finish the more laborious manual tasks in record time. Good thing too, because Kate was exhausted. But even though she dragged, watching the two of them as they worked was positively fascinating. There were good chunks of time when they were so focused on the task at hand that Kate could hardly see them at all. They moved with such speed she could only focus on them when they paused.

All the unknowns of becoming a vampire were still terrifying, but she had to admit, their speed was beyond cool. The need for blood was not. And while Kate had never seen them drink blood—Dr. Ramsey and Mr. Verde were careful to eat before they arrived at the lab—Kate still knew they did.

She had tasted her own blood from time to time like everyone else from getting small cuts on her fingers and sticking them in her mouth to prevent a drip, but the thought of gulping it for sustenance and actually enjoying it still made her a little nauseous.

As Kate typed away at the computer, entering data, she saw the two stop out of the corner of her eye. Dr. Ramsey and Mr. Verde stood hip to hip. Dr. Ramsey smiled with her head lowered and leaned her shoulder into him. Kate pretended not to notice and stared at her screen. Dr. Ramsey looked smitten. Why wouldn't she be? Mr. Verde was dreamy, like a dark-haired Fabio from her romance novels.

As they worked, Dr. Ramsey explained the process to Luciano.

"So, initially, Dr. Giffard— " Dr. Ramsey began.

"Kate, please," Kate insisted, although she struggled to call Dr. Ramsey by her first name as well. But they were colleagues, and the better Kate got to know her, and Mr. Verde, the more she felt at ease with them. Apart from the speed, it was easy to forget they weren't human.

"Kate tried to grow the virus in cells from tissues or tumors, which is the usual way virus cultures are started. But the Vampyre virus seems to infect the cells in the blood more quickly than the tissue. So, we decided to switch gears and grow the virus in the white cells, the cells that fight infection, in whole blood."

Luciano nodded.

Dr. Ramsey returned the many vials of chemicals and reagents they had finished with to their proper shelves in the refrigerator.

"Viral cultures can sometimes take weeks to grow, but the Vampyre virus seems to replicate itself as quickly as we can regenerate. Even though it has only been a few days, we already have enough virus to begin mapping..."

Kate felt a wave of dizziness pass over her and missed a bit of what Dr. Ramsey was explaining to Mr. Verde. She had felt drained for a few hours now. They had been in the lab from dusk until dawn for days, with Kate sometimes making a trip in during the daylight hours to speed the process along. She hadn't slept a full eight hours for a while and it seemed to be catching up to her.

"I just uploaded the information from the first batch. We should have some usable data in a few hours," Kate said, sitting down next to Mr. Verde.

"Are you feeling alright?" Dr. Ramsey asked. "You look a bit pale, and your cheeks are flushed."

"I'm a little tired, I think. We've been in the lab all night for several days now. I think I just need a little rest and fresh air," Kate answered. Surely that was all it was. She had taken the antivirals religiously, and her daily lab work had all been normal, even at dusk today when they had begun their work.

Dr. Ramsey glanced at Luciano, brow furrowed, teeth worrying her upper lip.

"Let's draw another set and take your temperature before you leave," Dr. Ramsey said.

Kate sat at her desk while Dr. Ramsey gathered the supplies. She used the ear thermometer on herself, studying the number on the screen after it beeped. "98.6 degrees," Kate said. "No fever here." While she still felt drained, it was a relief. Surely if she were beginning to change, something would show it.

The monkey she had infected had spiked a high fever before the change. His white count had spiked, but only just before he became unconscious to complete the change. He'd been injected with a sizeable dose of virus, though, compared to his body weight, so his little body had been quickly overwhelmed. Kate's exposure was small. As with other viruses, she would expect the viral load to rise more slowly and trigger a longer response. But it was all a guessing game. This virus was unlike any other she had dealt with and they just didn't have the data to predict her response.

Dr. Ramsey gathered a blood sample and had it on the machine in record time.

"Well, it's midnight now. The computer's going to be churning through data for hours yet. Let's call it a night and meet back tomorrow after dark," Dr. Ramsey said.

Kate nodded slowly. "You're right, we can't start the next steps until we see the sequencing data anyway."

The hematology instrument beeped, signaling Dr. Giffard's CBC was complete. Dr. Ramsey retrieved it and gave it a quick glance. "All normal here. The chemistries should be finished in about fifteen minutes."

"If the CBC looks good, I doubt the chemistries will show anything. I'm going to head out and get some sleep," Dr. Giffard said.

She rose slowly, and Dr. Ramsey and Luciano followed her toward the door. She removed her lab coat, placed it on one of the hooks beside the door, and wriggled into her jacket.

"We'll make sure everything is put away and locked up," Dr. Ramsey said.

"Thank you. I'll see you tomorrow evening," Kate said.

———

BETH

As soon as the door closed, Beth's expression changed, showing the worry that she felt but tried to hide from Dr. Giffard. "Luc, is she starting to turn? Is this how it begins? Have you ever seen a person turned this way?"

"It could be, Beth, or she could just be tired. As you said, her lab work is normal. I don't know of a way to tell the difference. We just have to wait and see," Luc replied.

Beth began to pace, a habit she had when she was worried. "Maybe I should go home with her, just in case."

"One thing we do know from the rhesus experiment is that the monkey acted sick before becoming unresponsive, and then it took more than twenty-four hours to complete the change. Dr. Giffard says she's tired, not sick. We want to help her, but we don't want to scare her any more than she already is."

"I just wouldn't want her to change and wake alone... thirsty. It has been nearly nine days. I started to believe the antivirals had worked against the small amount of virus from the bite."

"And we don't know that they haven't. We can check on the lab cameras tomorrow evening as the sun is setting. If she isn't here by sundown, we'll go straight to her house to check on her."

Beth grudgingly agreed. Her guilt was like a heavy weight on her heart. If Dr. Giffard turned, it would be her fault. And hers would be one more life ruined by Beth's pursuit of the truth.

CHAPTER II

KATE

KATE CRASHED AFTER LEAVING Dr. Ramsey and Luciano at the lab the night before. She had tried to get in a few chapters of her latest romance novel, *Breathless in Boston*, but awakened a couple of hours before dusk with the book open on her chest. She felt exhausted, as if she hadn't slept at all even though she had indeed slept, and for nearly seventeen hours.

She felt feverish, and looking in the mirror while she brushed her teeth, she was even more pale than usual. Some of her dark blonde hair, cut just below shoulder length, was sticking to her forehead and neck. Her head swam a bit when she moved too quickly and throbbed like she had a hangover.

She showered quickly, determined to meet Dr. Ramsey and Mr. Verde at the lab and see if the results of their experiments gave them something to work with.

She tried to focus on brushing her hair and applying some mascara so she looked like her eyes were at least open but couldn't quite squelch the nagging anxiety building inside her. She tried to dismiss her symptoms as nothing but a common cold.

Apart from the coffee shop days ago, Kate hadn't been around anyone, let alone someone who was sick. But viruses could be passed from such small things, even the doorknobs leading into the research building. She had been taking the maximum antiviral dosage every day since the bite. It would have helped against many viruses, but certainly not all.

From what Dr. Ramsey had told her, Luciano had never turned anyone purposefully before Dr. Ramsey. While he did know of another turned from his bite when he had chosen not to kill them, he hadn't observed the change. They were in unchartered territory, at least for the three of them.

When she had decided to study the Vampyre virus, she had known it was dangerous. But she'd been worried about someone tracking her down and killing her for what she knew. The chances of being infected herself had just never seriously crossed her mind.

She leaned forward with her elbows on the sink, fingers on either side of her nose, hands cupped around her mouth. She closed her eyes and breathed deeply, fighting back against the fear that threatened to take over. She was no good to herself or anyone else if she panicked now.

She had mapped the genome of many viruses. This was her wheelhouse, and she had yet to fail. She could do this, and she knew it. If she did turn, and survived it, she would find a way back.

Kate stepped away from the sink and pulled a thermometer and a bottle of ibuprofen from the medicine cabinet. She placed the thermometer under her tongue and waited for the beep.

101.4 degrees. *Bugger!*

She cupped her hand beneath the running faucet and drank from it, swallowing two of the little brown tablets along with it.

CHAPTER 12

BETH

Luc and Beth were waiting for Dr. Giffard outside the rear entrance to the research building, just beyond the view of the security cameras.

Dr. Giffard arrived just before sunset, and as soon as the last of the light was gone, returned to the entrance. She opened the doors and walked to her car, pretending she had forgotten something inside. When she returned to the door, she opened it wide and looked up, as if admiring the stars. Moving too fast for the cameras to pick up more than the breeze on Dr. Giffard's clothes, Luc and Beth entered and went directly to the lab.

Beth met Dr. Giffard at the door to her lab as she returned.

"How are you feeling?" she asked.

"Exhausted, feverish, a little lightheaded, and I have a headache worse than any hangover I've ever experienced."

Beth blanched. It was not what she'd hoped for. Dr. Giffard looked pale but with flushed cheeks and overly red lips.

"Have you been taking the antivirals?"

"Yes, every day since the bite."

Beth nodded. She wasn't sure it would make any difference, but it was all they had.

"Let's check your temperature," Beth said, moving faster than human eyes could follow to the cabinets beside Dr. Giffard's desk and back, tympanic thermometer in hand. She gently inserted it into Dr. Giffard's ear and pressed the button. After it beeped, Beth withdrew it and glanced at the reading, her heart sinking.

"102," Beth said. "You do have a fever."

"It was 101.4 at home. I've probably picked up a bug. It's fall and all of the usual viruses are starting to circulate. Just because I study them doesn't mean I'm immune," Dr. Giffard said, attempting to sound lighthearted. But Beth wasn't fooled. She could see the worry in her eyes.

"Let's get another blood sample, just to see if there are any changes there," Beth said. She was back at Dr. Giffard's side with collection supplies before she could sit down.

"I know you two can't catch whatever it is, so let's keep working," Dr. Giffard said when Beth had finished. She moved to her computer and began pulling up the data from last evening's run.

"So what do you do for fun, when you're not unraveling the secrets of the viral genome?" Beth tried to distract Dr. Giffard and herself from the worries over her illness.

"Not much, actually. I haven't taken more than a day or two off from my research in five years. It seems like there's always something important that I just can't leave alone. But I'm going to do it someday. And I'm going to travel. There's an island in the Caribbean called St. Lucia that I read about in a novel. Have you heard of it?"

"No," Beth replied, "I'm afraid I'm not much better. What's it like?"

"It is just gorgeous. It stays in the mid-eighties almost constantly. It's tropical, so it rains frequently but only in a short little burst about the same time each day. Then the rest is just warmth and sun. The water is a crystal clear blue-green that you only see on postcards, and I'm pretty sure the resorts have handsome cabana boys to bring you drinks with little umbrellas while you listen to the waves." She peeked sideways at Beth with a sheepish smile that didn't quite reach her eyes. "I hate cool weather, so some winter, I'm going to go and rent a little villa on the beach for two weeks and do nothing but swim, sunbathe and read a suitcase-full of romance novels."

"That sounds fantastic," Beth said. "I haven't been to the beach since I was a girl. I have to admit, feeling the sand between my toes again and hearing the waves would be so relaxing. Maybe I could even have a drink with one of those little umbrellas." She laughed for Dr. Giffard's benefit but couldn't help thinking that she could never again see the beach in the daylight and feel the warmth of the sun on her skin unless their research came to a successful end.

"And long walks on the beach in the moonlight after the sun went down," Luc added. Had he heard her thoughts or at least sensed her mood? He was right though. Beth could imagine long romantic walks hand in hand with Luc, the sounds of the waves crashing around them. She wondered how it would feel to make love to him in the ocean and glanced at him, imagining him in a Speedo as she looked him up and down, giving him a wicked grin which he returned in kind. As if she needed another reason to get the cure in a hurry.

"Well, look at that," Dr. Giffard said, excitement in her voice. "This is far better than I had hoped. The rapid growth of the virus yielded a robust sample. The computer was able to sequence over eighty percent of the viral RNA. We should have the entire thing in a couple more runs."

They turned their focus on setting up another round of samples using the most recent set of viral cultures. Dr. Giffard loaded the finished samples on the instrument and picked up the tray of reagents to return to the refrigerator. She took two steps and then started to lean to her left. Beth watched as though she were in slow motion. The glass bottles on the tray slid to the side and fell, turning end over end in the air as Dr. Giffard's body went limp and began to collapse. Beth was at her side, with Luc close behind, catching her and the bottles before either could hit the floor.

Beth scooped Dr. Giffard into her arms and laid her gently on one of the empty benches. Even though she could hear her heartbeat, she reflexively felt for her pulse, which was thready and rapid. Her face was ashen and covered by a dew of sweat. Her eyes fluttered, unfocused, and then closed.

"Kate, can you hear me? Kate?" Beth said, shaking her gently. But Dr. Giffard didn't respond.

"Oh my God, Luc, what are we going to do? Should we take her to a hospital? What if it isn't the virus? What if she *is* sick from something else and she dies from an illness that could have been treated?"

"Beth, you must consider the other side too. What if it is the virus and she turns in the hospital? How could we explain that and her need for blood? They would want to run tests and may find things they can't explain, things that we don't want them to find. That would put even more lives in danger."

They had only just begun to know one another, but Beth had started to grow fond of Dr. Giffard. The thought of not having more time to explore a blossoming friendship stung.

"I don't know if I can take it if we're wrong. I don't know if I can just watch while she dies." She looked up to see Luc's face, wrenched with pain to match hers. She reached her hand out to him. He took it and pulled her closer, wrapping his arms around her.

"It's the virus, Beth. She *is* turning," Luc whispered into her ear, voice rough with emotion.

"How can you tell?" Beth asked.

"Listen to her heart. It was irregular and slowing, but now it's racing, growing stronger and more regular, and it's quieter with each beat, more like ours. Her body is changing."

But while her heart became silently regular, she began to twitch and gasp, writhing on the bench top. Beth pulled free of Luc and reached out to hold Dr. Giffard from falling off the table.

Her medical training kicked in and she yelled at Luc, "Hold her down so I can protect her head."

With Luc in place, Beth grabbed Dr. Giffard's head. Her teeth were tightly clenched, but at least her tongue wasn't between them.

"It shouldn't last long," Luc said, his voice heavy with emotion.

"How do you know?"

"Because it's exactly what happened to you," he rasped.

And just as quickly as it had begun, Dr. Giffard's writhing stopped. Beth rearranged her limbs to lay straight, arms beside her. To anyone looking on, she was dead. She lay completely still, not even breathing. Only the faint whisper of her rapidly beating heart remained.

Beth felt the adrenaline slowly subside, and her thoughts turned to preparing for whatever came next. "Is that it, or is there more to come?"

Beth looked to Luc to see tears welling in his eyes and his hand raised to cover his mouth. He shook his head. "No, now we wait to see if she wakes," he croaked out.

Beth understood. He had watched her change the night they had broken free of the train car. Luc had watched her jerk and twitch, had listened as her heart slowed, caught, and raced. He had watched alone, having no idea if she would survive.

"I never thought about how it must have been for you watching me change. I am so sorry."

She gently touched Dr. Giffard's arm, assuring herself she was indeed stable, and then went to Luc, wrapping her arms around him and laying her head on his chest. He returned her embrace, nuzzling his face into her hair. As agonizing as this was, she knew Luc had endured worse. He had watched her alone all night, bearing the guilt of turning her, uncertain if he would ever talk to her again.

She knew she'd remained unconscious the remainder of the night and the entire next day after she turned, waking ravenous with hunger that could only be satisfied with blood. Luc had stayed by her until she awakened and fed, and she would do the same for Dr. Giffard.

Chapter 13

Luc

He thought surviving the death of his wife at his own hand was the worst thing that could have ever happened. But watching Beth turn after he willingly fed on her to save them both was worse.

He had just found her, just accepted his love for her and the thought that he could have a chance at life with another, even if she was human. To risk losing all of that was overwhelming. When he had burst free of the train car, he ran at top speed, Beth in his arms, getting as far from the train car as he could. All the while, he had listened to Beth's heartbeat, sluggish, slow, and growing slower with each beat.

When he was several miles away, fearing he could wait no longer, he stopped in the middle of a field and laid her gently in the grass. Biting into his wrist to open a vein, he held it to her lips, letting it drip into her mouth until she swallowed, choking a bit on the thick liquid. He raised her head and continued to hold her mouth to his wrist. He had no memory of what he had drunk from the Master and had to be certain she got enough to make the change. When she stopped responding, he removed his arm from her mouth, smearing the blood into the wound which had already begun to heal.

Her heart slowed further as he listened, her breathing more irregular. "Beth, Beth, wake up. Talk to me," he begged, but there was no response. He shook her gently, panic rising in his chest. He heard the sound of an engine in the distance and feared the Master could have somehow followed them.

Taking Beth in his arms, he again ran, her head and arms hanging limply in his grasp. He had to get her somewhere safe, somewhere they would not be discovered, and pray she would make the change. Luc remembered an abandoned farm, just east of St. Louis, Missouri he had found on an evening run. There was an old barn on the property that could provide cover until they were ready to move on.

He covered the distance in record time.

The old barn was as he remembered it, wood weathered with only an occasional hint of red to suggest it had once been painted. The field had grown up around it with large clumps of fescue surrounding maple and elm saplings. The doors hung askew but were still hinged. They creaked loudly as Luc wrenched them open.

Inside the barn, the smell of decaying hay was strong, combining with the earthy scent of the dirt floor. A plow was in the corner, partially covered by a vinyl tarp. The edges of the tarp were frayed, but the center was still intact. Cradling Beth in one arm, Luc grabbed the tarp with the other and shook it roughly to dislodge the years of dust clinging to the surface. Turning it upside down and doubling it, he at least had a semi-clean surface to lay Beth on.

Her heart had grown quieter during his run here, though the rhythm was more regular, faster. But her breathing had nearly stopped, with her taking only an occasional gasping breath. Luc carefully laid her arms beside her and stretched out her legs, hoping to make her more comfortable. But no sooner had he positioned her than she started to jerk and shake, almost as though she was having a seizure.

"Oh God, Beth, please don't die. Please, God, don't let her die," Luc chanted, pleading, and after what seemed like an eternity Beth stilled.

Her breathing had stopped entirely, but he heard her heart, rapid now but much quieter. Luc prayed this meant she was turning, prayed it meant that she was going to make it through this and wake up, prayed it meant he would have a chance to hold her, kiss her, and tell her how much she meant to him.

As the hours passed, Beth remained silent and unmoving. Luc held her hand, kissed her forehead, paced around the barn, and prayed some more. He had no idea when or if she would awaken. He had risen at dusk when he turned, but did that mean all new vampires did? How in all his years had he never asked these questions of the vampires he had met along the way?

And then it occurred to him that if she awoke... no, *when* she awoke, she would be as thirsty as he had been, blindingly hungry and ready to drain anything she could get to. If she came across a human, she would kill, and he knew Beth would never forgive herself for that. He needed to get blood, and fast, before dawn came and he had no way to leave.

Luc kissed Beth once again. "I have to leave for just a little while to make sure you have what you need when you wake up. I will be back as fast as I possibly can. I don't know if you can hear me, Beth, but I love you." He ran the backs of his fingers gently down her cheek. She was much cooler to his touch now than she usually was, paler, but beautiful.

It tore at his heart to leave her alone and unprotected, but she would need blood and plenty of it. He looked back once more as he closed the doors behind him and disappeared into the darkness.

True to his word, he had returned in record time. The Community Blood Center had a collection site in St. Louis. Moving faster than the video cameras would be able to record, he had broken through the metal door on the rear of the building, pulling a large chunk of the door frame free of the wall. He had grabbed a transport cooler from the processing area and filled it with ten units of O-positive, the most common blood type and easiest to replace. He had no idea how much Beth would need. But he knew he had taken his wife's entire blood volume when he had turned and wanted to be sure there was enough.

The trip there had been difficult, knowing every second he was away from Beth she could be in danger or dying alone, but the trip back had been worse still, knowing he was getting closer with every step and wondering if it would be enough.

Luc nearly tore the door from the barn upon entering, being so eager to get inside to see her. But there she was, just as he had left her, unresponsive to his voice and touch. Her heart was nearly silent now. Only vampire hearing would be able to detect it at all. She was indeed turning, and it gave him hope she would wake at dusk.

He could feel dawn coming and looked to the ceiling, only now thinking about protection from the sun's deadly rays. The roof was mostly intact except for a hole in one corner. Luc moved Beth as far from that area as possible and laid the tarp out flat, clean side up, so that they could lie beneath it while they slept. He pulled the cooler next to the tarp, lay down next to Beth, pulled her close to him, and folded the remaining half of the tarp over them.

The daylight hours always made him groggy and weak, but having a patch of sunlight so close made it more difficult still. His worry for Beth made any rest he would have had even more fitful. The day seemed endless as he lay, praying constantly, waking frequently, and holding her close.

Finally, Luc could feel his strength returning. The angle of the sun's rays through the hole in the roof had lengthened and dimmed. He shook the tarp off them and sat up, watching Beth's face intently. The sunlight through the roof changed from yellow to orange to red.

Luc began to tremble and tears began to sting in his eyes. What if she stayed like this? What if she had turned never to awaken? What had he done wrong? What piece of information did he not know that would have made the change incomplete?

Luc closed his eyes to say another silent prayer, begging God to bring her back to him.

He opened his eyes to see Beth staring back at him.

Luc's heart soared and a smile jumped to his lips. She bolted upright, eyes wide and wild. And he remembered the thirst. He had almost forgotten in his joy at seeing her awake. In an instant, he had the cooler open and a unit of blood in hand.

Clearly, Beth could smell the blood, even through the bag, and grabbed for it. She tore through it with her teeth and fangs to get to the blood inside. It gushed into her mouth and down her chin, dripping to her chest and dotting her shirt. As she gulped, Luc grabbed a second unit, tearing away all but a short segment of tubing from the unit for her to drink from.

Beth dropped the empty bag to the ground and grabbed the second unit from Luc's hand, drawing deeply on the short straw of tubing. Beth barely paused from drinking until she had finished the fourth unit. She looked at the empty blood bags on the ground, at her bloody hands and her blood-stained shirt, then up at Luc.

A slow smile spread across her blood-covered face. "It worked. We made it."

Luc nodded. He was so relieved to see her standing before him, so overwhelmed by the emotion of the last twenty-four hours, he had no words.

Beth raised her hand, touching the blood on her chin, and used her shirt to wipe it away. She reached for Luc, wrapping her arms around his neck and pulling him close.

Luc's worries about harming her as a human were in the past. He still hated that it had come to this, but his relief and joy at the thought of their lives together, the hope growing inside him for a future he never thought he could have, washed over him. The tears he had held back for so many hours finally fell.

Beth saw his tears and kissed each one, trailing slowly to his lips, molding her body to his. He felt the heat growing in his abdomen, the longing he had for her, and he felt his fangs begin to lengthen. Instinctively he pulled back and looked at Beth, only to find hers extending beyond her upper lip as well.

The dam of emotion he had held back for so long now poured out of him, and he crushed her lips and her body to his.

There was nothing more between them, and there was no holding back.

Chapter 14

Beth

Beth ran her hand gently down Luc's cheek, and his eyes turned to meet hers. He had been quiet for a long while, and the caress gently brought him back to her. He kissed her hand and held it to his mouth, eyes closed as he breathed in deeply.

"I'm going to check the refrigerator just to be sure we have all the blood we need," he said.

Beth followed him with her eyes. She wasn't sure why he'd been so distant but wondered if he was again thinking of the night she had turned. He had been lost in his thoughts off and on for the nearly twenty-one hours since Dr. Giffard had slipped into what Beth could only call a coma. She was unresponsive to voice and touch, her skin pale and cool. She wasn't breathing, but when Beth listened closely, she could still hear the whisper-quiet, rapid beating of her heart. It was a small bit of comfort in the process. Yes, Dr. Giffard had chosen to continue the research of her own accord, but Beth couldn't help but consider what she could have done differently.

She should have contacted Dr. Giffard sooner so she could have intervened with the infected monkey, or saw to it that Dr. Giffard found a stronger cage in the first place. Or maybe she could have supplied Dr. Giffard with additional samples to make infecting the monkey at that time unnecessary.

But she couldn't go back. What was done was done. She would focus on nothing else until she could right this wrong and return Dr. Giffard to her human life.

"There are twenty units of blood. That should be more than enough. I suppose Dr. Giffard had stocked up for the monkey," Luc said, returning to Beth's side. He put his arm around her waist and pulled her to his side to gently kiss the top of her head. His body against hers and his kiss, even on her head, warmed her from head to toe, comfort amid all the uncertainty.

Luc had seen to it that Beth had never fed on a human after she turned until her thirst was under control, and she would do the same for Dr. Giffard. They both had spent their short lives in study of things to help people, not harm them, and she knew that neither of them could live with taking a life to continue their own.

It was a risk to spend the daylight hours in Dr. Giffard's lab, even with it being a Saturday. Beth was thankful they were less likely to encounter any cleaning or maintenance staff to have to explain the situation and their presence in the lab with an unconscious Dr. Giffard. And while Dr. Giffard used to allow graduate students in the lab to assist in her research, clean and care for the animals, she had dismissed them and managed the lab's cleaning herself since she had begun working on the vampire virus. Normal janitorial staff were not allowed inside the lab. She typically worked with far less infectous viruses, but the risk to them without proper training was too great.

The timer near the desk beeped, and Beth kissed Luc on the cheek before rising to turn it off. It was time for another set of labs and observations. She collected the necessary supplies. Dr. Giffard's bloodwork had shown a steep rise in her white cells in response to the infection just after she became comatose. Since then they had shown a fairly rapid decline until, like the initial labs she had run on Luc, the red cells had lysed and the CBC had become useless. Dr. Giffard would be interested in the results when she was conscious again.

Luc and Beth had discussed moving Dr. Giffard to Luc's house, but Beth felt strongly that everything that could help if complications arose was already here. They could both feel the drain of being awake during the day and knew being discovered there would leave them with few options to escape. But they would not rest until Dr. Giffard awakened.

Beth walked to Dr. Giffard's side and paused. "Kate, in case you can hear me, I'm going to draw another blood sample to see if anything has changed." With this, she wrapped the tourniquet around Dr. Giffard's upper arm. She felt for the vein and inserted the needle, blood flashing in the hub. She popped the tube onto the vacutainer and drew up another sample that looked like red Kool-Aid. After filling another tube and removing the needle, she watched the tiny wound heal, another good sign that Dr. Giffard was indeed going to come through this. She labeled the tubes with Dr. Giffard's initials and the date and time. While they didn't have a test to measure viral load yet, Beth hoped the samples she had collected and frozen could be used later to give them more information about the change as well as the virus.

While Beth had no memory of turning or sleeping the entire day before waking, she did remember rising that evening a little disoriented and very hungry. As sunset approached, Beth removed a unit of blood from the refrigerator, cut open the tubing about six inches from the bag for Dr. Giffard to use as a long straw, and returned to her side. Luc rose and joined her. Beth could feel the relief of the setting sun, like a refreshing second wind, a weight lifting from her heavy chest. At that moment Dr. Giffard's eyes opened.

She was Dr. Giffard but not quite the same, paler but with smooth supple skin. Her hair, always well groomed, seemed more lustrous and full, her lips were plump and pink, and her lashes seemed longer and thicker around her hazel eyes. The veins beneath her skin were more prominent, probably because of her paler complexion. But the most telling feature of the new Dr. Giffard was her rapid movements. Her head snapped to the left, looking at Beth with wild eyes.

Beth raised her hand slowly, palm flat, and said, "Kate, it's okay. You're in your lab with Luc and me. I know you're hungry. I have something for you to eat." Beth lifted the bag slowly to her and held the makeshift straw up for her to drink from. Beth could smell the blood even from the small opening, and it made her stomach tighten.

Throwing her legs over the side of the table, Dr. Giffard yanked the blood from her hands, drawing deeply from the tubing and gulping. She sucked and drank so quickly that drops escaped her lips and trickled down her chin. The unit was gone in seconds. Dr. Giffard's eyes, closed in revelry as she drank, opened and looked again at Beth.

"I'll get you another," Beth said. But before she could get up, Luc stretched out his hand, another unit already ready to go. Dr. Giffard drank it nearly as quickly as the first.

"More," Dr. Giffard rasped, and Luc, surprisingly already ready with the third bag, handed it to her. This unit, Dr. Giffard drank more slowly. She licked her lips and dragged the back of her hand across her chin, partially clearing but mostly smearing the blood drops there.

"Thank you," Dr. Giffard said, finishing the third unit and appearing calmer now. Her voice was more full and musical than Beth remembered. Had her own voice changed as much?

"No more ice cream for me, I guess," Dr. Giffard said, seeing the concern on their faces and sending a crooked little smile their way. Her teeth were still stained pink-red from the blood, but she was clearly trying to lighten the mood. She wiggled her lips and then ran her tongue over her teeth, a puzzled look on her face. Then she raised her hand to her mouth and touched her extended fangs.

"I am so sorry, Kate. I never dreamed—" Beth started.

"You couldn't have known, Beth," she said, dropping her hand. "This isn't your fault, either of you." She looked from Beth to Luc, meeting their eyes, a slight waver in her voice. Then Dr. Giffard gave a single nod and sat still for a moment, clearly trying to gather herself. "So, only blood to drink and no sunlight. Is there anything else I should know?"

"Avoiding humans for a few days, until you have a better grasp of your thirst and new abilities, would be best. You move much more quickly now, often faster than human eyes can follow. You need a little practice not to stand out amongst them," Luc offered.

With this, Dr. Giffard flexed and extended her arms at full speed, trying them out and looking a bit like a bird flapping its wings at a hummingbird's pace. A grin spread across her lips. She stood from the bench and made a full lap around the lab in well under a second. A girlish giggle escaped her lips, and Luc and Beth couldn't help but join her. She began a second lap but slipped going around a table and slid on her backside into the wall. She was back on her feet in a blink.

"Bugger," she whispered under her breath. "I'm okay. I guess some things haven't changed."

Beth and Luc couldn't hold back. They belly laughed at the fall but also just to relieve the stress of the night before. Dr. Giffard joined in, her laughter like bells. Beth prayed she really was taking this as well as it seemed.

When they had all settled down again, Beth added, "You'll need to at least pretend to breathe when near humans. An occasional sigh is useful too."

With this, Dr. Giffard inhaled deeply. Her eyes widened. "My God, I can smell the pine trees on Williams Street. They have to be at least a half mile away and we're inside. I smell the spearmint gum in my messenger bag inside my desk drawer, and each of you has your own scent. Um, not that you smell bad or anything."

Beth chuckled. "I know what you mean. And you will find that humans smell entirely different. You can smell their blood from long distances, and body odor is especially pungent."

"Something to look forward to," Dr. Giffard said. "This is all a little overwhelming. My hearing and vision are also far more acute. It's more than a little distracting." With this Dr. Giffard became quiet and Beth again worried that she wasn't doing as well as she seemed.

"Thank you for staying with me and for being here when I woke up," Dr. Giffard said, tears threatening in her eyes.

Beth reached her hand out and laid it on Dr. Giffard's arm. "We wouldn't have had it any other way." After all this brilliant woman had endured, her kindness and concern for them were endearing.

After a moment, Beth broke the silence. "Wait until you see your night vision." She remembered her first night as a vampire and how it took her several weeks to feel truly comfortable with her new abilities, but the night vision and the breathtaking view of the stars was something she would never forget.

"I would love to go outside and stretch my legs," Dr. Giffard said. "But first, I would really like a little more blood."

CHAPTER 15

PETER

"BASED ON THE RESEARCH Beth... Dr. Ramsey... completed before she ran, I believe she would try to reach out to both virologists and geneticists to study the information within the virus itself and how to replicate it, as well as to understand the modifications to Mr. Verde's DNA. I had compiled a list of the top virologists and geneticists around the world," Peter said to the Master. "But with the additional information you provided from the lawyers, that leaves four virologists and three geneticists at Tulane in New Orleans; four virologists and six geneticists at the University of Chicago, and another two of each at the University of Illinois College of Medicine at Chicago; six of each at the University of New South Wales in Australia; three virologists and four geneticists at Sapienza University of Rome; and five virologists and two geneticists at the University of Rome Tor Vergata."

The Master sat as he always did in his study, leaning back in his leather desk chair, elbows on the armrests, fingers splayed and steepled together in front of him. The fire popped in the fireplace behind him, warming the room in stark contrast to his frigid demeanor. Peter stood in front of him as usual; there was no chair opposite the Master's desk, and Peter was never offered one.

"Nearly fifty. We must shorten the list. It will look suspicious if too many die at once."

"And if Dr. Ramsey and Mr. Verde get wind of the deaths before we reach the correct scientists, they may take those involved and go further underground, making them even more difficult to find," Peter said.

"So, how do you intend to narrow the field, Peter?"

A knock at the study door was followed by the voice of one of the Master's humans, a giant of a man in a pale blue polo shirt that looked as though the ribbing of the short sleeves would burst open at any moment from being stretched over his sizeable biceps. Peter couldn't remember his name. It was unimportant anyway. He was as dumb as a rock but followed orders without question. And he knew his place, which was another useful quality. When Peter assigned him a task, he carried it out just as if it had come from the Master.

"Master, Detective Handler is here to see you," Biceps said.

"Show him in," replied the Master.

Detective Handler entered the room, his usual disheveled self. Peter couldn't believe the Master tolerated him with his cheap and moth-eaten suit, grimy fedora, and constant stench of cigarette smoke. He did know better than to light up in the Master's home. He would reach for his pack and tap it down in his hand, even removing one now and again to put behind his ear or to pinch between his lips like an adult pacifier, a constant tremor in his hands, making it obvious how much interacting with the Master got under his sweaty skin.

He nodded quickly in Peter's direction. "I got eyes out for Dr. Ramsey and Mr. Verde in each of the four cities like you wanted, but nothin' yet. I'm also gonna put a man on each of the plasma centers after hours to see if we might pick up their trail that'a way. There hasn't been any additional activity on Dr. Ramsey's accounts or phone. The house Mr. Verde was livin' in was owned by a trust under the family name of Ragonesi. Italian, I'm guessin'. There are several other local holdings that I'm gonna check out startin' tomorrow. Maybe they've holed up in one of 'em."

The Master's cold gaze moved from the detective to Peter and back again.

"Very well, gentlemen. Track them down. I do not intend to be disappointed."

Peter heard the detective swallow before they both turned for the door.

CHAPTER 16

BETH

BETH WAS BEGINNING THE necropsy on a monkey that had not survived the change when Dr. Giffard arrived at the lab. Beth had set up a makeshift autopsy table with a large metal pan propped up slightly and angled to drain into the sink.

"Good morning?" Dr. Giffard called to Beth, a questioning tone in her greeting.

After another attempt to infect guineas and rats failed, Beth and Dr. Giffard had found suitable heavy-duty cages and inoculated another two rhesus monkeys with the original virus to observe and study. Luc and Beth had stayed in the lab overnight to monitor.

"Unfortunately, we lost one of the monkeys. You can see all of the data there on the clipboard," Beth said, nodding toward Dr. Giffard's desk. "The rhesus never appeared to make the change. His temperature was right around 105 before he died. I thought a necropsy might tell us more." Beth was glad to be back in her wheelhouse, even if it was an animal she was working on. It felt good to use her skills to help their research.

Dr. Giffard walked to the desk, donning a lab coat from a wall hook on her way, and flipped through the paperwork on the clipboard.

"The second rhesus woke at sunset and was wild with thirst after the change. I was worried that he would be too violent to work with.

But after his second unit of blood, he returned to his usual docile self and let us examine him," Beth added, continuing her work on the necropsy.

Just as she would perform a human autopsy, Beth made a cut from each shoulder to the top of the breastplate, then straight down to the pubis. She used some large shears to cut along the center of the ribs on either side of the breastplate and lifted it away.

Dr. Giffard walked to Beth's side and looked over her shoulder at the monkey's internal organs. "They're nearly liquified, just like the guineas and rats."

"Sure looks like it. I drew labs at the time of death. It showed severe anemia just like the other animals that didn't survive," Beth said. "The white cell count was through the roof, but the surviving monkey had similar counts. I don't know if this organ liquefaction happened to the others that made the change but was repaired by their rapid healing after the viral RNA was incorporated, or if there was something about these particular animals that didn't allow the incorporation and resulted in these signs of infection," Beth said.

"We will have to take some biopsies of the internal organs of any future animals we infect," Dr. Giffard suggested. She walked to the surviving rhesus' cage to give him a quick exam.

Beth didn't have the equipment to make slides from the tissues in Dr. Giffard's lab, but she took samples and placed them in formalin in case she had a chance to process them later. Seeing what had happened to the tissue on a cellular level could tell her what had caused the change in the tissues and why the change had failed. It may help them avoid future mistakes and unnecessary deaths. Unlike tissue from Luc, what structure of the rhesus tissue remained didn't further degrade in the formalin, which also supported the hypothesis that the monkey had suffered from overwhelming infection but never turned.

As Beth completed the necropsy, Dr. Giffard moved on to the computer to look over the last set of results. Luc, who had been resting in the corner, was up at the sounds of their conversation.

"Could either of you use some help?" he offered.

"Sure," Dr. Giffard said. "The first batch of new test viruses is ready to inject tonight. You can help me draw them up."

As she showed Luc how much to draw up, she explained the process. "We took the individual fragments of the viral genome and loaded them into empty virus shells. While the Vampyre virus is a retrovirus, the empty virus shells are from a different virus called Adeno-associated virus that is easier to grow and manipulate. Since we're using only small fragments, we may be able to figure out which fragment is doing what."

Beth had finished her work with the monkey and was placing the remains in biohazard bags and disinfecting her makeshift table. She chimed in, "If we can narrow down what's causing the sun sensitivity and requirement for blood for nourishment, then perhaps we can target them specifically to be removed or blocked in vampire DNA."

"And if we can find the fragment or fragments that allow us to regenerate, we could isolate just that portion to use to help people regrow organs and limbs like never before," Dr. Giffard added.

Her tasks done and the paperwork completed for the incineration of the monkey, Beth and Dr. Giffard proceeded to inject the next round of monkeys. Luc took the animal's remains to biohazard disposal. There were no security cameras in the lab besides the ones she and Luc had installed, but there were cameras in the hallway. With Luc's speed, however, they would never pick him up. He was gone and back nearly before the lab door had a chance to fully close.

Dr. Giffard, one of the syringes in hand, depressed the plunger with more force than intended, shooting liquid up to the ceiling. "Bugger," she said, then giggled. "I still forget sometimes how much my strength has changed."

Beth smiled at her, marveling at how well she was doing. It had been nearly a week since Dr. Giffard had turned, and, all things considered, she was handling it very well. Beth and Luc had helped her in every way they could, providing information for her new life, including how to safely obtain blood from a plasma center in a neighboring town. Dr. Giffard was still getting used to her new abilities, especially strength and speed. Beth remembered the feeling and still struggled some with her own. It was like going through puberty all over again and feeling as though your body was not your own.

Like Beth, Dr. Giffard had been amazed at how quickly she could read and absorb information. She had commented that it would have made graduate school so much easier. Now though, it allowed them to process the data from their gene sequencing in record time.

"That's the last one," Dr. Giffard declared. "Now we wait. I'm guessing we'll have about twenty-four hours before we see a change in the newly injected monkeys. Since you and Luciano covered yesterday, I'll stick around today to monitor and catch up on some reading."

She and Beth exchanged a grin. Dr. Giffard's bag, still on her desk, was bulging, and Beth guessed it was packed to the brim with romance novels. She was a hopeless romantic, and while Beth couldn't entirely relate, a little alone time with Luc sounded wonderful.

"It's only 3 a.m.," Beth said, checking her watch and looking up at Luc. "Race you home?"

CHAPTER 17

PETER

NARROWING DOWN THE SCIENTISTS that Beth had chosen to continue her research was no easy task. Peter had been sitting at his charcoal-gray wood plank desk in his home office for over an hour. The room was starkly modern, with pale gray walls and ceramic tile floors, patterned to look like wood, in a neutral tan.

He leaned back in his black mesh desk chair, fingers clasped behind his head, and looked out the wall of floor-to-ceiling windows in front of him. It was night, and he could see the lights of the city like stars below him.

He knew two letters had been sent to each of the four cities. Each had one or more large universities with a robust list of research scientists. He knew from the Master that Beth had discovered the virus that caused humans to turn into vampires and that she wanted to use it to help the human race by enabling rapid healing and regeneration. He also knew she wanted to turn Luciano and other vampires back into humans.

He couldn't understand why Luciano would ever want to be human again. To have such raw power, speed and near immortality was a gift. He had waited his entire adult life for the opportunity to become a vampire, following the Master's every command. He would do and give anything to be turned. When the Master said it was time, he would not hesitate to take the power and position he had earned through his service.

Perhaps over time, he would give even the Master a run for his money and take what was rightfully his after all these years of service. And even though Beth didn't seem to want power for herself, at some point she would have to respect his. She would eventually grow weary of running, bored of Luciano, simple and tiresome, and seek out a more stimulating life with someone who could understand her, challenge her and help her use her considerable skills.

When he found Beth's scientists, he would press the Master for the gift he deserved.

The desktop before him contained only his laptop, the screen giving a faint glow to his face. Peter stared at it, Beth's picture in its center. Her eyes stared back at him, taunting him, daring him to figure out what she had done. What he could do with that smart mouth of hers. He sighed loudly.

The partners at the morgue still talked about her disappearance. They knew her work ethic and reputation and didn't think that she had gone willingly. They supposed she had been kidnapped or murdered, not believing she would otherwise leave her post. They were, of course, right. Until now they had left her desk undisturbed, awaiting either her miraculous return or a declaration of death, but not willing to act without more information.

Beth was incredibly bright and resourceful but inexperienced in evading the Master. Luciano, however, had evaded him for centuries. The two together could prove very difficult to track.

Peter knew Beth was fond of Luciano, and, imagining the two intimately involved, he felt surprisingly jealous. Beth was a far better fit for someone equally brilliant like him. But he supposed there was some degree of bad boy-like draw given Luciano was already a vampire. When the playing field was level, he would show her what she was missing.

To understand the virus and manipulate it, he had assumed Beth would need the help of a virologist and perhaps geneticists if she hoped to identify the regions in vampire DNA that allowed for their special abilities. Perhaps researchers in infectious diseases as well.

When she had come to the Master, attempting to bargain for Luciano's useless life, she had to believe she would most likely die. It had been noble but stupid, especially for her, believing she could bend the Master to her will with threats. But Beth wasn't stupid, was she? She had to have known her survival was unlikely. The research alone she'd sent the other scientists wouldn't be enough to study the virus. They would need samples. Ah, yes, samples.

Beth would have to have sent the scientists samples or given them access to them somehow. Something like the vampire virus, hazardous material, was not an item you would send to someone's office with a note. She would have needed to ensure that it was handled appropriately to prevent others from being infected. And any fresh tissue samples would likely have been frozen for transport.

Peter placed his elbows on his desk and rubbed his temples slowly for a moment. Then he sat up straight, hands open on either side of his head. "Of course, a tissue bank!"

He really should have thought of it earlier. Beth would have left tissue samples, either in her name or—more likely—the scientist's name, at tissue banks near them. So he would have to identify the tissue banks in each city, hack their databases, and see what names of local scientists popped up, particularly virologists and geneticists already on his list.

Now he was getting somewhere, and he knew the perfect hacker for the job.

"It won't be long now, Beth," he spoke to the screen "Not long now."

CHAPTER 18

KATE

KATE SAT ACROSS FROM Beth, both reviewing the data from their recent inoculations along with their notes. Beth had shooed Luciano from the laboratory, telling him she needed a couple of hours to concentrate. Kate could understand why he could be a distraction given the attraction she sensed between them. Perhaps the love of her life would one day soon walk up to her outside her lab as they had and whisk her away to a life of romance and carnal pleasure. But those were thoughts for another time. She sighed and refocused.

In a few short days, the progress had been remarkable. All but one of the rhesus monkeys had survived the initial inoculations, and Kate was thrilled. Five of them seemed to have been unchanged, but examination of their blood had shown active viral replication. Kate and Beth assumed this must mean that they'd received only part of the required genetic material, that the RNA had to be combined with another segment to have the full effect.

The sixth monkey, who had received the segment at the tail end of the RNA, had gained significant speed and strength along with a voracious appetite that increased whenever his activity levels spiked. But the appetite was only for normal food, not blood. On a whim, Kate had inoculated guineas and naked mice with the same adeno-associated virus, and to her delight, they, too, survived. Kate supposed that either the different viral vector had helped or perhaps it was the fact that it was far smaller bits of genetic material. Whatever the case, it would allow them to study multiple animals at the same time, and, in the case of the mice, genetically identical animals.

"Since five of the monkeys showed viral replication but no physical changes," Kate said, "I think we should pair the segments they were injected with in all combinations to see if some of the fragments need two segments to have an effect. We can eliminate the strength and speed since we already identified that segment. If we assume first that the genes need to be combined in the same order they are sequenced within the vampire virus and that the genes that work together are next to each other, then we have four possible combinations of the five remaining unknowns. If we assume they have to stay in order but don't have to be next to one another, then there are ten."

Beth, who had been nibbling her pencil and deep in her own thoughts, raised her head and gave her a sideways grin.

Kate was so excited with the results so far she'd spoken with a speed that any radio announcer reading the legal requirements at the end of an infomercial would envy. Since she had become a vampire, she could do everything faster. While her parents had passed and wouldn't know of her research, they would have been proud of what she'd accomplished and certainly the good that would come from it. She had followed in their footsteps by going into the research field, and like them, she would not fail. It wasn't as though they had ever told her failure was unacceptable, but they lived it in everything they did, always striving to achieve at the next level. It was a behavior she learned to mimic. Regardless, she was on track now. They would have their answers and a cure. She was certain of it.

If the legend was true, the Vampyre had tried to impart their enhanced abilities to the helpful village men but had failed miserably, leaving them with bloodlust and severe sun sensitivity in addition to the desired strength, speed and regeneration.

"If we assume the Vampyre put the segments in that sequence for a reason, I think we must also assume for now that they must be next to one another," Beth said. "So, I would favor the first four combinations. However, for the sake of time, it may be better to run all ten combinations. We know the Master is searching for us. Whatever we can do to make the process go more quickly, we should try."

"What do you know about him?" Kate asked, setting aside her notes and meeting Beth's eyes. She knew there had to be more that Beth and Luciano hadn't yet shared. It was time she learned more about this villain that seemed to loom in the background of everything they did. Clearly, Beth and Luciano were afraid of him, and they, especially Beth, didn't seem like people who feared much of anything.

"I met him only once," Beth answered. "He's a small man, with Egyptian features and complexion but otherwise plain. His head was shaved, and he wore small round silver spectacles. He was cold and calculating. Luc has told me that he's very old, many centuries if not millennia. He enjoys the pain of others and has no value for human life. He murders at will, refusing to provide for his need for blood in any other way. Because of his long life, he has amassed sizeable wealth, which he uses, along with violence or whatever else is necessary, to get whatever he desires. He surrounds himself with humans, loyal to him for the benefits they receive in return. He's feared by the few humans who know him, but also by vampires. The Master is ruthless and will not hesitate to take what he wants regardless of the consequences to others."

"So basically evil incarnate with limitless resources, and he's after us. Got it. Great," Kate said flatly. Beth's description gave her goosebumps. She had led a good life, albeit sheltered. People like the Master existed only in movies and books. Sure, she knew there were bad people out there, but knowing one was after them now made it real. "When we figure this out and free ourselves from the need for blood and darkness, what's to stop him then? What will make him ever stop hunting us?"

"We have to release it to the world. We have to offer the cure to the vampires and share the benefits of our research. If vampires no longer require human blood, they are less of a threat. And if we can offer regenerative healing to those who need it, I'm hopeful the Master will have no way of containing it or the vampires that want it. But Luc feels the Master's hatred for us, especially if we best him in this, won't just be forgotten. He doesn't believe the Master will ever stop coming for us and that one day we will have to face him, hopefully beside the vampires and humans we help."

They both sat for a moment, letting the words sink in. Kate had always hoped for some excitement, some amazing discovery from her research that would change the world. The stakes were high, yes, but she was already as far in this as she could possibly be. Turning back would leave her alone with lifetimes as a vampire and Beth and Luciano still on the run with no cure. Perhaps the Master wouldn't discover her or her involvement if she stopped, but there was no certainty in that. And could she really walk away from this now?

She shook her head. No. This was her chance, and she wasn't turning back.

She looked back at Beth, exhaling a deep breath. "All ten it is."

CHAPTER 19

LUC

FOR LUC, NEW ORLEANS was heavy with memories, many good, some bad. They washed over him as he strode through the Quarter and the old Storyville district on his way back to the lab. He had been wandering the Quarter and indulging old memories since Beth had asked for a couple of hours alone with Dr. Giffard.

He passed the Basin Market, which was all that remained of Lulu White's saloon. Luc had spent many an evening there drinking with friends, reveling in the jazz music of players like Jelly Roll Morton and Louis Armstrong. But as he walked, his curiosity got the better of him and he made a detour down Bienville. There, close to the corner of Bienville and Bourbon, was a saloon called the Old Absinthe House. He was surprised it still stood and looked none the worse for the years either. Patrons sat on small round stools around the old wooden bar. The bar looked familiar, but the big screen TVs hanging above it reminded him how much time had passed since he last strolled past its doors.

How many times did I walk down Bienville and over to Dauphine and Conti to see Cora? Cora West. That was a name that had occasionally crossed his mind in the seventy-plus years he had been gone from Louisiana.

As he walked, the images of 1931 New Orleans overshadowed what stood before him and he was there once again. New Orleans was suffering, like the rest of the country's big cities, from the Great Depression. Poverty was extensive, but as Billie Holiday would sing a few years later, "them that's got shall get," and those that had in New Orleans still wanted their jazz and booze, even if the booze was still illegal.

Luc was dressed in his best, a light gray pinstripe three-piece suit with a clean white shirt and broad navy blue patterned tie. His fedora was cocked just slightly to the right, and as he walked he could hear the tap of his black leather shoes on the pavement. The night air brought a refreshing caress to his skin. A few couples milled about, arm in arm, and the occasional Ford Model T was parked along the street. Along with the light through the windows of the West Hotel, jazz music spilled onto the street in front of him, Louis Armstrong's "Mahogany Hall Stomp." Cora loved Louis Armstrong and frequently requested his numbers.

Cora had been born Eliza West, a slave in Louisiana and rumored to be the daughter of the slave owner she and her mother served. Freed by the death of her owner at the end of the Civil War, Cora was penniless and hungry and decided to use what she called her "considerable assets" to become a prostitute. Turned by one of her patrons, she had risen through the New Orleans Storyville district to become a madam of her own house.

Luc had worked as a musician in her establishments, playing with his saxophone alongside Harold "Slim" Scott for patrons as they waited and spending his nights with Cora when the music stopped.

At 417 Dauphine, Luc paused in front of a business and was jarred from his memories of the past but also overcome by déjà vu. The sign read, "West Hotel and Saloon." A smile crossed his lips. The building was familiar but had been updated to current standards. The signage and style were classic 1930s New Orleans but restored to a perfect replica of the times, down to the color of the entryway rug.

As he stepped through the doors, he could remember the first time he had crossed the threshold. He had caught Cora's eye from the piano while she stood at the bar back then. As he entered today and looked to the long mahogany bar at his left, he was certain it was his imagination and not reality when he saw her there once again.

Instead of the slim cut but gently draped gold satin one-shoulder gown she had worn that first night, she now wore a tight-fitting rose-red dress, ruched from bust to knee with a deeply plunging neckline, highlighting her "considerable assets." She was already tall, and in red stiletto heels, she was nearly eye-to-eye with Luc.

Her black hair was left to its tight ringlet coils, chin length at their longest, creating a halo around her heart-shaped face. Her full lips were painted a matching red around a broad smile, highlighted by a narrow gap between her front upper teeth. Her eyes, a beautiful warm brown, held his gaze, unblinking, eyebrows dipping then rising as she scanned him from toe to head, lingering along the way. Her lips slowly curled into a smile, her tongue escaping and making a complete arc across her upper lip.

Luc crossed the room to the bar, still not entirely sure he wasn't seeing a hallucination.

"Luke Green," she said, eyes lingering on his lips.

"Hank, actually, his grandson."

She pouted her lips and nodded.

"Cora West," Luc returned.

"Lilly West, illegitimate niece."

Luc also nodded. Both knew the difficulties but also the necessity of plausible explanations for their appearance. While most who knew them would be long gone, a good story was vital.

"Nice to meet you, Hank. Have you returned to New Orleans looking for anything in particular?"

Luc didn't think her glances could be more forward and lewd than when he had walked to the bar, but he was wrong. He had to admit, it was flattering to be admired by such a beautiful woman, but it ended there. His heart was solely Beth's, and his body knew it.

"I'm actually visiting with a close friend."

"This friend have a name?" Lilly asked.

"Janice," Luc said, nodding slowly.

With a small *humph*, she turned her attention to rearranging a few glasses on the shelf next to the bar, grabbing one and filling it with a shot of whiskey to set before Luc. "How long will you be *visiting*?"

"I'm not sure." Luc wanted to keep the conversation general in case anyone was listening in. He lowered his voice, knowing Cora, *Lilly*, he corrected himself, would still hear him without difficulty. There was a man about four seats down who seemed keenly interested in their conversation. Given the color in his cheeks, Luc suspected he was interested in Lilly and irritated with the attention she was giving him. "How have you been these last many years?"

Lilly crossed her arms on the bar and leaned forward, showing even more cleavage, though Luc wouldn't have thought it possible, and looked at him intently. "Business was slow for a time after Luke left. Aunt Cora's... services... were frowned upon by the local authorities and she had to... renovate... the hotel rooms. But she managed to turn things around by the late '60s and was making a considerable profit in the late '70s. She hired a manager for several years, running things from afar until handing over the reins to me in 2008. The West Hotel has been voted the best in the Quarter for the last five years running."

"Your Aunt Cora would be proud." She shot Luc a wicked grin, and he returned it. "Did you want to come to New Orleans to run the hotel or was it a favor to your aunt?"

"I spent my teen years with Aunt Cora in New York City. It's an amazing city with a robust nightlife. But Cora always longed to go back. She told me stories about your... *grandfather*... that would stop a girl's heart. Life for her in New York never held a candle to her years here. The charm of the Quarter, jazz around every corner, creole cooking, and handsome musicians in jam sessions in the parlor in the wee hours of the morning looking to stumble into the nearest bed that would welcome them."

Luc remembered those late nights too, playing his saxophone and pretending to drink whiskey until the doors closed; Cora watching him from the bar and giving him a "come here" nod toward her room upstairs. Many an evening he had excused himself from the last songs of the night to join her before the rest of the band either wandered home to family or down the hall to indulge with the ladies.

The memories were comforting, but now that he had Beth, they seemed somehow empty. While Cora had been a welcome distraction, she could never take away the longing for his wife. He would always love her, but Beth had healed the emptiness inside him and so much more.

"*Granddad*... shared similar memories with me. He and Cora were good for each other then, it seems."

"Perhaps time brings things full circle?" Lilly looked him square in the face, an undisguised and open invitation to pick up where they had left off.

"Or perhaps a once-in-a-lifetime thing."

"Hmm," Lilly said, drawing back. "Maybe I would like to meet this *friend* of yours. She must be something."

"She is, Lilly," Luc said with a soft smile. "She would have to be to hold a candle to a gal like Cora." Lilly lowered her head and peeked at him from under thick lashes. A warm smile spread across her lips.

"Enjoy it. The good things never seem to last." Luc knew she meant the relationship between the two of them but couldn't help but think about his wife, lost to the Master, and Beth, now hunted by the same.

The thought of losing Beth took his breath.

He recovered enough to say, "I hope you're wrong, Lilly."

Chapter 20

Beth

Dr. Giffard and Beth had anesthetized the animals they needed to examine, although Beth suspected it would not last long given the increased metabolism the virus caused. Dr. Giffard began to open the first animal's cage.

"Maybe we should leave it closed for the initial observations, Kate. The mouse may wake up and then we could be chasing it around the lab," Beth said.

"Good point. Let's not do that again," Dr. Giffard replied.

This mouse had been wildly agitated and aggressive when they arrived at the lab. They both suspected it was suffering from the bloodlust of turning, so they had filled an automatic waterer with blood. It had clawed at the cage trying to reach it before they even had it in place, then drank greedily until it'd had its fill. It had taken several attempts before they were able to properly anesthetize it, but after its feeding it had settled some.

"Do you still have the camera on?" Beth asked.

"Yes, still rolling," Dr. Giffard said.

"Here goes nothing," Beth said, turning on the UV light. Slowly and carefully, being certain she, Luc, and Dr. Giffard wouldn't be exposed, she aimed the light toward the animal's tail. Dr. Giffard stood nearby with a large cup of water and a fire extinguisher. Beth moved the UV light onto the mouse's tail. No sooner had she reached the tip than it began to sizzle. Beth jerked the light away, but the tip of the mouse's tail was already ablaze.

Dr. Giffard jerked backward and then threw the water at the mouse, dousing his entire body along with the flames at his tail and splashing both of them. Beth nearly dropped the UV light but managed to hold on, hands shaking as she flipped it off. In an effort to help Beth catch the light, Dr. Giffard had taken a step to the side, slipping in the water and landing on her backside on the floor, sprawled and looking up at Beth wide-eyed.

"Holy crap!" Dr. Giffard said. "I saw that with the first rhesus, but I wasn't any more ready for it this time."

Luc could remain quiet no longer and burst into laughter having watched the entire process.

Beth shot him a fierce look with squinted eyes but couldn't help the nervous laughter that bubbled up from her chest any more than he could. The scene had to have been comical. It felt good to laugh and warmed her heart to hear Luc's laughter. Calming, she turned back to Dr. Giffard, who had regained her feet and was smoothing her clothing and hair, also chuckling.

"I'm fine," Dr. Giffard said, making Beth stifle another giggle before regaining her composure.

"When I tested a tissue sample from Luc, it showed the same reaction. I should have been ready for it, but I'm not sure I'll ever get used to that," Beth said.

"I wonder if it will heal. Maybe the genes for bloodlust, sun sensitivity, and regeneration are tied together somehow." Dr. Giffard leaned forward to see the tail more clearly. The tip was dark gray ash, and the skin above that was red, weeping and blistered. After a full minute, there was still no change.

"Nope. It looks like the bloodlust and UV sensitivity are tied together, but regeneration must be separate. This little guy is going to have a sore tail for a while."

Beth felt bad for the little mouse, remembering Luc's burns and how long it had taken for him to fully recover.

"I have some antibiotic ointment that won't harm him if he licks it. We can at least soothe some of the tenderness with that," Dr. Giffard offered.

After applying the ointment, it was time to move to the next mouse. One of the animals hadn't survived, leaving eight more to test. The deceased mouse had received the first half of the genetic material given to the first mouse they tested but a different second sequence. A third mouse had received the second portion of the genetic material given to the first mouse but an entirely different first sequence.

Beth again turned on the UV light and this time inched the beam over to the tail and quickly jerked it away. No reaction. They looked at one another, still gun-shy.

"Once more to be certain," Beth said. This time she brought the UV light beam onto the tail and held it in place—still nothing.

Beth flipped off the light. "Either we have the wrong sequence, the wrong combination, or the genes this mouse was given are not for sun sensitivity." With this, she removed a scalpel from the instrument tray near her and made a small and superficial incision into the mouse's tail. After a full five minutes, there was no change in the wound. They cleaned it and closed it with super glue. The next three mice showed similar results.

Beth's confidence was beginning to waver, even though she should be focusing on the victories. Finding the sequence to remove the bloodlust and sun sensitivity was a huge help to them, but she worried they wouldn't be able to isolate the sequence to help with human regeneration.

"We still haven't seen any regeneration. What could we have missed?" Dr. Giffard asked, apparently having similar thoughts.

"There are still four to go. I'm not giving up yet," Beth said.

Beth exposed mouse number 7 to the UV light, again with no response. She moved on to make the incision in the tail. As they stared at the wound, the bleeding quickly stopped and the wound closed.

Dr. Giffard and Beth couldn't help the wide smiles that spread across their faces.

"We found it!" Dr. Giffard nearly screamed.

"Thank God!" Beth said, exhaling deeply with relief. "Okay, let's check the rest."

They continued the process with the remaining three mice, all showing no sensitivity to UV light and no regeneration.

"So, the genetic material for bloodlust and UV sensitivity are tied together and need to be in the proper sequence to have their effect," Dr. Giffard said. "Also, the regenerative abilities seem to require two sets of genes and also need to be in the proper sequence. The fifth segment we still can't identify an effect, whether it's in a combination of genes or alone. The previous round of tests showed the last segment for speed and strength to be expressed alone. Could the unidentified segments enhance the speed and strength? We didn't test that combination since we already had an effect with it alone. Or maybe it's something we don't know to test for. What other abilities do vampires possess that it could code for?"

"Hypnosis, perhaps? Or telepathy? Many vampires can do both to varying degrees," Luc offered, sauntering over to join them. He was wearing the blue jeans Beth had given him, slung low on his hips, with a rust-orange long-sleeved cotton pullover that clung to his chest highlighting the muscles beneath.

Beth couldn't help thinking about him earlier in the evening, rising after dusk to shower and walking through the bedroom to get his shirt with just a white towel tied around his waist, chest still glistening with beads of water. Though she felt strongly about waiting for sex until she could be certain of his feelings apart from the bloodlust, she couldn't help imagining sliding off those blue jeans.

Having cared for him while he was regenerating and comatose, she knew what she was missing.

The telepathy between them had become much stronger since Beth had turned. He could read her loud and clear, and, for the most part, she could hear him. He lowered his head to look at her now through his long brown lashes, a seductive grin on his lips. His thoughts in return brought color to her cheeks.

"Hypnosis? Telepathy? Why haven't you told me about this? I haven't heard anything." Dr. Giffard crossed her arms and moved her weight to one hip.

"I didn't hear thoughts right away either, Kate. It took concentration and practice. And I still haven't tried hypnosis," Beth replied, realizing she had become quite comfortable feeling Luc's emotions and hearing most of his thoughts. They were sometimes difficult to block out, which distracted her, but on the whole, she enjoyed being able to project hers and share with him privately.

"This is something you definitely have to teach me," Dr. Giffard said. Beth could already feel some of her emotions and occasionally caught a word when she thought it with intensity. For now though, she thought it may be best to keep that to herself.

"We'll work on it in between experiments. But if Luc's right, I don't know how to test it in these animals. Even if we could read some basic thoughts or feelings from the mice, it wouldn't mean they could sense us," Beth said.

"And even if they were capable, if it takes time and practice, how would we teach them to do it?" Dr. Giffard asked.

"I'm not sure that's a skill we would want to give the world anyway. It could be a huge advantage for the telepath but a distinct disadvantage for those who don't possess it," Luc added.

Beth agreed. She wouldn't want just anyone hearing her thoughts and made a mental note to practice blocking more when she wasn't busy at the lab. If the Master, or a vampire loyal to him, were to capture her, she wouldn't want to give away secrets that could endanger others.

"Okay, so maybe let that one go for now. Are there any other secret skills you two haven't shared with me? Can we fly or turn into bats?" Dr. Giffard asked, eyes wide.

Luc and Beth laughed aloud.

"No, I am afraid that's it," Luc answered.

"Darn. Oh well, at least we've identified the bad stuff." Dr. Giffard sighed, shrugging. "If we can figure out how to block the genes for bloodlust and sun sensitivity, we can free ourselves from those. Then we can focus on the regenerative genes and how to use them to help humans." Dr. Giffard smiled and looked up at Beth. "But first, teach me how to turn on the telepathy!"

Chapter 21

MASTER

THE MASTER STOOD UNMOVING, more still than a human could ever manage, his chest like stone, unbreathing. His eyes, though unblinking, shifted as he surveyed the moon and stars through the windows of his den. The fire crackled, as always. He enjoyed the sound and the earthy smell of the wood with just a hint of smoke. It was a comfort, reminding him of simpler days more than four thousand years ago when he slept near the warmth of the fire with his wife, his son not far away. But the comforting memories were fleeting, followed by those of death and loss and millennia of guilt. But now was not the time to think on such things.

He clasped his hands behind his back, a position he often took when considering new information and deciding on next steps.

Peter had informed him of his most recent efforts, that he believed Beth would have stored blood and possibly tissue samples at organ and tissue banks within each of the cities. He believed he could track down the involved scientists by using the banks' computer records. The Master had given approval for him to work with Detective Handler and a human hacker with appropriate computer skills for the job.

Peter had done well. He was a useful pain in the ass. The Master would have loved to have been rid of him, but he was just too valuable at the moment. His medical knowledge was helpful in understanding and perhaps predicting Dr. Ramsey's next moves. And he fulfilled his original purpose in the morgue, covering up the Master's predilection for drinking human blood from the source when he was careless and his "donor" didn't survive. He would string him along, intolerable as he was, until he was no longer useful.

Detective Handler, at the Master's request, had been gathering information on the falsified autopsies Peter had performed to cover up the Master's indulgences. He kept the files handy to be used against Peter if he became too insistent one day. The Master kept files on all who worked for him. One often needed a bargaining chip to keep an errant hired man in his place. He knew the names of every bookie Handler was indebted to. While he found it useful to keep them at bay for now, that would quickly end when the detective had outlived his usefulness.

Humans were so very tedious.

A knock was followed by a male voice through a crack in the door, "Master, a Miss Thomas is here to see you."

"Show her to the bedroom. I will be there shortly." Tedious, but useful for a few moments of pleasure or a meal when it suited him. But for tonight, he would try to keep this one alive. He wouldn't distract Peter with another body; he needed Peter focused on finding Dr. Ramsey.

CHAPTER 22

BETH

"I FEEL LIKE THOMAS Edison inventing the lightbulb," Dr. Giffard said, elbows on the table, fingers holding up her head. She let out a deep sigh.

Beth knew what she meant. She had been so elated when they discovered the gene combinations that produced the desired effects and had mistakenly thought the rest would be the easy part. After two nights of new experiments, they were still right where they'd started.

"We're missing something obvious. We have to be," Beth said.

"You both need to clear your heads. The answer will come to you," Luc said.

"He's right, stepping away might help." Beth thought for a moment and then grinned at Dr. Giffard. "Feeling up for a run?"

"A run? Are you serious? I hate running. I've always tripped over my own feet. And sweating, I hate sweating," Dr. Giffard said, wrinkling her nose.

Beth laughed aloud. Luc tried to hold it in but failed.

"Vampires don't sweat, Kate," Luc said with a huge grin across his face, a playful glint in his eyes.

Beth loved the sound of his laughter and could never keep from answering his smile with one of her own. She hadn't realized how lonely she really had been before she met Luc. She really had believed she was happy on her own, self-sufficient and confident. But Luc had completed a part of her she hadn't realized was missing, and it made her feel like she could conquer the world with him at her side. She hoped, with the bloodlust removed, he would still feel the same.

"Come on, Kate. When I need to clear my head, a run always helps. And if you haven't tried running outside at vampire speed, you're missing out!" Beth could tell she was skeptical. "Just a short one."

With a deep sigh, Dr. Giffard said, "Okay. A short one. And if I trip and fall on my face as the world's most awkward vampire, you must never tell a living... or undead soul."

"Deal," Beth agreed before turning toward Luc. "Are you coming?"

"I'll let you two ladies go without me. I'm not certain I could keep that promise," he said.

Dr. Giffard threw him a fake glare as they stepped through the lab door to leave.

It was just after midnight, and the early October air was cool against her skin. Beth could smell the scent of pine trees and breathed it in deeply. They were too close to the lights of the city to see the stars well, but she could tell the sky was cloudless. She would head away from the city into the more rural areas so that she and Dr. Giffard could get a good look.

"Do we need to stretch or something first?" Dr. Giffard asked.

Beth chuckled. "Nope. Ready?"

"As I'll ever be."

Beth started off more slowly than her usual pace. She knew there were some variations in speed between vampires. She was faster than Luc—something she was proud of—but not by a lot. Whether it was because she had done so much running before being turned or just something innate to her vampire DNA she didn't know. But whatever the reason, she relished the speed.

Dr. Giffard was keeping up easily, so she sped up, pushing her to go faster. Dr. Giffard matched her speed. Beth could see a grin spreading across her face, and after just a few minutes she heard her laughing aloud.

"This is amazing!" she yelled, running with her arms out to her sides and then trailing behind her like a happy toddler.

They had reached the countryside, and Beth slowed, coming to a stop in the center of a freshly cut field. The smell of the dry hay filled her nose, earthy and a little dusty. The trees in the nearby hedgerow had their own warm smell and Beth caught the musty scent of a pond in the next field over. The sound of the crickets was like a chorus of high-pitched voices, rising and falling.

Beth looked to Dr. Giffard, who stood with her mouth wide open, and followed her eyes to the sky overhead. It was breathtaking. There was no light pollution here to distract from the heavens. With her enhanced vision, it was like the stars were all around them, three-dimensional, coming down within reach above them.

"I've never seen anything like it," Dr. Giffard whispered, a hushed reverence in her voice.

"I know. I sometimes just lie in a field and take it all in. It's the most peace I've ever felt. When I look at that, I realize how small we really are, how small our problems are, in comparison to the universe."

"It's humbling."

They both lay down in the cool grass, watching the stars for several minutes and letting the joy and wonder of the moment pass over them. Then Dr. Giffard spoke up. "You've never told me how it all happened. You meeting Luc and becoming a vampire, I mean."

Beth considered for a moment but decided it couldn't hurt to tell her. It might be nice to have another person in the know about what they had gone through, and Dr. Giffard was certainly trustworthy.

"I was working one night, the graveyard shift as usual. They brought in this charred body. No human could have survived such severe burns, so I was shocked when I started the autopsy and he bled and then the wound started to heal."

"I think I would have panicked," Dr. Giffard said, eyes wide, but still staring at the stars.

"I thought I was hallucinating from sleep deprivation, but the doppler showed his heart beating even though I couldn't hear it. I debated on what to do. If I had turned him over to the clinicians, I figured they would either have killed him while treating him as a human or discovered what he was and exploited him for science. I couldn't accept either of those, so I chose a third... I took him home with me."

Dr. Giffard's jaw dropped. She leaned up on one elbow and shook her head. "Seriously?" She paused for a moment, brow furrowed, then asked, "How did you feed him?" She leaned forward, waiting for the answer.

"I made up a fake experiment and used my university appointment to get expired units from the blood bank."

Dr. Giffard shook her head again, staring intently without blinking, not speaking, so Beth continued. "I debrided his wounds at home and kept giving him blood while I watched him heal. I know now that he would have healed more quickly if I had been able to get him more blood, but I didn't have that knowledge or a way to get additional units at the time. He was comatose for a while and then pretended to be afterward, first because he was too weak to care for himself, then because he was uncertain about how I would react. He had no other place he could safely go in his state."

Beth lowered her head, a little ashamed of the next part, but she felt she could trust Dr. Giffard.

"I talked to him the whole time, telling him stories about my life, things I'd never shared with another human soul. But I thought he was in a coma and wouldn't really hear them. So, when he *woke up*, he knew a whole lot more about me than I intended." She looked up at Dr. Giffard from beneath her lashes.

"Wow." Dr. Giffard said the word as if it had two syllables, eyes again wide, eyebrows raised and her mouth still formed around her last word. "How did you find out? Did he just *tell* you?"

"I didn't know for quite a while, but then he slipped while talking about something I said that I didn't think he could hear and told me he had been awake nearly the entire time. I was so completely embarrassed I didn't talk to him for several days."

"I would have felt violated. I know I don't know him well, but it doesn't seem like his nature to purposefully eavesdrop," Dr. Giffard agreed.

"He didn't know me when it began, didn't know he could trust me. He was safe at that time, and I was giving him blood, so it was more self-preservation than anything else. It's my own fault for being such a Chatty Cathy, but I was just trying to pass the time."

"It sounds like neither of you intended for it to happen, but he must have liked what he heard, because he fell in love with you," Dr. Giffard said with a sly smile. "It's really romantic if you think about it."

Beth had to smile at that one. Dr. Giffard could find romance in almost anything. She supposed she was right, but it had been a hard pill to swallow at the time. She still flushed when she thought about the blue jeans comment. Maybe someday she would have the guts to tell Dr. Giffard about that one, but today was not that day.

Beth shared the rest of the story, including Peter and presenting herself to the Master. "I couldn't just let Luc die. I was already falling in love with him."

Dr. Giffard's face was a wash of emotions as she nodded and bit her lip.

"He held us both for days until Luc was starving and then put the two of us together in a train car with the doors chained shut. He knew by then that Luc cared for me. Luc was so ravenous and weak that the Master thought he would kill me in hunger then take his own life out of guilt for killing someone he loved. But I convinced Luc to feed on me, break us free of the train car, and turn me before I died." It was the first time Beth had shared her story with another. Reliving the memory brought back the fear and helplessness but at the same time pride and confidence over the fact that she and Luc had found a way free of the Master together.

"I remember how I felt when I first woke up after turning. I couldn't think about anything except blood," Dr. Giffard said. "He loved you enough to stop feeding on you even in that state. That says a lot."

Dr. Giffard was right. Beth hadn't completely understood then how much strength it had taken for Luc to stop when he so desperately needed her blood. But she did now and it made her smile.

Dr. Giffard lay back to stare at the stars for several more minutes, not pressing for more, leaving them both alone with their thoughts until she spoke again. "I've been thinking about the telepathy lately. I can't hear anything yet, but I've seen telepaths in movies where they become overwhelmed with all the noise. Does that happen to you?"

"It was a little distracting at first, hearing and feeling Luc's thoughts. But I was even more embarrassed for him to hear mine. I didn't know how to block them from him. I'm still working on it, but I'm learning to tune him out and turn off the noise," Beth said. She continued to get glimpses from Dr. Giffard now and then too, but was still working on honing in to hear her clearly. She supposed her skills had progressed so quickly with Luc because they spent so much time together and were so close.

"Turn off the noise," Dr. Giffard repeated. "Turn off... I've got it! I've got it!" she screamed. She jumped up and turned to run back toward the lab. She took four or five quick steps, tripped, and rolled head over feet to the edge of the field.

Beth was instantly at her side, doubled over and belly laughing. Dr. Giffard looked back, a bit bewildered at first, freshly cut hay hanging from her shirt and stuck in her hair, then started laughing too. She stood and dusted herself off.

"Well, if I hurt anything, it must have already healed because I can't feel it," she said. "Let's try that again," she said, breaking into a run.

"But what? What have you got?" Beth called after her before finding her stride.

Take two of the run was much less eventful. And Dr. Giffard, clearly excited to get back to the lab and begin working on her idea, was running at top speed. It allowed Beth to really stretch her legs, and all the pent-up tension ebbed away. They stopped and began walking in the shadows beyond the reach of the research building and stepped into the pool of light at normal human speed.

"One sec," Beth said before Dr. Giffard scanned into the door. She reached up and pulled the last couple of lingering blades of hay from Dr. Giffard's hair. "Better hide the evidence." She gave Dr. Giffard a sideways grin.

"Thanks," Dr. Giffard said and turned to open the door.

"How was the run?" Luc asked as Beth and Dr. Giffard returned to the lab. They were already engaged in conversation, talking about the next round of experiments.

"It was fantastic! Just what I needed. Who knew I would ever enjoy running? And lying in a field looking at the stars, the ideas just started popping into my head," Dr. Giffard said, words falling out her mouth as fast as her lips could move.

"I'm glad it helped. While you two were out, I reset everything so it would be ready to go when you got back," Luc said.

Beth walked to him, held his face in her hands, and kissed him on the mouth. A short kiss but with her whole heart. With her nose to his, she whispered, "You're the best." His boyish smile in return made her smile all the more.

Dr. Giffard, unable to contain her excitement, continued. "So, we've been trying to modify the gene therapy virus to go into the host's cells and cut out the segment of mutated DNA. But what I realized is that we don't have to remove it. All we have to do is turn it off so it's not transcribed into a workable gene as the cells replicate."

Beth had begun nodding at "remove it," already making the leap with Dr. Giffard to the next logical step in the process. "Yes! We should have thought of it before. We were just too wrapped up in making what we were doing work to think about another approach. You start programming in the sequence, and I'll get the equipment ready."

CHAPTER 23

BETH

LUC AND BETH HAD hardly closed the door to the shotgun house before they were in each other's arms. Beth had been looking forward to some alone time with Luc, and evidently, he felt the same. It was no more than an hour before dawn, and they had hurried home to steal a little time together before spending the daylight hours resting.

Luc's kiss was deep and urgent. Beth returned it in kind, running her hands over his shoulders. They had felt like steel when she was human. They still felt like he could lift an ox—well, he probably could—but now they felt more normal under her vampire touch. His skin was no longer cool to her but exactly the same temperature as her own.

She had just moved her hand to Luc's neck to tangle her fingers in his hair when they heard a knock, loud and insistent. As they broke off the kiss, Beth's hand moved to rest on Luc's chest, and they stared at one another while Luc let out a deep sigh.

"It's Cora... er, Lilly," Luc said.

"Lilly?" Beth asked, sure she didn't know anyone named Lilly and certainly not in the mood for visitors at the moment.

"I'll introduce you and explain more later," Luc said, turning the doorknob.

"Lilly," he said as he opened the door, uncertainty in his voice. Lilly flashed through the door and was immediately behind Luc and between him and Beth. She was gorgeous, a tall, athletically built black woman who looked like she was born with perfect skin and lipstick on her full lips. She moved with a confident gracefulness that any model would envy. Beth didn't think she could be any more attractive until she smiled, beaming with blindingly white teeth at Beth. A small gap between her front teeth was the only thing that might be called an imperfection, but honestly, in her face, it made her features even more alluring.

"You must be Luciano's friend," Lilly said, placing a great deal of emphasis on the word *friend*. "I'm Lilly. He didn't mention how beautiful you were. What was your name again?" She held out a hand with perfectly manicured nails, and Beth accepted it. The smile and offering seemed genuine, and Beth met it with one of her own. *She seems likable enough, and she knows Luc's real name.*

"Janice. Pleased to meet you. Are you a friend of Luc's?"

"Oh, yes, we have a lot of history together," she said, turning that smile back to Luc with a bit more familiarity than Beth would have liked. *Maybe I won't like her so much after all.*

Luc walked to Beth's side and placed his arm around her waist.

"What brings you out so close to dawn?" he said.

"After you stopped by the other day, I heard from an old friend in Kansas City."

Beth willed herself to not appear surprised. Luc hadn't mentioned meeting Lilly. She felt an unfamiliar pang of jealousy but reminded herself that this was Luc. She didn't believe he would be unfaithful to her but couldn't help but wonder why he would keep his meeting with another New Orleans vampire a secret.

"He said the Master has the word out that he's looking for you and Dr. Elizabeth Ramsey. I assume that is also you?" Lilly looked at Beth.

She felt Luc tense and tighten his arm around her. She nodded.

"As you can imagine, those who know you or who are not fond of the Master aren't talking. Even those who would declare loyalty don't seem in a hurry to help him, but if the time comes that he forces the issue, well..." Her smile was gone and she leveled her gaze on Luc. "You need to be careful. I thought you would want to know. My contact in Kansas City didn't suggest he knew you were here, and, of course, I would never mention it. You and I had some good times together, and with our long lives, you just never know when our paths might cross again." And again the broad smile just for Luc.

Okay, now I'm pretty sure I don't like her.

Lilly's gaze returned to Beth. She was trying her best to keep her face neutral but didn't feel it. She tried to focus on the fact that Lilly was here to warn Luc. Even if she was hitting on Luc every chance she got, at least the loyalty meant something.

"Thank you for the warning and your friendship. I won't forget it," Luc replied, keeping his arm around Beth's waist.

"I'm sure you will return the favor one day," she said as she turned and opened the door. She shot Luc one more sultry smile. "Luciano... Dr. Ramsey."

Beth made an attempt at a smile before the door closed but was certain it looked forced. Her curiosity was piqued and she wanted to know more about Lilly and Luc's history together, but at the same time wasn't entirely sure she wanted more than the broad strokes.

Beth turned to look at Luc, who was eyeing her beneath his lashes, a comical crooked grin on his lips, hands in his front pockets. He looked like a schoolboy caught red-handed. She considered her next words. She had little relationship experience, but in her heart, trusted Luc. She decided there must be a good reason he hadn't mentioned his meeting with Lilly. She would give him time to explain after they'd discussed the more urgent matter. "So, what's important first. We know the Master is looking for us and spreading the word. Do you know of any vampires here loyal to the Master that we may need to worry about?"

Luc exhaled as though he had been holding his breath, apparently relieved to talk about something besides Lilly. "Not that I know of. New Orleans is a favorite for many vampires, however. Many come here to the Quarter because it's such an easy place to blend in. And with the constant flow of tourists, a few missing ones aren't surprising. The city comes alive at night, just like we do. If there were any vampires of concern, Lilly would know and would have shared it with us."

"So we're basically where we already were except we know to be more cautious of other vampires that might be loyal or somehow indebted to the Master. Are there a lot of those?"

"More than a few, I'm afraid. There aren't nearly as many who are willingly loyal as there are those who owe or fear him. He has helped many become wealthy and powerful in their cities, running marginal or downright illegal businesses, but they know he could just as quickly return them to nothing if he desired. The fortune he has amassed over many centuries means he can buy almost anyone or anything."

"And as for the other part, Lilly, what is her place in the pecking order?" Beth said with a little more snark than she intended. If Luc noticed, he didn't let on.

"Lilly is self-made. She was born a slave and worked her way to where she is now. Some of her business dealings were not exactly legal, but her current business is legitimate. She owns the West Hotel on Dauphine and has since the early 1900s. She doesn't owe anyone anything as far as I know, but many are indebted to her."

Beth nodded, considering. "And when did the two of you meet?"

The sheepish look returned to Luc's face. "Initially in the thirties when I was playing saxophone in some of the local... establishments. Lilly went by Cora then and hired me to play."

"To play for the hotel?" Luc's hesitance over the "establishment" hadn't been lost on her. The '30s were an interesting time in New Orleans and even the carriage driver that had shown her the Quarter had commented on Storyville and the many brothels in the area just prior to that time.

Luc's shoulders tensed a bit. "It was a brothel then. Cora owned and ran it and hired jazz players to keep the patrons entertained while they waited. Prostitution was illegal then, but she catered to a very wealthy clientele that made sure she stayed under the radar."

Beth's mind was racing. There was so much about this man she didn't know. Her jealousy was piqued because of Lilly's beauty, feeling plain in comparison. And if she was a prostitute, like it sounded she might have been, it would imply Luc may have tastes well beyond what her experience could provide. It made her worry that her waiting for sex would sound all the more ridiculous to him. She wondered how long he would remain patient.

"Did Cora... um, have clients of her own?"

"She started out as a prostitute after the Civil War when there were no jobs for freed slaves. She had some loyal and well-to-do clients that helped her earn the money she needed to start her own business."

It was hard for Beth to take in. While she, too, was a vampire, she had only been alive for thirty-two years. She tried to push her fears aside and understand what it must have been like for Cora, free but penniless, female and discriminated against for race and gender at every turn in a white male-run country that could not yet think of her as an equal. It would have been a nearly impossible situation. Lilly seemed bright, and Beth tried to imagine the desperation that would drive her to the same choices. She would never understand completely, growing up as she had. But her heart softened a bit toward Lilly, and she could admire her drive and business achievements. *Until you've walked a mile in their shoes...* Beth recalled the old adage.

Beth must have taken a little longer than she intended mulling it all over.

"I didn't frequent her employees if that's what you're wondering. Cora and I met when I joined Slim Scott, a jazz player back then, on a gig one evening. We talked a bit and she hired me to play regularly. We became close over the years."

"I know I shouldn't be jealous of a girlfriend you had before I was born, but I can't help but feel just a little. She is beyond gorgeous, but more importantly, she knows you well and more of your history than I do." She couldn't bring herself to mention sex right now and, trying her best to block him mentally, hoped he wouldn't pick it up in her thoughts.

Luc walked toward Beth and held both her hands, making sure she was looking him in the eyes before speaking. "I should have told you about seeing her again. But I just didn't think it would be important. I had no intention of seeing her again. Lilly is a long-time friend, yes, but that's all she will ever be. Our relationship is in the past, and even at its best, it couldn't hold a candle to what you and I have had in just the few short months we've been together. We may not have a long past, but I want us to have a long future."

Luc continued, "And you say Lilly is beautiful. She is, but you don't see yourself for what *you* are. You don't notice the men who turn their heads as you walk or those who stop and blatantly stare, but I certainly do. You are oblivious to it all, and it's another reason I love you. When

Cora called you beautiful, she meant it. You are beautiful, Beth, and I am so thankful you have chosen to be with me."

Beth knew now that vampires could blush, and she did. She felt the emotion behind his words and it rang true. Everyone had a past, and with Luc's spanning three hundred years, there was bound to be some baggage. The feelings of jealousy were hers to control. Her heart and mind told her Luc loved her, and she chose to let it go. Luc wanted her, and that was all that mattered.

CHAPTER 24

KATE

"IT'S JUST NOT WORKING. I don't even see evidence of the virus being present in his blood," Kate huffed as Beth and Luciano entered the lab. Every day seemed to her like one step forward and two steps back. Of course, she'd had difficulty with experiments in the past, but this was the one that would allow her to leave her mark on the world. Having an answer at her fingertips but just out of reach was killing her. And while they had no clear evidence the Master was hot on their heels, she could tell Luciano and Beth were more anxious the longer they stayed.

"When we used the Adeno-associated virus on the mice, the blocking sequence we inserted worked like a charm. The virus infected the hosts, and the viral genome was inserted into the hosts' DNA, turning off the genes for bloodlust and UV sensitivity. But after two attempts, Reese doesn't even look to have been infected with the new Adeno-associated virus at all."

They had grown fond of the little rhesus monkey that had been infected with the bloodlust and UV sensitivity portion of the vampire virus and had begun calling him by the nickname. He seemed perfectly healthy and completely unaffected by their attempts to remove the undesirable traits from his genes.

After reviewing Kate's notes, Beth sat down at one of the nearby lab benches with her fist closed and leaning against her chin. She stared for several minutes in Reese's direction, but her eyes were unfocused, lost in thought. Slowly she sat more upright in her chair, laying her forearms on the bench top. "Luc, you said we could eat any of the units at the blood centers, even the ones that might be infected with other viruses."

"Yes, we seem to be immune to things like Hepatitis and HIV," Luciano said.

Kate looked at Beth, following her train of thought, slowly nodding and thinking aloud. "If we are immune to other viruses, maybe Reese's body just fights off the foreign virus before it can even enter a cell to do its thing." Kate was elated at the epiphany, but then her spirits fell just as quickly.

"That could certainly explain it," Beth agreed.

"But if he's immune to our usual viral vectors, what can we use to get the information in there?" Kate said. She was talking to herself but speaking aloud as she considered the possibilities. "The vampire virus itself," Kate said with a finality to her voice and a slow smile. She had her answer. She was used to working alone or with graduate students where she was the one with the brilliant ideas. But she had to admit working with Beth, someone who clearly functioned at the same level and shared ideas freely, was exhilarating.

"If the vampire virus is the only thing that can penetrate the vampire defenses, then we're going to have to modify it and use it as our vector," Kate said. But her moment of triumph faded with realization, her smile disappearing and her brow creasing. "That's not going to be an easy task."

CHAPTER 25

HANDLER

HANDLER'S PHONE VIBRATED IN his pocket. He fished it out and glanced at the screen. Grimacing and sighing deeply, he answered, leaning back in his desk chair and holding his forehead in his hand. The voice on the other end began speaking before he could.

"Detective Handler? Dr. James. Our computer specialist has identified two scientists in Chicago who accessed tissue and blood samples from a tissue bank in the Chicago area, Precision Biological Services. Both samples were deposited anonymously and could only be accessed by the designated scientist. The Master requests you go to Chicago to locate them and investigate. We need to know if they're researching the provided samples. I have the names. Are you ready?"

Pulling his notebook and pen out of his jacket pocket and leaning forward to write, he said, "Go ahead."

"The first, a virologist, Dr. Julianne Riley. The second is a geneticist, Dr. Liam Henri, H-e-n-r-i. They're both at the University of Chicago."

Dr. James always sounded irritated and terse to Handler. But he supposed working for the Master would make one feel constantly anxious. It did him. He knew when he took the first job that he was dancing with the devil. But he needed the money badly to cover his gambling debts until his luck turned. And once he was on the payroll, he realized he would have a hard time leaving. As long as he could do the investigating himself and not have to witness another bloody interrogation with the Master, he could handle it.

"Got it," Handler said.

"Keep your eyes and ears open for any clues as to the location of Dr. Ramsey and Mr. Verde. Report back to me daily with your findings." With that, Dr. James ended the call.

Handler didn't expect more. He knew Dr. James thought he was beneath him, a disposable resource to use at his whim and discard. It was nothing new. P.I.s were often treated this way. No one wanted to be associated with him, but they sure sought out his services when things got messy.

Handler turned on his dinosaur of a computer—complete with a monitor that weighed at least fifteen pounds—and searched for flights from Kansas City to Chicago. He hated flying, but with gas prices, it might be cheaper than making the drive. Chicago had a robust subway system, so he would likely be able to get away with not renting a car. Parking was hell there anyway. He found the cheapest flight which left at 6 a.m. the following morning and booked it.

James had mentioned a virologist and a geneticist. Handler had no idea what either of those were and decided he should probably do a little research before heading out. He knew the Master would stop at nothing to find Dr. Ramsey and Mr. Verde, but he didn't know why. He was usually able to contain his curiosity and perform the requested duties without being nosey. But the Master had torn apart the lawyers he had tracked down with his teeth. Whatever they had done, they had made a horrible enemy. Just thinking about that night sent chills up his spine.

He regretted their deaths, or at least his part in them. Would he have nabbed them if he knew the Master would kill them? He wasn't sure.

The bookies had been breathing down his neck and he feared for his own life if he didn't come up with the money he owed them. Even though he hadn't killed the lawyers, he felt responsible. He hoped the fate of these scientists would be different. Dr. James had only asked him to investigate. That he could handle.

He began his search for the two scientists, finding their university appointments and staff pictures easily. Dr. Liam Henri was a male, mid-forties by his picture, who had assisted with the original human genome mapping project. Dr. Julianne Riley was an attractive fifty-ish female with an interest in retroviruses, *whatever the hell those are,* and had done extensive research on the HIV virus. That one he recognized from the news and the headlines with Magic Johnson. He had made some money betting on his games before the infection made him retire.

So whatever Dr. Ramsey and Mr. Verde were up to, they needed these scientific specialties to pull it off. He knew Dr. Ramsey was a kind of doctor who did autopsies for a living. While he thought it sounded disgusting, he wondered what she could have found in an autopsy that would put her on the Master's shit list and require a virologist and geneticist, which must be even bigger eggheaded doctors than she was, to figure it out. And how did Verde fit into all of this? He wasn't a doctor.

Handler leaned back in his chair, placing his feet on the shabby wooden desk, and lit a cigarette.

Dr. James had mentioned tissue banks meaning Dr. Ramsey left something for the scientists. Why would the Master care about their research?

He took a long draw on the cigarette and then tapped the ashes off into an overflowing cigarette dish on the desk.

He had seen enough of the Master to know he was not a normal human. He looked like one, except the way he moved too fast for human eyes to follow, and then there was the fact he only conducted his business at night. And the fangs Handler had seen when the Master had murdered the lawyers were not normal. The only blood-eating or drinking creatures with fangs he could think of were vampires. But vampires weren't real. He knew there had to be another explanation. Psycho? Serial killer with weird teeth? Some kind of freaking alien? He didn't know. But whatever Dr. Ramsey and Mr. Verde had done, they had pissed off one bad dude.

CHAPTER 26

HANDLER

FLYING INTO O'HARE, HANDLER opted for a forty-minute taxi ride to the Pritzker Medical School campus rather than a two-plus hour trip on the L-train, although it would have been cheaper. It may not have smelled better, but it was probably close. The cab stunk heavily of cigar smoke, pungent even to Handler, who was used to a constant cloud of his own cigarette smoke. The back seat smelled like B.O. and coffee, some of which had been spilled on the seat judging by the brown stains. At least, that's what he hoped it was. The cabby had his window down, but it did little more than blow his cigar smoke into Handler's face. He scooted as far to the passenger side of the back seat as possible and lit up. He puffed on his cigarette, took a deep drag, and tried to enjoy the scenery along the way.

To Handler, a city was a city. I-90 could have been I-70 in Kansas City, with miles and miles of concrete road, overpasses and congested traffic. He was nearly fifteen minutes into the ride when he started to see the high rises of downtown. It reminded him of downtown Kansas City, only bigger. The skyscrapers were cold and grotesquely large against the skyline, and he couldn't help but think of gravestones sticking up from the ground in rows in a cemetery. As they approached Hyde Park through Washington Park, there was at least a bit more green, the trees still heavy with leaves. He'd been to the University of

Chicago once before, but it'd been many years ago. He remembered its gothic architecture with tall spires, steeply arched windows and limestone facades. Pritzker was next to that campus, but the building they approached held none of the gothic architectural charm.

As they approached the Arthur Grady Biological Science Center, Handler could see its mirrored windows reflecting the sunlight. It nearly blinded him. It reminded him of a rectangular disco ball, stark in its contrast to the rest of the University of Chicago campus. He was not a fan of the more modern building styles. They looked stuffy, cold and institutional, but he supposed it *was* an institution, so that fit.

The cabby dropped him off at the curb in front of the building, and he shelled out $75 for the trip plus a $5 tip. The cabby gave him a frown, but the cab was dirty and stunk. What did he expect?

The entrance was mirrored just as the rest of the structure, the large double doors reflecting Handler's image as he walked toward it. His hat was askew, his suit rumpled. Sure the trip had added a few wrinkles, but Handler was never much for ironing, and dry cleaning was pricey. He supposed he could have shaved, but he honestly didn't care. His job was to get information, not look pretty.

Handler entered through the double doors, pressed the automatic door button, and closed his eyes at the refreshing blast of cool air that met him. It was an unseasonably warm day in Chicago for early October, and sweat had begun to trickle down his back in just the few steps between the cab and the door.

Just to his left was an elevator as well as a directory. He scanned the list of labs and doctors until he found Dr. Julianne Riley. The list showed her lab to be on the main floor, room 145. Dr. Henri was on the third floor in 313. *That's about as unlucky as it gets.*

Handler headed down the main hall just to the right of the

elevator. The floors were white linoleum and looked relatively new, but the lights overhead were old fluorescents that buzzed through their yellowed plastic covers as he passed. The rooms were in order and he easily found 145. There was a narrow vertical window in the door, and as he walked slowly by, he saw a young male, mid-twenties, wearing a light blue lab coat and gloves as he looked through a microscope on the counter. Behind him, through another door, he could see someone in what looked to Handler like a hazmat suit, white from head to toe, working under some kind of metal hood. He supposed it was for safety like he had seen on television. When the person turned toward the door, he could see Dr. Riley's face, wearing the same somber expression as her recent driver's license photo, through the plastic mask. *Bingo!*

To the right of the door was a magnetic badge-scanning pad. The door also had a key lock, but he doubted it would work without a badge. He continued down the hallway which split into two additional corridors at its end. Turning right, about halfway down, was an open door revealing a break room complete with two small round tables surrounded by mismatched molded plastic chairs. The counter in the back held a sink and coffee maker, the pot looking like it hadn't been washed in the last decade. An old white refrigerator covered in yellowed comics clipped from newspapers stood on the left wall. Two doors further down was a swinging door labeled "Men's Locker."

Handler checked the hall behind him and, finding it empty, pushed the door aside. It opened to a wall blocking the view of the locker room behind the hallway. He rounded it slowly, hearing no movement, and saw three rows of lockers. Most had locks, some keyed, some combination, but a few did not. He opened those without locks, finding old scrubs, shoes, and gum wrappers. The third one he tried was labeled with a plain white stick-on mailing label with

"STUDENT" in black Sharpie.

A sneer curled his lips as he opened it to find a short white lab coat. A small alligator clip hung to the inside of the pocket attached to an ID badge. The picture was a young red-headed male, early twenties, with prominent freckles and very crooked teeth clear in his broad smile—"Lawrence Reed, Medical Student."

Handler checked the remaining lockers, but no others held any treasures he was interested in. He didn't know if the badge would allow passage into Dr. Riley's lab so he could have a look around later, but it would be easier than breaking in if it worked.

Next was a visit to the third floor which held an identical layout to the first. Room 313 was similar but contained no separate room in the back, just multiple lab benches with sinks, computers, and microscopes. The lights had been left on but no one was in the lab. As he peered in the door, he heard footsteps approaching him in the hallway.

"Can I help you?"

It was Dr. Henri, who looked just like his online picture, only about ten years older. He wore a long white lab coat with coffee stains on the lapel and had a laptop in hand with a stack of papers on top.

"No, no, I'm just wandrin' and biding time until my son's finished workin'. He's a medical student assisting with some research to pad his resumé. He said he'd be finished in fifteen or twenty minutes and then we could get an early supper."

"Visitors are supposed to remain in the lobby on the first floor," Henri said stiffly, walking past him to swipe his badge at the door to his lab.

"Oh hell, sorry, I just got bored and started explorin'. I'll head back there now."

Henri didn't bother responding, seeming far more interested in the papers in his hand than Handler, who turned and strode slowly down the hall toward the elevators.

He left the building the way he had entered, checking the halls and entrance for cameras, but found none. Just down the sidewalk and right toward the center of campus was a tall shade tree with a cement bench. Handler looked at his watch: 4:35 p.m. It would be a decent place to park until Dr. Riley decided to call it a day, just far enough away she wasn't likely to notice him so he could follow her home.

***

It was 8 p.m., and Handler stood in front of the door to Dr. Riley's lab. He had walked back to the lab building after tailing Riley to her apartment just a few blocks away. She hadn't stopped working until nearly 6 p.m. His ass had felt as flat as the cement bench by then, and he had been running low on cigarettes. He knew where she lived from his online research, a short walk from the lab, but needed to gather information about how she got to and from for his report to the Master. The DMV showed no vehicle registration, so he had expected she would walk, carpool, or hire a ride, but the Master paid him for details.

He pulled the stolen ID badge from his jacket pocket and tapped it on the scanner. The red light at the top of the box turned to green as the latch released. He opened the door and quickly went inside, not wanting to hang out in the hallway any longer than he had to. The lights were off in the lab, but small ceiling lights on either side of the emergency lighting were enough for him to navigate to the desk on the far side of the room.

A nameplate on the desk identified the owner as Dr. Julianne Riley. There was a cleared space in the middle of the wood-topped metal-framed desk, but the rest of it was covered in stacks of scientific journals and piles of paper. A single photograph of a fluffy white cat with big yellow eyes and a pink collar sat next to the monitor. He would wait to poke through all of it after he got into Dr. Riley's computer.

He was no hacker—searching the internet and checking his email were the extent of his usual computer skills—but his computer geek had sent him with a device to get into the machine. He hooked it up as instructed, plopped down in the squeaky desk chair, and turned it on. After a few minutes, the computer accepted its login and began loading.

I'm in. Now what? Handler texted the geek. He followed his instructions to find the computer's name and IP address, and in seconds the mouse began moving on its own across the screen. Files opened and closed as the geek hunted for anything related to the tissue samples Dr. Ramsey had left behind.

As the geek worked on the computer, Handler began riffling through the papers on the desk. Much of it seemed like daily temperature charts, supply lists and checklists for something called reagents, but nothing looked like reports on viruses. Dr. Ramsey and Mr. Verde weren't listed anywhere. He searched the drawers but found nothing except office supplies and more journals. There were no flash drives to gather, so if she had any she'd taken them with her. Several filing cabinets stood between the desk and the wall of the isolation lab. The computer monitor showed files being downloaded as he stood to check the cabinets out.

They held more reams of paper within folders labeled with the names of various grants. Some of the files were labeled as teaching and testing files, CME—which he discovered stood for continuing medical education—and one labeled memberships. He thumbed through anything that looked remotely related to viruses other than journal articles, but again found nothing out of the ordinary and no mention of the tissue bank.

He turned to the isolation lab, which was surrounded by windows, and pressed his face to the glass. There were several refrigerators and large round waist-high canisters. Clipboards hung on the walls containing graphs and handwritten notes. Handler didn't know what was in there, but since the doc had been in there in a hazmat suit, he wasn't chancing it. There was no way the Master was paying him enough to go in and check it out.

As he was finishing, his phone buzzed. The geek had texted back.

Finished. Nothing here, but I downloaded all the files to look at more thoroughly offline.

Handler removed the device as the computer was already shutting down.

One down and one to go.

On the third floor outside room 313, he tried the ID badge again. The red light on the scan pad flashed blue and red but didn't open. The geek had given him a device for this as well. He had hoped to use a stolen card so as not to immediately arouse suspicion with an unidentified entry. But at least this hadn't been necessary on the first lab to risk cluing someone in before he could look around.

He held the gadget up to the scanner, pressed the scan button as he had been instructed, and waited. As he did, he heard faint whistling from the opposite end of the hall. *Shit!*

He heard wheels and the sound of dripping water. Little beads of sweat broke out on his forehead as he willed the device to work faster. The whistling turned to singing and then more squeaking wheels. It was getting closer. The lights went on at the far end of the hall.

Handler was just ready to remove the device when the light turned from red to green and the lock clicked open.

Jerking the door open, he went inside and slowly closed it to make sure it made no noise. The person at the end of the hall kept right on singing as the door fully closed.

Handler leaned his back against the solid part of the door, head back and eyes closed. *I'm getting too old for this shit.*

This lab contained the same meager lighting as the last. The left side of the room was lab benches with all types of research equipment and machinery he didn't recognize strewn across it, with refrigerators and freezers in the back.

The right side contained two desks. One was neatly arranged with a computer monitor and keyboard in the center. The second and furthest from the door was a total disaster. The surface of the desk wasn't visible apart from a small rectangle the size of a laptop. The rest was haphazard piles of paper and journals in no discernable order. There were at least ten dirty coffee cups and candy wrappers.

Handler hooked the computer device up the computer on the neat desk just as he had before and texted the geek. When the computer booted, Handler gave him the necessary information to hack in. The drawers on this desk had a few office supplies but were mostly empty. He suspected this desk belonged to whatever medical or grad students assisted Dr. Henri in his research.

He moved on to the second desk and quickly found several documents addressed to Dr. Henri but again, nothing related to his investigation. The drawers were as disgusting as the desktop, filled with trash, old food and papers in no particular order. The top drawer, however, held a crumpled envelope beneath other old mail with a sender address that caught his eye. It was from the law firm of

Williamson, White and Martin, the very same law firm that he knew
was now short three lawyers.

He pulled the envelope out of the mess and looked inside.

May 4th, 2023

Dear Dr. Henri:

*My name is Dr. Elizabeth Ramsey. I am a forensic pathologist
and until just recently worked with Heartland Forensic Specialists in
Kansas City, KS. We have not met, but I have studied your work. I
am enclosing a record of my recent observations on a most unusual
patient. I have discovered that his DNA has been modified through the
use of a novel retrovirus causing numerous chromosomal alterations.
Some of the alterations have resulted in unique abilities such as increased
strength and rapid healing, as well as negative side effects such as extreme
sensitivity to UV light. I have sent this same information to seven
additional virologists and geneticists.*

*I must tell you that if you are receiving this information, I am likely
dead for knowing what I now share with you. Those who would have kept
the information silent are powerful and resourceful. Study this material
and make your own decision about whether or not to proceed. Should you
choose to pursue it, I have stored tissue and blood samples in your name
at Bioscience Organ Procurement (see attached account information).*

*I believed, and still do, that the knowledge to be gained is worth the
risk.*

Sincerely,

Elizabeth Ramsey, M.D.

Handler stuffed the letter back into the envelope and shoved it into
his inside jacket pocket. He now had proof Dr. Henri was one of the
scientists that Dr. Ramsey had chosen but nothing that showed he
had acted on it to further the investigation. He didn't know what a

retrovirus was, but clearly Dr. Ramsey felt it was something the Master didn't want her to know. And who was this patient whose DNA had been messed up by it? Could it be the Master? Surely, the "powerful and resourceful" people she referred to included the Master.

It also confirmed the information that the lawyers had given up during their torture sessions and meant he had six more scientists to find and investigate. While he would be grateful for the money, he didn't cherish the thought of a longer working relationship with the Master. After what he'd witnessed, he had no doubt that the Master would get rid of him the moment he stopped being useful.

His phone buzzed.

Nothing here. No one has logged on to this machine since May.

Handler wasn't surprised. From the vacant laptop spot on the desk, he was pretty sure Henri kept his laptop with him. But was it so he could work from home, or to protect a secret?

There was a loud bang from the end of the hallway. Handler froze. He heard footsteps outside the door and hurried to press himself to the wall next to it, out of the line of sight of anyone looking in. As he did, he saw the glow from the computer monitor wink out as it shut down and hoped the person hadn't seen the flash of light from the hallway. But the footsteps turned and went back in the direction they had come from, and after a few more seconds, the light at the end of the hallway went out.

Handler sighed. Hearing nothing more, he turned toward the refrigerators and freezers. The refrigerator had a clear glass door, so he could easily see the containers within. He couldn't make much of it. All of them were labeled with multiple reference numbers and dates but no names or locations. Some of them looked to contain clear fluid and tissue fragments while others contained blood.

The freezer door was solid with no windows. A temperature readout on the top read -22. Handler opened the door and looked around. Fog formed as the cold air met the room air and Handler waved it away with his hand. The freezer contained many bottles similar to those in the refrigerator, but all were in plastic bags with orange biohazard symbols. He noticed one toward the back looked different from the others, containing what looked like frozen blood rather than fragments of tissue or tinfoil-wrapped mystery items. He grabbed a glove from one of the lab desks and slipped it on. Picking up the bag, he could see the frost-covered label.

Bioscience Organ Procurement.

He snapped a picture with his phone and returned the sample to the freezer. Not knowing what was in it or how dangerous it might be to handle, there was no way he was taking it with him to melt and release whatever might be in it.

Just as he was closing the door, the freezer began to beep loudly. He shut the door more abruptly than he had intended and again plastered himself against the wall. The freezer quickly stopped beeping and returned to its regular hum.

Handler waited for a full minute but heard nothing from the hallway. Having found what he had come for, he hurried to retrieve his equipment and headed out the door.

CHAPTER 27

LUC

"LUC, WE'RE UP TO our eyeballs here. Are you sure we can't do this in a couple of days?" Beth asked.

"Nope, it has to be tonight. We've got tickets to Preservation Hall and can't miss it." Luc hadn't told Beth that he'd been asked to join the Legacy Band. He wanted to surprise her. She had heard him play at the shotgun house a few times and seemed to fall in love with the music.

"Do either of you know anything about the history of Preservation Hall?" he asked. Both shook their heads. "Preservation Hall was opened in 1961 by Allan and Sandra Jaffee. They fell in love with the music and wanted a place where the old masters could play and where people could go to hear the original jazz in its pure form, untainted by the emergence of rock and roll. So many of the greats have played there over the years and still do. I met many of them back in the '40s before Preservation Hall even opened. It completely changed the way I looked at music." He knew he was talking quickly in his excitement, but he wanted them to understand what this meant to him. And it would mean a lot to have Beth there to share it with him.

"I don't think I've ever seen you quite this excited about anything." Beth glanced at Kate and then back at Luc. He was careful to hide his thoughts, but he was sure his excitement was still coming through. He watched as a small grin appeared on Beth's lips and knew she was going to agree, making him return the grin with a broad smile of his own.

"Well, I suppose a break might be good for us, and a little time out on the town with the two of you sounds wonderful."

"Perfect, I'll meet the two of you there at nine." Luc leaned in to kiss Beth gently before turning and disappearing out the lab door, which slowly swung closed after him.

Luc strode over to Kate and Beth at normal human speed. It was hard to go so slowly with all the excitement he felt, but he had to reel it in, both to blend in and so he wouldn't tip them off that something special was happening.

He saw Beth the moment he stepped outside the building. He couldn't imagine who wouldn't notice her. She wore a simple fitted dress with cap sleeves and a rounded neckline. Though the dress itself was unremarkable, the way it fit her curves was not. It stopped just above the knee, but the bit of femininely muscled leg that extended below and flashed between the kick pleat in the back would make any man catch his breath imagining what the rest of her runner's body might look like. She moved gracefully, milling with the crowd and examining the outside of the Hall.

It didn't look like much from the outside, the paint peeling here and there with past colors showing through. Faded wood shutters covered the windows, and the entrance was gated by a fan-shaped ironwork window above doors with vertical bars, see-through from top to middle, and heavily rusted solid metal from the middle to the floor. A faded blue sign hung in two parts from under the eave, the top one shaped roughly like a trombone case and declaring the building to be "PRESERVATION HALL" in block letters.

Luc saw Beth look down from the sign as he approached. He was dressed in his navy blue suit and jacket, closed with a single button over a pale blue dress shirt. His tie was a swirl of blues in paisley with just a bit of orange which matched his pocket square. He had chosen it knowing how much Beth liked him in blue.

He watched as Beth looked him up and down, an approving smile on her face. She whistled. "I've never seen you in a suit. You look devastatingly handsome."

"I was going to say hot." Kate grinned and wiggled her eyebrows at Beth, who laughed and nodded, eyes wide.

"And now I feel underdressed," Beth said.

Returning their grins, Luc said, "I'm glad you both approve. And you couldn't look more beautiful," he said, staring into Beth's eyes. "Ladies?" He held out his elbows for each to take and walked them in through the front door, the doorman giving him an approving nod as he passed. Luc led them to two saved seats in the front row of the Hall.

It was a small space meant for intimate exposure to the musicians and a very personal, interactive musical immersion. The front of the Hall contained an old upright piano to the left and some plain and well-worn wooden chairs on either side of a simple drum set bearing the words "Preservation Hall Jazz Band" on the bass drum in red and blue. The audience seating consisted of a hodge podge of benches and chairs packed in as tightly as they could go, starting about eight feet in front of the band with room for standing in the back. Packed in like sardines, the whole venue couldn't hold more than a hundred people. Luc watched as Kate and Beth sized up the place.

After they were seated, their legs touching and nearly pressed against the people on either side, Beth's brow furrowed, "Where are you going to sit?"

Luc couldn't hold it in any longer. Smiling at Beth with a childlike grin, he pointed to one of the wooden chairs to the left of the drum set and said, "Right there."

He turned and strode to his seat, not giving her time to respond, the look of surprise on her face leaving him with a grin from ear to ear. He sat in the simple wooden chair, and, like the rest of his bandmates, began warming up. He glanced at Beth, talking to Kate and gesturing toward him. He stayed focused on his warm-up, not prying into their conversation, but was pleased that a smile never left her face. When she looked forward, catching his eye for just a moment, she beamed at him, her hands clasped together just beneath her chin in a look of joy and anticipation. And, Luc thought, pride.

His attention was pulled back to the music as the trumpet player, their band leader, opened the show with, "One, two, one, two, three, four."

The set opened with "This Bucket's Got a Hole in It," and after several bars playing in unison, the members began their short solos, first the trumpet player, then the pianist, then the trombone, and fourth was Luc. Eyes closed, he let the notes wash over him, playing within the musical key but creating his own melody. He had played for so many years that his fingers seemed to act without him willing them to play. He thought the melody and his fingers made it happen. And in a few short bars, his solo ended to cheers and clapping from the crowd, none louder than Beth and Kate. Beth beamed at him from her seat, hands once again clasped together and held at her chin. She looked delighted, and the pride in her eyes swelled in his heart, nearly bringing tears to his eyes. He wanted to share this with her so badly. He wanted to share everything with her, now and in whatever years they had to come.

He watched as her expressions changed with the music, and she even closed her eyes and swayed to the slow-driving melody of "Just a Closer Walk With Thee." Luc was in his element, forgetting about the Master, being a vampire and time in general as he played for himself and for Beth. He could see the joy on her face and on the faces in the crowd around her. There were few things better than the emotional ride of the music. Luc loved it with every fiber of his being. There was only one thing in this world that he loved more than that right now... Beth.

He kept time, tapping his toe during a drum solo, and again met her eyes. It was all there. While Beth was usually reserved with her emotions, when she looked at him there was no hiding her feelings. They flowed through their bond. Her feelings of love and pride wrapped around him like a warm blanket. That combined with the music moved him in a way he had never felt before. He could see the love in her eyes and hoped that she saw the same reflected in his.

He wanted this cure now more than ever so that Beth would know without question that his feelings for her were untainted by the bloodlust. While he had been hesitant about proceeding with finding a cure just weeks ago, he wasn't now. They would do what they needed to solve this, and then they would begin their long lives with nothing between them.

All too soon, they reached the final number, "When the Saints Go Marching In," and halfway through they began their solos, the main vocalist and trumpet player announcing Luc last as Hank Green to the cheers of the crowd. The music rose in intensity, the notes flying from his fingertips as all of them improvised the final bars. When the last note fell, the crowd once again erupted in cheers and clapping. Kate whistled with her fingers while Beth's eyes glinted and she bit her lip as if choking back happy tears.

The applause lasted for several minutes, everyone on their feet, the band members taking a final bow before it began to fade. While the approval of the crowd was pleasing to Luc, seeing Beth's reaction was what mattered most.

Luc placed his saxophone in its case and shook hands with his bandmates, congratulating them on their performance. Then he walked to Kate and Beth, where he was met with a bear hug.

"You were absolutely amazing," Beth said. "I've heard you play at the house, but never like that. You stole the show with that final solo. It took my breath away." She hugged him again even tighter and whispered in his ear, "*You* take my breath away." She pressed a kiss to his neck and nuzzled in close. It sent shivers through his entire body as he could both hear and feel the meaning of her words.

As she released him, he said, "Thank you." And turning to include Kate with Beth's hand still in his: "Thank you both for coming. I apologize for the secrecy and insistence. I wanted you here for my first night but didn't want to spoil the surprise."

"I'm glad you insisted. We wouldn't have wanted to miss a single moment," Kate said.

"I'll walk you both back to the lab after I stash my sax."

As he turned with the two ladies and headed toward his instrument, he saw an elderly gentleman dressed in a navy blue suit and wide matching tie, his shoes nearly glowing they were shined so perfectly. He wore a black pork pie hat with a flat rim and black ribbon band. A small amount of carefully combed gray-black hair poked out around his ears. His lips were full and almost pouty, cheeks full, the tale-tale features of a trumpet player. He looked so familiar, and he was looking, staring really, mouth partly open, straight at Luc.

He stepped slowly with his cane blocking Luc from his path. "Hank Green?" the man asked. "You are the spittin' image of Luke Green, but that would be impossible since I played with him in this very town about seventy years ago and you don't look a day older than he did then."

Luc extended his hand, already knowing this was Gerry "Gator" Jones before he spoke, a trumpet player he had played with for nearly five years. He had to be in his late nineties, and Luc assumed he would have passed by now.

"Yes, Hank Green. Luke Green was my grandfather." He felt Beth's hand in his and could sense her anxiety. "And what is your name?"

"Gerry Jones. They called me Gator back then. You could not look any more like your grandfather if he cloned you," he said.

"It is an honor to meet you, Gator. I hope it's okay to call you that. My grandfather told me stories about you before he passed. He taught me everything he knew about playing the sax and said you were the best there ever was at the trumpet. I had no idea I would ever have the chance to meet you." Gator and Luc had been bandmates but also friends. He hated lying to him but also couldn't imagine a good way to tell him the truth.

"Let me introduce you to my girlfriend, Janice Gates, and our friend, Dr. Katherine Giffard."

Gator held out his hand and shook each of theirs. "Pleased to meet you both. Hank, your granddaddy would have been proud of the way you played tonight and impressed with the level of company you're keeping." With this last phrase, he winked at Beth and tipped his hat to Kate. "Luke always did have a soft spot for the beautiful ladies."

Luc caught a glance from Beth, eyebrows raised and a crooked smile on her lips. He was sure he wouldn't escape that comment without an explanation later.

"Are you still playing?" Luc asked Gator.

"Every chance I get, but I'll be settin' up with the Legacy Band next Tuesday."

"Well, I'll be here. Meeting you is like meeting a legend and I will not miss an opportunity to hear you play."

Gator tipped his hat and nodded his head. "I would be pleased to hear about old Luke's last years. Spittin' image," he said, shaking his head. "I look forward to seeing you again. Goodnight, ladies."

While Luc wished he could tell Gator the truth, he was pleased his old friend had lived a long life and was still doing what he loved. Having another chance to hear him play and share in his life was a treat he had never imagined. His heart was full tonight and lighter than it had been in a while. The last three hundred years had been rocky, but now with Beth, his music and a cure so close on the horizon, he allowed himself to finally feel hopeful.

CHAPTER 28

HANDLER

HANDLER WALKED IN THE door and tossed his duffle on the bed. There was hardly room to walk around the bed in the tiny hotel room, but it was cheap. He sat down on the mattress, which dipped under his weight, and pulled out his pack of cigarettes and lighter. He tapped the pack on the bedside table, got one out and flicked his lighter. When it wouldn't light, he tossed it on the bed then pulled a book of matches from another pocket and struck one. When the butt of his cigarette glowed red, he drew deeply. Holding the cigarette between his lips, he dug for his phone and flipped it open. *Time to check in.*

He punched in Dr. James' number.

"Did you find anything?" Dr. James asked, not wasting time on greetings.

"I tailed Riley from the lab to her apartment, which I'll check out tomorrow. The initial sweep of her lab and computer were clean, although your computer geek has the files to do a more thorough check tonight. She had an isolation room in the back of the lab which I couldn't get into. I went through her desk and files though, and nothin' looked suspicious."

"But there's no way to be certain she doesn't have the samples unless we can get into the freezers," Dr. James said, irritation in his voice.

"She was in there today in a hazmat suit. I'm not trained for that. If you want to check those out, then get someone with a medical degree to do your snoopin'."

Handler paused, expecting backlash. But Dr. James responded with, "And Dr. Henri?"

"Henri is another story. I found a letter the lawyers sent from Dr. Ramsey wadded up in his desk. The man's a slob."

"Is there any more information in it that would lead us to the other scientists?"

Handler pulled the letter from his pocket and unfolded it, holding the flip phone with his chin and shoulder. "Says Dr. Ramsey sent the same information to seven additional virologists and geneticists, but no names or locations. She mentions the samples at Bioscience Organ Procurement. I found one of them in his freezer but couldn't make anything of the specimens in the refrigerator."

"Did you keep the sample?"

"No, it was in a biohazard bag. Again, I'm not equipped to deal with the medical crap. The freezer alarm went off and housekeeping was down the hall so I had to be quick."

Dr. James said nothing, but Handler heard an irritated sigh.

"I found a home address for Henri while I was rummaging around the office. I'm going to check out both apartments tomorrow after they leave for work."

"Very well, see if you can find any evidence that they've made contact with Dr. Ramsey or Mr. Verde. Since we know Dr. Henri is involved and can't confirm Dr. Riley is not, I am certain the Master will want them both taken care of."

"Taken care of? But it looks like she isn't involved."

"The Master won't want to take that chance. Get rid of them after you see what information you can extract and report back to me."

"Now wait a minute. If you want me to find people and get information, no problem. Hell, I even kidnapped a couple of folks for the Master. But I draw the line at killin'. I'm no assassin."

"I'm sure he will be interested to hear you are a man who lives by such high moral standards."

"That was never part of the deal. I'll finish my job here, but if the Master wants them dead, he's gonna to have to send someone else." With that he hung up, his hands shaking so badly he nearly dropped the phone as he tried to return it to his pocket. He took off his fedora and ran his hand through his greasy hair then took a few quick puffs on his cigarette. He needed the money, sure, but he had to live with himself. If the Master wanted to tear them apart with his teeth, that was up to him, but he wasn't killing anyone. He hoped he had been enough of a help that the Master wouldn't decide he needed *taken care of* too.

It was just after 9 p.m., and there was no way he would be able to sleep anytime soon. He returned his hat to his head and walked to the door. Maybe he could find a poker game to blow off a little steam before he headed off to his next assignment. Peter and the Master would no doubt send him to New Orleans, the only city on Dr. Ramsey's list that was still in the US.

Chapter 29

Handler

THE PIPE AND CIGARETTE smoke clung to the air. The thickness of it made the neon "High Roller" sign above the entrance to the high-limit poker room fuzzy like faraway headlights in a dense fog. The sound of slot machines dinged and rang in the distance. Handler watched the server's ass in her short pleated black skirt. It hung just low enough to cover her cheeks as she shimmied away from his table to retrieve yet another Jack and Coke.

He had bought into the game with $5,000 even, the payment for his most recent job. Hell of a job, that one, watching someone bite chunks of flesh off another person. It still gave him the willies. But the money was good and the victims were blood-sucking lawyers, after all.

Tonight was his night. Lady Luck was with him and he had grown his $5,000 into $25,000.

The stupid schmuck across from him had lost nearly every hand. He had bought back in three times so far, all told, about fifteen grand Handler reckoned. Served him right with his fancy clothes and Rolex watch. He might look good, but he was a crap poker player. Handler had taken him to the cleaners all evening.

The dealer shuffled once again and dealt each player two cards, placing the five cards typical of Texas Hold 'Em face down on the table in front of him. Handler chewed on the lit cigarette between his lips and turned up the edges of his cards, just enough that he could peek at them. Yes, tonight was his night. Pocket kings looked back at him. He kept his face stone sober, but inside his heart raced.

His bet. "Five thousand," he said pushing a stack of poker chips forward toward the dealer.

Two of the other players at the table called, including the schmuck, pushing forward $5,000 in chips each, and the remaining two folded.

The dealer turned over the first three cards, the six of hearts, the king of spades, and the two of diamonds. Trip kings after the flop. It just didn't get much better than that.

"I raise another five thousand," Handler said, meeting the eyes of the other two players. The first folded, but the clueless schmuck on the end called... again.

Handler laughed inside, knowing he would soon be raking in another $15,000. Easy money. It would go a long way to pay back the loans he had from his most recent streak of bad luck. But all of that had turned around tonight. He was rolling in it now.

The dealer flipped over the next card, three of clubs. Handler raised another five thousand, and the loser on the end called. The guy had bet on stupid stuff all evening and probably had a low pocket pair, maybe even the last king, but it would not beat his three beauties.

The river card was another three, this one the three of diamonds, and Handler nearly wet himself. A full house on the river, kings over threes with a healthy pot to boot. This really was his night.

"All in," he said as he pushed the remaining wall of chips he had collected forward, all $25,000 now on the table. It was all he could do not to laugh out loud. The schmuck on the end didn't have enough chips on the table to call. He motioned to his concierge and requested an additional $10,000. The concierge made a quick call and nodded to the dealer, who provided the chips. Normally Handler would have found this delay of the game annoying, but not this time. It was like watching an ATM spit out free money. After this hand, he would be up $45,000 and this poor schmuck would be wondering what hit him.

The loser received the chips and pushed them to the middle of the table to call.

Handler flipped his cards over, revealing his pocket kings. "Full house on the river, kings over threes," he gloated, banging his hand flat against the table, drawing deep on his cigarette and blowing it out.

The schmuck on the end flipped over his cards as well. "Quad threes," he said.

Handler's jaw went slack, and he felt the color draining from his face, cigarette stuck and hanging from his bottom lip. "Fuck me."

CHAPTER 30

BETH

LUC STEPPED AWAY TO gather his things from the back room of the Hall. Beth stood next to the side door, enjoying the moment and watching Luc disappear. Hearing him play had touched her heart. It wasn't just the music, but watching this gentle, handsome man glancing only at her, feeling his joy and love as he played, had nearly brought her to tears.

She waved and smiled at Dr. Giffard, who had moved across the room to talk with another of Luc's bandmates. She gestured in Beth's direction, evidently telling them who she was.

The research was difficult but moving forward faster than she'd anticipated. She found joy in working again, even if it was outside of her chosen field. They were getting close, she could feel it. She had the utmost confidence in Dr. Giffard. She and Luc would soon be either vampires who could eat and walk in the sun or humans spending whatever life they had together. She felt elated, and whether it was entirely her emotions or the shared feelings with Luc, it didn't matter. She would revel in it as long as it lasted.

But just as she completed the thought, Beth felt eyes upon her. It was more than that though. It made the hairs on the back of her neck stand up. The feeling was eerie and odd. She couldn't quite put a name to it. It was a bit familiar but still foreign. She wracked her brain for what it reminded her of while she began to scan the crowd, resisting the urge to do it at vampire speed. And just then, she had it. It was similar to when she spoke with Luc in her mind. A vampire was scanning her thoughts, or at least attempting to. She was definitely improving at the telepathy but not enough to pick up clearly where it was coming from. She quickly blocked her thoughts as best she could.

As her eyes continued painfully slowly around the room, she saw her, there in the back of the room. She was partially covered in shadow but stepped forward when Beth's eyes met hers. Lilly. She was dressed to kill in a blood-red dress that hugged every curve of her body. It rested with a thin strap over one shoulder, hugging her chest and making it obvious there was no room for a bra. She turned to the side to step in front of a man blocking her exit, revealing the back of her dress, which plunged so low that Beth was also sure she didn't have room for panties. And the worst part was she owned every inch of it.

She strode seductively toward Beth, all the while holding her gaze. While Beth would have to admit she felt just a wee bit plain in her presence, she wasn't about to show it. She put her shoulders back and straightened her back. Maybe Luc had been interested in Lilly in the past, but now it was her he wanted, and that made her feel both bolder and more confident.

When Lilly stood just inches from her, Beth met her gaze full-on.

"So lovely to see you again," Lilly said, her words like sugar but her stare like ice. "Elizabeth, wasn't it?" she said.

Beth was certain she knew her name quite well. "Janice, thank you. Cora was it? Or no, Lilly, since Luc last *left* New Orleans?" Beth knew she shouldn't be baiting her but just couldn't help herself. She saw the corners of Lilly's model-worthy smile twitch ever so slightly.

At that moment, Dr. Giffard returned to Beth's side, no doubt seeing them looking at one another a little too intently. She extended her hand toward Lilly. "Hello, I don't believe we've met. I'm Kate."

Lilly neither took her hand nor broke her eye contact with Beth. "Pleased, I'm sure."

Turning to look at Dr. Giffard, Beth said, "Kate, this is Lilly, Luc's... *old* friend. Would you mind giving us a moment?"

Dr. Giffard looked at Beth intently, and Beth was certain she was trying to read her thoughts. Beth tried to send her an "It's okay, I've got this" message. She must have at least understood the overall feeling because she nodded and stepped away, even though she did scrunch her brow.

"I'll go wait for you by the door," Dr. Giffard said.

Beth returned to level her gaze on Lilly. She had blocked her thoughts since the moment she realized Lilly was attempting to read them. She put on her best smile and said, "I assume you came to tell me something?"

If Lilly was surprised by Beth's boldness, her years as a vampire helped her keep the visible emotions at bay. Her perfectly painted lips parted to say, "Why, yes. I wanted to speak with you about Hank. To the point, *you* and Hank."

"I'm not sure what business that is of yours."

"We have been... friends... for a very long while. I know him far better than you ever will. You are just one in the line of many. And when this fling between the two of you ends, I'll be the one he comes back to."

"So if you're the one he truly wants, why would he choose to be with me? Boredom?" Beth could tell her comment hit home. Lilly's composure slipped for a split second, her nostrils flaring and her eyes flashing wide before the model-worthy smile returned.

"Boys will be boys. Sometimes they need to go slumming for a bit before they realize how good they have it."

"Yes," Beth said staring at her intently, "sometimes they do."

Beth's inference was not lost on her. This time, Lilly's eyes narrowed and the grin turned to a sneer. "Hurt him, and you won't survive your first decade as a vampire," Lilly seethed.

"I have no intention of hurting him, only keeping him."

With this Lilly huffed, a wicked grin on her lips. "Good luck with that." And she turned on her stiletto heels and swished her perfect hips toward the door. Beth didn't miss the eyes of many of the men following her backside until she left.

Beth wasn't sure if Lilly was right or wrong. She and Luc had been together such a short time. Perhaps she wasn't all he needed. And if she wasn't, she didn't know how to be more. This insecurity was new to Beth. Her lack of experience in relationships made her question herself. Maybe she was wrong to have irked Lilly since so far she had been loyal to Luc, but she had certainly asked for it.

Dr. Giffard returned to her side as she saw Lilly leave, asking with raised brows if she was okay. Beth nodded as she reached her side then turned her eyes to Luc as he returned.

"Ladies, are you ready?"

Beth smiled at Luc. She didn't know if she could keep him, but she certainly was going to try. "More than you know," she said, trying to send him emotions of love and pride to be at his side.

Chapter 31

Handler

Handler had waited across the street from Riley's apartment until she left for work. Her door opened to an outside stairwell, so it had been easy to pick the lock and enter without being seen. The apartment was a small one-bedroom. *Evidently, research doesn't pay well either.* Just inside the door, he stood between the living room and dining room, a small bar and kitchen beyond him to the left. A tiny balcony was to the right through sliding doors. There wasn't much of a view through her third-story window, but it let in a good amount of light. Ahead of him was a short hallway that opened to a bedroom at the end. There was an additional door on the right side of the hallway that he assumed was a bathroom.

Riley's place was impeccably clean and neat although a little outdated. As he stood getting a general feel for the place, he heard a soft mew. The fluffy white cat he had seen in the picture on Riley's lab desk walked down the hallway.

Handler ignored the cat as it sidled up to him and rubbed against his pant leg. But he had to step over her to head for Dr. Riley's desk. Instead of a TV and entertainment center, Riley's desk filled the wall across from the living room couch. It was completely clear apart from a laptop, a mousepad with a pink mouse, and what looked like yesterday's mail. He flipped through it—a utility bill, an envelope from

First Bank of Chicago which looked likely to be a bank statement, and a flier for hearing aids addressed to "current resident."

He plugged in the hacking device and once again texted the geek so he could access her laptop. As the computer logged in, he searched the desk drawers for anything suspicious. There were only three drawers, the top containing the usual office supplies and the bottom two holding clearly labeled files for bills, taxes, insurance, and even one labeled "WILL." A twinge of guilt hit Handler that she would likely need that soon if the Master had his way.

The second hallway door was indeed a bathroom. The medicine cabinet contained nothing interesting, not even prescription meds. There was a bottle of multivitamins but no supplements to suggest Riley was a health nut. Cleaning supplies and towels were the only items under the sink and the only two drawers held toiletries and a blow dryer. Riley was a Plain Jane in every sense of the phrase. She didn't seem like someone who would be mixed up in something involving the Master. But then, neither did Dr. Ramsey.

Moving down the hall to the bedroom, he saw a neatly made bed covered in a pastel flowered duvet with matching pillows. There was a single bedside table with a drawer and a shelf below. The shelf was piled with books, all neatly stacked. At least four were cheesy romance novels. Handler got the feeling Riley didn't get out much. Shame, she was a nice-looking woman. He would have been happy to take her for a spin if given the chance.

The cat leaped onto the bed beside him as if wondering what he was up to and mewed again. Handler reached over and stroked her back. She arched upward toward his hand. Purring and seeming satisfied with his response, she flopped down in the center of the bed and began to stretch. She was a nice cat, and he figured it would be easy for her to find a new home. He certainly didn't need a pet to care for since work often took him away from home, but he had to admit, having a little furball to greet him when he returned might be nice. But another mouth to feed on his already unbalanced budget was something he did not need.

Her closet was as dull as the rest of the apartment, her clothing almost school marm-ish in all dark colors except for a couple of white dress shirts to go with the skirts and jackets. A few sweaters were folded in a hanging drawer system. He inserted his hands in between and behind them but found nothing hidden. The gray bins above were extra seasonal clothing items and a box of old photos of Riley graduating from high school and college and a few snapshots along the way. The dresser drawers were the same, not even money hidden in her underwear and sock drawer. There was no safe, no guns and absolutely no evidence of anything relating to Dr. Ramsey's research.

Handler gave the cat a final pat on the head and left the apartment, beginning his walk to Dr. Henri's place. It was thankfully only a few blocks away. He didn't much care for walking, but it was free. He paused to light a cigarette and took a long deep drag before moving again.

Riley was as clean as they came. He didn't understand the Master's beef with Ramsey and Verde, but it must have been something horrible considering he was willing to kill them and anyone assisting them. *What could Ramsey's research hold that would make her and other doctors targets?*

He mulled over the possibilities, stepping wide around an entrance to what looked to be an empty apartment building, windows broken out and a bum sleeping near the door, one arm slung over a grimy backpack at his side. Handler figured he was probably a drunk or a druggy, neither of which he wanted to meet.

The letter from the lawyer had mentioned speed and healing. While running faster and healing more quickly could be advantages, he couldn't imagine killing over them. Considering the Master was willing to kill them all over the information, he supposed it might be better if he didn't know the specifics.

The walk took nearly twenty minutes, and as out of shape as he was, he could feel the flush of heat in his cheeks and the strain on his lungs. He was relieved when he finally reached the entrance to Henri's apartment. He stomped out his third cigarette since leaving Dr. Riley's apartment and tipped his hat low as he entered in case security cameras were mounted inside. The place had no elevator, so he had to hoof it even further up two flights of stairs, pausing to pant at the top before picking the door lock into Henri's apartment.

Henri's place was a striking contrast to Riley's. It looked like a tornado had gone through. Nearly every available surface was covered in papers, old mail, dirty dishes and coffee cups. Books were piled on the floor here and there with no discernable organization. The living room and kitchen were open, separated only by the line made by the kitchen tile and living room carpet, both a light beige in the small areas where they were visible. Handler knew he wasn't a neat freak, but this was bad, even for his standards.

Henri's apartment had a short hallway as well, but it opened into two identical bedrooms, one with a queen-sized bed and the other made into a home office. In the middle of the usual stacks on Henri's desk, Handler noticed the same empty laptop-sized space he had seen at Henri's lab. This room, however, was different than the others. Not only were there stacks of paper, but here stacks of papers had been knocked over onto the floor and spread, as though Henri had been searching for something. One of the splayed piles of paper caught his eye. It contained the Bioscience Organ Procurement logo.

Picking it up, Handler realized it was a letter to Dr. Henri "in response to his request," stating that he had received all of the samples left for him and that the depositing agency had left no additional contact information. No doubt Henri had been studying whatever samples Dr. Ramsey had provided and been looking for more.

The bedroom was in the same state of disorder, but it also appeared that Henri had left in a hurry. Apart from the dirty laundry, the drawers were pulled open and clothing hung over the edges of the drawers as if pieces had been pulled out from beneath, the overlying clothing left where it settled. Not surprisingly, the bed was unmade, but pieces of clothing were also strewn over the linens. There was a shared bathroom between the two rooms, and once again the drawers were open. Searching them, Handler noted there was no toothbrush, toothpaste or deodorant.

He had searched enough apartments to recognize the signs. Henri had left in a hurry and was now on the run. But why was he running? Since Handler had seen him in his lab the day before, he knew he hadn't run before then. Could seeing Handler in the hallway have tipped him off? He thought he'd covered well, and Henri seemed to turn back to his paperwork almost immediately after questioning him. Could the freezer alarm or his unauthorized entry into his lab have set him off? Was he monitoring it for intruders? And if so, where had he gone? A university-level scientist living in a small two-bedroom apartment wouldn't seem to have the means to run effectively on his own, or the knowledge to pull it off successfully.

Handler texted the computer geek. *Henri may have run. Can you check for credit card activity?*

The computer geek, who had already been digging through all of Henri's financial data looking for any odd transactions that could lead them to Dr. Ramsey, texted back after a few short minutes.

He purchased a flight on American Airlines at 11:45 last night. Hacking their database now.

And a few moments later: *Redeye Flight #3827 O'Hare to Tampa, Florida, landed at 3:00 a.m.*

So something, either Handler's breaking and entering or the freezer alarm, had set him off.

"Damn it!" Handler cursed. The Master was going to be pissed.

CHAPTER 32

BETH

BETH SAT AT THE computer just after rising to read the news as she always did. The *Chicago Tribune* headline read "Scientist Killed in Hit and Run."

Beth read the article text to Luc. "Dr. Julienne Riley, PhD, a researcher at Pritzker Medical School in Chicago, was killed last night on her way home from work. Dr. Riley was hit by a vehicle in an alleyway just outside her apartment building near 57th and Kimbark, around 7:00 p.m. Police say there were no witnesses to the crime and the driver of the vehicle fled the scene. Dr. Riley's body was discovered by another tenant several hours later. If you have any information about this event please call the tip line…"

Beth turned away from the computer to look at Luc, who had just entered from the bedroom to stand behind her. She felt like she just had the wind knocked out of her. Things had been going so well. "My God, Luc. Do you think it really was an accident, or could this be the Master's handiwork?"

Luc reached over her arm to move the mouse and open a couple of files. "No way to tell for certain, but there hasn't been a recording from Dr. Henri's lab for the last two days." He looked through his computer files. "I'm going to pull up footage from the day before."

The cameras they had set up in the laboratories of the scientists who retrieved the tissue samples were triggered by motion. They had long since stopped watching Dr. Riley's lab camera, checking in only periodically. After she had accessed the tissue Beth had left for her, they had followed her research for a few weeks. But there was no evidence that she had begun working on the samples.

Beth moved aside to allow Luc better access to the computer, then stood to begin pacing as she waited. Her mind raced trying to imagine how they could have been discovered. She had been so careful. She wondered if it could have been something Dr. Riley or Dr. Henri had done to draw attention.

Dr. Henri had initially studied the information Beth had provided but, to their knowledge, had never initiated animal studies. At least, if he had, it was not at his university lab. They checked in on him from time to time but hadn't seen any changes. Perhaps they'd missed something.

"Here it is," Luc said as he pulled up the last footage from Dr. Henri's lab the night before Dr. Riley's death. Beth was immediately behind him, watching over his shoulder. A recording had posted at 11:20 p.m. There was minimal lighting, but they could see a large figure enter the lab and access the resident's computer. Dr. Henri used a laptop, which didn't appear in the footage. The intruder also accessed the refrigerator and freezer. He faced away from the hidden camera, but they could easily make out the silhouette of a hat. When he had later turned to leave, the light on his face was too dim to make out facial features, but the person was clearly too large to be Dr. Henri.

Luc turned to face her as she spoke. "We need to go and see what happened. Do you think that could have been one of the Master's men?" Beth twirled her hair in her fingers, her nervous tick.

"How would they have tracked them down? The only people who

knew which scientists you contacted were the lawyers you hired, and the Master wouldn't have known about them to investigate," Luc said, turning back to the computer to look at additional footage.

Beth resumed her pacing and wracking her brain for what she thought could have gone wrong until Luc spoke. "The overseas scientists are fine; there has been no change in their schedules. I haven't been watching Dr. Royle's lab here in town since he moved without accessing the tissue samples a month ago, but I checked his lab anyway and there has been no activity since a couple of days after he left. The lab is still empty."

Beth breathed a sigh of relief but continued to search her brain. The lawyers had shredded everything she gave them at her request. She was one of many clients. They surely wouldn't remember all of the details and certainly wouldn't share them—unless they were coerced. She stopped pacing and turned back to Luc.

"Even you have said the Master's resources are nearly limitless. I covered my tracks as best I could, but maybe he found something. Let's check the Kansas City papers for anything about the lawyers."

Luc accessed the *Kansas City Star* web page and searched for the name of the lawyer she had spoken with, Henry Williamson. Beth watched over his shoulder, chewing her lower lip. The first article in the list was an obituary from about two weeks prior. Mr. Williamson, along with both of his partners, had been murdered. From the write-up, it sounded violent.

She shook her head. "It's too much of a coincidence. He found them. I have no idea how, but he did. What if he knows the location of all the scientists? And Dr. Riley wasn't even actively working on the virus as far as we could tell. Why kill her?"

Luc stood looking Beth in the eye and placed his hands on her upper arms as he spoke. "I need to go there and see what happened. I agree it is unlikely, but it could still be a freak accident and Dr. Henri may just be on vacation. We can't know any of that or who the man in the lab is from just the footage. And assuming it is one of the Master's men, there may be clues to how much the Master knows or what his next steps will be."

The thought of Luc going there alone was too much. They had come this far together, and Beth wasn't letting him go anywhere near the Master without her.

"I agree that I want to find out the details, we *need* to find out. But I don't want you to go alone. We'll be stronger together." Beth shook free of his hands and walked to the bedroom, grabbing a duffle from the closet. Luc followed close behind, sighing deeply.

"But you need to stay here with Kate. Not only would you lose time on the research, but if she is in danger, she is in no position to defend herself from the Master. She doesn't even know what he looks like. She needs you here. And I'm very careful. I can leave tonight and make the outskirts of Chicago by morning. As soon as dusk falls tomorrow, I'll investigate and be home before dawn. If I can't make it back before dawn, I will call you, stay the night somewhere safe along the way, and be back the following night."

Beth paused from her packing and looked at him. If he was concerned about Dr. Giffard's safety, why didn't they all stick together? She wasn't crazy about dragging Dr. Giffard further into this, but there was no way to know she was any safer here.

"What if all three of us go? Dr. Giffard and I could take care of the animals at the lab and then go with you."

Luc once again moved to stand in front of her, taking a pair of jeans from her hands and placing them on the bed before taking her hands in his.

"Beth, you and Kate have no experience with this sort of thing. Kate wouldn't know what to look for and would just slow us down."

We would both slow him down. Beth didn't want to admit it, but he was right about this. She was new to the Master's tactics as well as vampire life, and Dr. Giffard had almost no knowledge of them whatsoever. One vampire snooping might go unnoticed, but three, two of them novices likely to make mistakes, were far more likely to draw attention in a place where the Master was already keeping tabs.

"Okay, okay, I get it," Beth relented, dropping her head. "But if we're going to do this, please call me or text me every couple of hours so I know you're alright."

"And you the same," Luc said. "Perhaps you and Kate will have unraveled this and be ready for vampire trials by the time I return. Then we can begin the next steps of getting the information out to the world. Proof we exist and proof we will no longer be a threat."

Beth wrapped her arms around Luc's neck and pulled him to her. She had no more words and didn't know how to say what was in her heart. *I love you* just wasn't enough. It was so much more than that. He had taken what she thought was a good life and made it exceptional. Even living on the run from the Master, Beth loved every minute.

She couldn't help thinking of Lilly's words, though, and wondering if his feelings were the same and if she was enough to keep him.

CHAPTER 33

LUC

POLICE TAPE MARKED THE area where Dr. Riley had died. While the blood had been washed away, Luc could still smell the drops that bled into the cracks in the pavement along with those embedded in the brick wall above them. The force from the impact of the vehicle must have been tremendous, as it had left an indention in the brick facade. Luc didn't know how fast that suggested the vehicle had been traveling, but there were no skid marks on the pavement to suggest they had tried to stop or swerve to avoid her.

Perhaps they hadn't seen her in the dim evening light or the driver had been too drunk to notice her. While Luc wanted to believe one of these scenarios could explain the scene, he hid himself in the shadows as best he could, knowing that it could just as easily have been the Master's thugs and they might still be watching the area.

Bits of glass, also still covered in blood, littered the ground, probably from a headlight. A few strands of hair were also stuck to the brick where Dr. Riley's head had likely struck the wall. With the look of it, she would have died quickly from massive internal injuries. At least she hadn't suffered.

They had been able to find Dr. Henri's home address online using one of the paid public records search engines, but Dr. Riley's address had not been listed. The news article had given him the intersecting streets 57th and Kimbark. While there were smaller residences nearby, there was only one large apartment building. From the cross streets, the smell of blood had easily guided him. Now that he knew her scent, he could follow it from the lobby of the building to her door.

Dr. Riley's apartment was sealed with police tape and the lock had been broken, looking as though it had been kicked in. The small space was a mess. The arrangement of furniture was neat and orderly, but every drawer, cupboard and door had been opened with the contents searched and thrown to the floor. There was no TV, but it didn't look like there was a place for one rather than it having been stolen. There was a stereo and some modest jewelry, moved but cast aside. This didn't appear to be a robbery but someone looking for something in particular.

There were several scents here. That of Dr. Riley was the strongest, as one would expect. Luc could also easily smell her cat. But in the midst of it all was a heavy smell of sweat, cheap aftershave and cigarette smoke. He could track it from room to room. The remaining smells were faint, perhaps representing police looking for anything to suggest foul play as opposed to an accident, or the Master's men looking for clues to find him or Beth. But police would have been respectful of the property and not have turned the place upside down.

Luc looked for a computer but saw none, although a cord was plugged in beneath the small living room desk and strung along the floor. It looked like a computer was the only thing missing from the apartment, again suggesting the intruders had been looking for something in particular. Whoever they were, they were human but certainly could have been the Master's men.

After completing his pass through the apartment, Luc left to phone Beth, walking in the shadows and keeping to the alleys as he went. "Hi, just checking in. Is everything okay there?

"Yes, Kate and I are in the lab working. Have you found anything?" Beth answered. They hadn't discussed the death of Dr. Riley with Kate yet, and he knew if Beth was with her now, her comments would be guarded.

"I can't say if Dr. Riley's death was intentional or not, but there is no indication that the driver tried to stop or veer away from her. And her apartment has been turned upside down. It doesn't look like a robbery. Her laptop appears to be the only thing of value that is missing. Several humans have been in there recently. And if there was anything related to your research here, it's gone now."

"That doesn't sound good."

"Yeah. I need to see Henri's place. Perhaps it's unrelated and he's just away for other reasons, but it feels like the Master's work. If he is away for other reasons, we need to warn him somehow."

"Are you heading to Dr. Henri's place now?"

"Yes, I'll call you after I check it out. Stay safe."

"You too. And, Luc?"

"Yes?"

"I love you."

Luc couldn't contain his smile. "Love you too."

Luc hung up, still grinning, and ran the rest of the way. It was only a short distance, and with his speed, he was there in seconds. While Luc didn't know Dr. Henri's scent, he could smell a stench behind the closed apartment door. Upon opening it, it was clear that Dr. Henri was a slob. The dirty coffee mugs, laundry and wrappers strewn about the house were a testament to that, but his apartment had also been ransacked. The cups and other items were tossed haphazardly around the floor. Books were knocked over and lay open. And if this weren't enough, Luc could smell the same commingling of human scents with that of Dr. Henri's stronger one. And stronger than all of those, the recent scent of sweat, smoke and aftershave. The same people or person who had turned Dr. Riley's place upside down had gone through Dr. Henri's apartment.

There was little doubt it was the Master's men. How had they found these two scientists? And was Dr. Henri dead as well and had not been found, or had they taken him to question him? If so, it was likely he would never be found. Luc doubted that the police would have any clear answers, but he thought it was worth a shot. He would see if he could get any information from them before sharing the bad news with Beth.

"Excuse me. I need to report a possible missing person," Luc said, getting the attention of the officer behind the desk. Thirty-something, he looked up at Luc without raising his head. His heavy eyebrows hooded his dark eyes. They met in the middle, giving him an almost comical appearance, and he imagined Charlie Chaplin with his wiggling eyebrows doing a silly dance. His expression, however, was not nearly as entertaining.

"Has the person been missing for more than twenty-four hours?" Eyebrows asked.

"Yes, I haven't seen him since the day before yesterday. We live in the same building and I get his mail for him when he is away. I noticed his mail is piling up and he didn't ask me to get it. I also noticed his apartment door was damaged and got worried."

"So you don't know for certain that he's missing."

"No, but it is very concerning. Have you had any reports of a break-in at 1530 West Monroe, Apartment 213? The man's name is Dr. Liam Henri. He is a scientist at Pritzker."

The officer typed into his computer. "Actually, Dr. Henri was reported missing just this morning by co-workers, but there's no mention of his apartment being damaged. I will add it to the record. And what is your name?"

"Brian Hoffman." The officer's words confirmed his suspicions. Dr. Henri was not on vacation, he was missing. He had hoped there would still be a chance to save him, but there was no hope for that now.

"And how can the detectives reach you if they have questions?"

"They can reach me at 555-249-6329." Luc knew this would be suspicious when they called and realized it was either a fake number or that it belonged to someone else, but he would be long gone by then. He thought it was unlikely they would ever find Dr. Henri. While he wanted to know how the two scientists had been identified, what he really needed to know was how close the Master's men were to Kate.

CHAPTER 34

BETH

"THAT'S THE THIRD TIME you've gone over the same instructions, Beth. You need a break."

"I know. I'm sorry. I'm having so much trouble focusing tonight. I'm worried about Luc and anxious for him to be back. He should be here by now. I don't know what I'd do if something happened to him." When he was here with her, she knew he was safe. It was also easier to squelch the uncertainty about their relationship and his feelings for her when she could see his face and feel the meaning in his words. But without him, alone with her thoughts, the doubts nagged at her.

"I imagine it's difficult to be separated from someone you love so much," Dr. Giffard said, "especially if you believe they're in danger."

"It is, but it's not just that. It's... complicated," Beth said.

"Complicated?"

Beth sighed deeply, not sure what more to share. She wanted Dr. Giffard's insight, but baring her soul and her deepest worries was uncomfortable.

"It's okay, you don't need to say a word. I didn't mean to pry," Dr. Giffard said.

"You're not prying. I'm just not used to talking like this... Sharing my insecurities with someone else feels very vulnerable."

"I can understand that. I'm terrible at it too. If it helps, I have very limited experience with the opposite sex. I'm more awkward with men than I am walking, and that's saying something." Dr. Giffard grinned wide, her self-deprecation endearing and clearly an attempt to make Beth more comfortable without pressuring her. "I have all these lines from romance novels running through my head and imagine when I speak it will be like a sonnet, drawing them to me with words. But then, when I get in front of one I like, I sound like a bad version of Dick and Jane."

Beth had to smile. She knew Dr. Giffard was trying to help and decided to let it all out. "When I was human and Luc was a vampire, he was afraid to get too... intimate, because the bloodlust is so strong. Vampires often drink each other's blood when they have sex. He was afraid he would hurt me or turn me by accident."

"I never thought about that," Dr. Giffard said. "I can see why he would be worried."

"Yes, so I thought after I was turned it would be better, but now I see how closely the bloodlust is tied to arousal and I question how much of Luc's feelings for me come from the bloodlust versus his heart."

"I haven't experienced that yet, but I do know what you mean about the blood. It's almost erotic when we feed."

"Yes, so as if I needed another reason to free us from the bloodlust, I would sincerely like to know that his feelings for me are unchanged when it's gone."

"I can understand that. Personally, everything about him says he loves you and I believe he does, but I'm not in your shoes. I see why you would be concerned about that. Do you think it clouds your feelings for Luciano now?"

"I knew I loved him before the change, so I don't doubt those feelings, but the bloodlust is a strong pull. When we're close and things start to heat up, out come the fangs. I can't control it and neither can he. I'm sure I would enjoy sex with him as a vampire but I would rather know for certain that his feelings are unrelated to the bloodlust. And beyond that, the fangs still feel unnatural. I just want us both to be human so biting one another could be a playful option and not a compulsion." Beth blushed as she realized what she had said aloud. "Is that stupid?"

"Not at all. Sharing yourself with someone completely is not something you should take lightly. I think it is fair to want to know his feelings for you match your own, with or without biting." Dr. Giffard shot Beth another playful grin and then became serious, reaching out to rest her hand on Beth's. "We're going to get there, Beth, I just know it."

"Thanks, Kate, for that, but also for listening. I appreciate it." And Beth realized that for the first time, she thought of Kate simply as Kate, her friend, not Dr. Giffard her colleague.

Kate smiled warmly. "Anytime, my friend. So what do you say I fix you a drink and we get back to work?"

"Sounds great. And when we get through this, we need to go out for drinks without a blood type like normal people." Beth suddenly stopped, sitting up and smiling broadly. "Luc's almost here." It was about an hour before dawn and the grin on Beth's face showed her relief. "I'll be right back." She headed out of the lab quickly and started to run. She wanted a chance to greet Luc in private before discussing his findings with Kate.

On my way! She sent her thoughts to Luc, just as he had shared his approach with her. *Meet you in the clearing just outside of town.*

Already there. Hurry up, slow poke.

Beth pushed herself as fast as she could go. Today's daylight hours had been the first she had spent without Luc since being turned. She had napped at the lab, sleeping restlessly when she did, worrying about Luc. She couldn't wait to see him.

And moments later, Beth was there, arms wrapped around his neck, forehead to his. "Who are you calling slow?"

Luc answered with a long and deep kiss that showed her just how much she had been missed.

She was a vampire that could run at amazing speeds and had the strength of more than ten men, and yet something as simple as a kiss from Luc could turn her to jelly. She felt her fangs pushing down into her lower lip, another reminder that blood and sex were irrevocably tied together no matter how much she tried to separate the two. She thought she had worked past a bit of the uncertainty with his reactions toward her at the concert, but she just couldn't shake that little niggle of uncertainty in the back of her mind. He had tasted her blood when she was human, and she couldn't help thinking that was what somehow tied him to her now. And perhaps Lilly was right and it wouldn't be enough to keep him.

She dropped her head to nuzzle against his neck and felt him rest his head against hers.

"I'm so glad you're back. I know we're nearly immortal, but last night seemed endless." She raised her head to look into soft brown eyes above those very tempting lips.

"As much as I want to stay here, dawn is approaching and we have much to discuss with Kate. She's in more danger than we thought. We can ask her to leave with us."

"Of course. I'm just not sure she will go. She has no family, so work has been her whole life. It's not like she can just show up at any university and start working. She will lose everything she's built over the years, including her lab. I know all of that isn't worth her life, but I know exactly how she'll feel. We're so close, Luc."

Luc loosened his arms a bit so he could look her in the eye but didn't release her. Beth lowered her hands to his arms where she could feel the firm muscles of his biceps beneath his shirt. He looked at her solemnly and said, "You have given up a lot to get to this point, but here you are, still standing. Kate will get through this too. And remember, it was her choice to move forward with the research. You have to remember that. It's exactly the path you chose."

"It is." Beth sighed deeply. "We have to figure this out, Luc. So many lives have been lost or impacted by the Master and his vindictiveness."

Luc pulled her into one more slow, deep kiss, making her feel like the only other person in the world. If she still breathed, she would have been breathless when they finally parted.

Reluctantly, she lowered her arms and clasped his hands, ending their embrace. "I suppose it's time to talk with Kate."

CHAPTER 35

KATE

DAY FOUR OF THE vampire retrovirus modification. It has been three days of constant work. Dr. Ramsey and I began as soon as the sun set and worked until just before dawn. Mr. Verde has been supplying us with fresh blood both for us to feed on and also to bathe the cells we need (those infected with the vampire virus) in a constant pool of blood. But today, finally, our efforts have paid off. We have created a novel retrovirus vector from the original vampire virus and have produced enough live virus to inoculate the affected rhesus monkeys. Results to follow.

"Okay, we're as ready as we will ever be," Kate said as Luciano and Beth entered the lab. "There is enough of the new..." She paused mid-sentence and looked at both of them, eyebrows furrowed. "What should we call it, this new virus we've created?"

"Vampire-lite?" Beth said with a smirk. Kate couldn't help a chuckle that ended with a soft snort.

"Seriously, it should have a name," Kate said.

"How about the Giffard-Ramsey retrovirus," Luciano suggested, walking to the refrigerator for blood to refuel after the long trip.

Beth moved to Kate's side. "I like the name, but usually the viruses are named after the disease they cause."

"So how about the Vampyre Retrovirus, GR version 1," Kate said, smiling broadly.

"Now you're talking," Beth said, returning her smile and nodding. But the smile appeared forced.

"We have enough for three doses. Let's see if we can turn Reese back to normal," Kate said.

Beth glanced nervously at Luciano and then dropped her eyes. "Kate, there is one more problem we have to discuss."

Kate's heart fell. Things in Chicago must not have gone well.

"It was the Master, wasn't it?" Kate asked. She could tell by the looks on their faces the news was grim, their suspicions confirmed.

"I believe so," Luciano answered. She had suspected as much. She had hoped the Master would never find out about her or that they would at least have more time to finish what they had started.

Beth sat at a nearby lab bench and motioned for Luciano to join her. Kate rose from her desk and came to sit across from them, folding her hands in front of her but fidgeting with her fingers.

"I can't tell if Dr. Henri is alive or dead, but I know Dr. Riley is dead, and Dr. Henri is missing, both because of the Master," Luciano said.

"It's just too much of a coincidence that both would be in jeopardy in the same twenty-four hours. There can't possibly have been something else they were both working on that would have put them in harm's way at the same time. And as far as we could tell, they never even worked together. We're the only link," Beth added.

Luciano nodded. "Best case scenario, Dr. Henri somehow got wind of the danger and fled. But without help, a human won't get far on his own running from the Master."

Kate knew the same could be said for her, even as a vampire. She had no experience hiding from anyone. If she had to run, it would have to be with Beth and Luciano.

"If the Master does have him, I don't believe he could have enough information to lead them here. He doesn't know about any of the other scientists, not even Dr. Riley as far as we can tell," Beth said, looking between Luciano and Kate.

"How did he find them in the first place?" Kate asked. If the Master had already come for them, why hadn't he yet found her? Maybe it was possible he didn't know about her after all.

"I have been thinking about the murder of the lawyers in Kansas City," Luciano began. "If the lawyers gave them everything, including the names, why wait over two weeks before acting on it? So, maybe the lawyers remembered some of the cities but not the names. With everything shredded, they would have to rely on memory, and the names of eight scientists would be hard to recall. What if the Master knows some or all of the locations but not the names and it's taking him time to track them down?"

Time, Kate liked the sound of that, and it made sense. Unless the Master was watching them to see what they knew, waiting for his moment. She decided to keep it to herself until she heard the rest of their thoughts.

Beth began nodding in response to Luciano's comments, her hand at her chin, elbow on the countertop. "That's a good thought. And if they had located you, Kate, or suspected we were here, why would they risk tipping their hand by taking out Dr. Riley and Dr. Henri rather than attacking all of us at once?"

Beth stood, pacing as she always did when thinking. She had told Kate before that she thought better when moving, like when she ran. Her pacing made Kate even more jittery, though, and she began to gnaw on a fingernail.

Beth gestured with her hands as she spoke and turned. "Peter has to be involved too. With no insight into which type of scientist would be useful, the Master would be killing randomly. But Peter would know as well as I do which specialties could help unravel the details about this virus. That would narrow the search. But there are more than thirty virologists and geneticists in Chicago alone. I checked. It would draw too much attention to start killing them all. How would they narrow it down to just those two?" Beth began twirling a lock of her hair.

"I believe they took Dr. Riley's computer. If they have Dr. Henri, they will have his too. I've never seen an image of him without it. If so, they may have found the email you sent them," Luciano said.

"Email?" Kate asked. "What email?" She had received an anonymous email shortly after she had withdrawn the samples Beth had stored for her at the tissue bank, but she hadn't known what it meant. It contained only an address, nothing else.

Beth returned to the table and sat across from Kate. "I sent the same email to each scientist that retrieved the samples I stored for them. It contained only an address. I hoped the scientists would put it together and reach out if they needed more samples. But I sent that from a new dummy Gmail account from a computer in a public library in North Carolina. The address is to a mail service, paid for in cash under a false name, that scans in anything I might receive. It emails it to another Gmail account that I never access from my own computer, or even the same computer twice, for that matter. There is no way the Master could trace that. Even if he knew I had set up the mail service, I don't see how he could use that to find us—wait." She raised her hands in front of her for emphasis.

"The computers. What about the computers?" she said, turning to look at Luciano. "Peter and the Master must have had someone hack into my dentist's files to get copies of my dental records. He'd matched my dental films to the fake ones I took to put in your file. What if they hacked each of the virologists' and geneticists' computers in the Chicago area to search for files related to the virus?" Beth said.

Kate replied, "That would take a long while." She raised a finger and tapped her chin. "What about the tissue banks? Peter was your pathology partner, right? Wouldn't he know they would need tissue or blood for their research? There are very few tissue banks in each city. If they hacked those records and then matched them with the virologists and geneticists in town, that would narrow it down in a hurry. They could probably even tell if they had accessed the samples."

Nodding his agreement, Luciano said, "That makes sense. It would allow them to narrow the field more quickly."

Beth added, "There are ten tissue banks in the Chicago area, but half of them are specialty centers only taking a few specific tumor or tissue types. So they could narrow it even further and search from afar with no one the wiser until they got a hit on a single geneticist and virologist. Since Peter would have narrowed the field of scientists to search for, it would be very simple as soon as a hacker gained access."

"So assuming the lawyers gave the Master the cities, and knowing that Dr. Riley died fourteen days after the lawyers did, they are moving quickly," Kate said. "If it were me, I would work through the US cities first because they're closer and have more familiar systems. That means they will turn their attention here next."

Kate paused and closed her eyes. They were so close. She couldn't stop now. There was no telling how long it would take for her to pick the research up again. They would need a new lab with new equipment that was crazy expensive, and they would have to get it all without being seen by the Master's watchful eyes. The high-level equipment alone was rare enough, made by only a handful of companies worldwide, that it could easily be tracked, not to mention the highly specific reagents they would need could be tracked as well. Here the orders were routine, but a new lab or a lab newly ordering them would raise eyebrows.

"We don't have much time, Kate. We all need to leave at sunset and live to fight another day," Luciano said.

"Leave now? We can't leave now. I don't have access to another lab and everything we need is *right here*," Kate replied, sitting back in her chair and crossing her arms in front of her chest.

Beth gave Luciano a knowing sideways glance. "I understand how you feel. I had to leave my practice behind. But you've almost lost your life to this virus once. We can't let the Master finish the job. Perhaps another of the scientists will open their lab to us to continue with their help."

Kate shook her head. That was easier said than done and Beth knew it. Plus, even if they did take the time to recruit another scientist and get them to agree to let them continue in their lab, what was to say the Master wouldn't be tracking all the capable labs by then? And, selfishly thinking, she and Beth would have to share claims to the research with another scientist after having nearly completed it themselves.

"A few more days, that's all we need, I can feel it—just a few more days. Once I have the solution, it will be easier to find a place to just reproduce it. But we have Reese ready *right now* to test. At least let me try to inoculate him," Kate pleaded.

Beth and Luciano shared a final glance. "One more day," Luciano conceded. "We are stuck here for the daylight hours already now that the sun has risen. Test the new virus on Reese. We should know by tomorrow if it works or not."

The previous day, they had inoculated Rhonda, a second rhesus, with the original Vampyre retrovirus. She had risen with all the effects of the full virus. After nearly a unit of blood, quite a lot for such a small animal, she had calmed and began to respond to them normally. Like Reese after the initial infection, it appeared the little monkey had incorporated all the viral genome into her DNA. They had collected tissue and blood samples from the monkeys that they might need down the road and frozen them.

"We should inoculate Rhonda as well. We had planned to wait and only test her after the results from Reese were complete, but time is not a luxury we have," Beth said.

That meant this version one of the retrovirus had better be perfect. Kate sent up a little wish that it was. "Okay, one more day," Kate agreed. "Let's do it."

Beth picked up the video camera and trained it toward Reese to get a video of the process. Both Reese and Rhonda were very tame, and Kate held Reese and cooed to him as she gave him the injection. He accepted it, only withdrawing slightly with the first prick of the needle.

Passing the camera to Kate, Beth removed Rhonda from her cage and held her. Rhonda seemed intent on grooming Beth, slowly picking up and smoothing small strands of her hair. Beth returned the affection, gently stroking Rhonda's small back and whispering to her that she was such a sweet little girl. And assuming the version one virus did its job, Rhonda would be back nearly to her old self in a few short hours.

Beth handed Rhonda to Luciano so she could use both hands. She unsheathed the needle and placed her thumb on the tip of the plunger.

"Here we go, Rhonda. One little poke—"

But Rhonda, seeing the needle, shrieked and kicked at Luciano.

Caught off guard, the kick knocked his arm back into the needle in Beth's hand. The momentum pushed both her hand and Luciano's arm back into her chest, depressing the plunger and depositing the contents into Luciano's forearm. As he righted himself and withdrew his arm, the empty syringe fell to the floor.

"Oh my God," Kate whispered, staring at the syringe.

Beth sat heavily in the chair beside her, nearly missing it and looking as though she would vomit. She raised her hands to cover her face.

Luciano, seeing the needle on the floor, looked back to Beth and reached out to her, placing his hand on her shoulder. "It was an accident. I should have held her more tightly."

Beth's head jerked up. "No, this is my fault. I should have been more careful and sedated her. Just because Rhonda had been calm until now didn't mean she would continue to be. She's a monkey. It's my fault." Her eyes were wild, bewildered. Kate could see the emotions as they crossed her face even if she couldn't yet feel them and didn't know what to say.

The virus had to be perfect. They had to have gotten it right.

Please let us have gotten it right.

Chapter 36

Luc

"Reese and Rhonda's temperatures spiked around six a.m. then came down around eleven a.m. Since then, their temperatures have held steady at what would have been their previously normal body temperatures," Beth said, recording the results on the clipboard at Reese's side. She had been working at top speed, non-stop, since he had been injected.

Luc sat at a lab table across from her, preparing samples and chemicals in case they were needed for further testing, but she didn't meet his eyes. He could feel the tension rolling off of her.

It was an accident and he knew it. Beth knew it too, but convincing her that it wasn't her carelessness that caused it was another matter. He could tell she was beside herself with guilt. Sure, he was concerned about it, not having intended to be a guinea pig, but he trusted Kate and Beth and their abilities. Three hundred years had made him less reactive when things went sideways. This wasn't the first time his life had been in danger, and yet, here he still was.

He had seen for himself the work they had done on the monkeys and believed there was a very good chance he would soon be free of the bloodlust and sun sensitivity. And if things didn't go as planned, who could be better than Beth and Kate to fix it?

Kate sat at her desk, going through what Luc knew was another set of data to analyze everything they could about the original virus and the new VR, GRv1 virus. She was as intense as Beth and wouldn't stop until she had as much information as she could possibly gather in case changes were needed.

"Do you think it worked?" Luc asked, trying to make conversation with her and not knowing what to say to make her more comfortable.

"The temperature spike suggests they were infected and the return to a normal body temperature is a good sign," Beth answered, still focusing on the clipboard. "I think we're ready for testing."

"Just let me get a drink first. I'm starving," Kate said. She walked to the refrigerator and grabbed a bag of O-positive. "I really miss coffee," she said with a deep sigh. Luc appreciated the attempt at lightheartedness even though her voice still sounded tense.

"If this worked, it may not be long before we can all try a cup," Luc said and then frowned. "I have no memory of the taste, though I'm certain I drank it."

"So what will you try first, if you're no longer dependent on blood?" Kate asked Luc.

"I'm not sure," he said. "It's been so long, I don't remember the flavor of any of the human foods. I have seen many commercials about french fries, and I know I once enjoyed fried potatoes. Perhaps that would be a good start."

"Beth, what about you?" Kate asked.

"M&Ms for me," she answered. "I used to eat them nearly every day."

Luc smiled at her, even though she barely glanced up, remembering her love for them and how pleased she was when he brought her a bag the night of their first kiss. He would bring her a bag every day for the rest of their lives if they got through this.

Kate finished most of her unit of blood in under a minute and poured the few remaining cc's into two small bowls for Reese and Rhonda. Beth gathered the UV light and prepared to test Reese for sensitivity.

"Well, let's see if Reese and Rhonda still share our taste for blood," Kate said.

Luc manned the video camera, watching intently. His muscles tensed in anticipation, and he said a quick prayer that it had worked. At least the monkeys looked fine, so even if they were still vampires and unaffected by the new virus, the pressure on Beth would be lessened.

Kate set one bowl of blood in Reese's cage. He wandered over to it, sniffed it, and turned away. Beth and Kate shot one another wide-eyed glances. To Luc, their expressions were comical, especially with all his nervous tension. He couldn't stifle his smile, but the excitement over their possible success kept him focused on the task at hand.

Beth turned on the UV light, being careful to angle it away from them, and ever so slowly brought the beam of light close to Reese. Having felt its burn before, Reese moved away from the stream of light but soon ran out of room in the cage to escape. The light hit his back foot, and he cooed nervously. Beth jerked it away quickly in case it burned him, but nothing happened. Her eyes were wide and riveted on his foot. She brought the light back to his foot and held it. Thirty seconds passed and still no flames. She swung the light so that his full body was exposed to it. Still nothing.

"Fantastic!" Kate breathed. Her excitement was clear as a look of relief across Beth's face.

Luc could barely contain his own joy over their success. He hoped this meant Beth would now relax and forgive herself for the accident. "Let's see if he can tolerate normal food now," he said, lowering the camera for a moment to get a banana from the supply of fruits and vegetables for the other animals in the lab.

With the camera again recording, Luc handed half of the banana to the little monkey. Reese took it, smelled it, and then took a small bite. He seemed pleased with the taste and continued eating in large mouthfuls until the banana was gone.

"Until now, he's refused anything but blood. We'll have to wait to see if he holds it in, but I would say that is a *very* good sign," Kate said.

Beth was nearly giddy, and her eyes looked damp as tears of relief threatened. She wrapped an arm around Kate and the other around Luc and squeezed. Then she turned to Luc, wrapping her arms around his neck and nuzzling her cheeks, now wet with tears, into his chest.

It's going to be alright, Beth. You did it.

Beth nodded against his chest in response to his thoughts and he could feel her relief.

Luc thought his heart would beat right out of his chest. He was so proud of Beth and her unrelenting focus on a cure. He realized he hadn't allowed himself to truly believe she would find a cure. And now, with the answer in hand, hope for a normal human life washed over him.

He wrapped his arm around Beth and pulled her closer.

CHAPTER 37

BETH

"REESE'S LAST SET OF vitals still look good. His liver enzymes were up slightly with the last draw, along with his blood sugar, but only barely above normal. Similar findings in Rhonda," Beth told Kate as she reviewed the last printout from the chemistry analyzer. Additional testing on Reese and Rhonda had shown that all of their other abilities were intact and that, when they used their strength or speed, their energy requirements spiked substantially. They nearly inhaled the food they were given and begged for more. But a diet nearly triple a normal rhesus caloric intake seemed to hold them for most activities.

Luc watched their progress intently, helping where he could. Though they were monitoring him closely, he hadn't yet shown any signs of infection. But the dose he received had been so small for his size compared with that of the monkeys they couldn't predict when it would kick in or even if it would, considering the differences in their DNA.

"The liver enzyme spike could have something to do with their increased metabolism," Beth offered. "I'll draw another set in a few hours to compare. He's been playing calmly since the last draw. Perhaps we will see a spike with each burst of speed or strength that normalizes when they slow to normal speed."

"I've been thinking about that too," Kate said, leaning back against one of the lab benches and crossing her arms. "He's undergone some major changes, and he may have some significant alterations to his nutritional requirements. We will need to draw blood after a few days to look for early deficiencies in vitamins and minerals that he may burn through more quickly than usual. I'm not entirely sure what to expect. I would assume that his increased speed and strength would tax the muscles, so an increased intake of calories and protein to replace what he uses would make sense. But the truth is, I don't know how much his physiology is altered. If it could handle all his bodily functions with only blood for fuel before, maybe the efficiencies of his metabolism will remain and the increased calories will be enough. It's just too early to guess."

Luc leaned forward in his chair, elbows on the table and hands folded in front of his chin. "The monkeys seem completely healthy. We agreed to one more day. We've had it, along with success. The sun will set soon, and as much as I like Reese and Rhonda, how are we going to run with them in tow? Three vampires and two rhesus monkeys are going to be difficult to hide. I'm injected, the new virus should be in my blood. You can study it more from my blood after we are reestablished," Luc said.

Beth put down the paperwork she'd been examining and moved to sit next to him. "Okay, you're right about traveling with the monkeys. Maybe we can stash or carry tissue samples from them when we do leave. But Master or no Master, I won't risk leaving the lab with you until I'm certain the new VR virus is safe or that you're not going to change from its effects," Beth said.

"How many tests will be enough, Beth?" Luc said, opening his hands and gesturing with his palms up to emphasize the question. "It could take weeks or months for you to be confident in the results. We don't have that kind of time."

Beth couldn't begin to consider leaving at this point. There were just too many unknowns, and Luc's life was on the line. Just because two monkeys looked okay didn't mean he would be.

"Maybe we could wait just a few more days, Luciano, at least until we know if you're going to be infected," Kate said. "We could inject multiple animals and see if we get the same results while we're here. We would still need long-term studies before we used it on anyone else, but there would be time for that later. And I believe you when you say the Master is powerful, but so are we. And there are three of us; it isn't like Dr. Riley by herself and being fully human. If they are hunting down scientists, they will be expecting me, human and alone. Doesn't that give us an advantage?"

"It is far too big a risk," Luc answered.

"But so is leaving now and having you get sick along the way, Luc," Beth said. "Kate's dose was small like yours and it took her a few days to change. We didn't have anything to test with then, but since we know the differences between the virus we made and the original, we should be able to test your blood and see if it's circulating. Maybe we can even get a titer to see if it's increasing, decreasing, or staying the same. In a couple of days, we should be able to tell if the new virus will take hold or if your immune system stops it before it can."

"I don't know if we have one day, let alone two. Either way is a risk, and I would rather risk my changing along the way than all three of our lives," Luc said, his gaze intent and going back and forth between Beth and Kate.

Kate walked to sit next to Beth, and both dug in with their arms crossed in front of their chests.

"I'm sorry, Luc. I understand, but I love you and I'm not going anywhere," Beth said.

"Me too... well, the not going anywhere part, you're my friend... you know what I mean," Kate said.

"The two of you are impossible," Luc said.

Beth hated going against his wishes, but the choice just made sense.

She supposed it was his turn to pace and said nothing as he made slow laps around the room waiting for sunset. Beth and Kate sat quietly, entering the most recent results into their notes. Beth could feel Luc was upset with her. She struggled to think of what she could say to make him better understand her point of view.

As the sun finally set, Luc announced, "I need some air."

"Let me get a blood sample, please, before you go," Beth said. Luc, looking none too pleased, sat on the benchtop next to her and waited for her to gather the supplies and return.

"Luc, I'm sorry you're upset. I know you're willing to risk your life for me, but you have to accept that I will also risk mine for you without hesitation. If we left now and something went wrong that I could have fixed by having access to this lab, I couldn't live with myself. I'm not trying to be reckless and I'm not being stubborn about finishing the new virus. I'm just not willing to risk the man I love."

Luc, who had been avoiding her eyes and radiating anger, exhaled deeply and looked at her from beneath his lashes. His eyes softened from the irritation they held earlier. She felt the anger dissipate as she finished the blood draw.

She offered him a hesitant smile, which he returned.

"Beth, you need to take a look at this," Kate said from across the room. She stood in front of Reese's cage, staring intently. Beth thought it strange she would interrupt the moment and figured it must be important.

"What is it?" Beth asked as she appeared at her side.

"Does Reese look different to you?"

After studying him for a moment Beth answered, "Are those white hairs on his chin?"

"Yes. I don't remember them being there before," Kate said, furrowing her eyebrows and glancing at Beth.

"How are his vitals?" Beth asked, trying to keep her anxiety at bay and gather all the information she could.

"Stable. He hasn't eaten in the last hour after munching on his fruit pretty regularly, but otherwise no change."

"Let's take a look at Rhonda," Beth suggested.

Beth scoured Rhonda with her eyes and then glanced back at Kate. "I know those white hairs weren't there before. And does she look like she has a little less muscle mass to you?"

"I was thinking the same thing," Kate answered. "They look like they're aging."

Beth looked across the room at Luc, her forehead creased. She chewed her lip but said nothing. She could see the concern mirrored in his own face and feel panic clawing at her mind but fought it back down. Losing her cool would not help anyone. She needed to continue to look at this logically and methodically as she always did with the problems she faced. Luc's life could very well depend on it.

Chapter 38

Beth

"I've started sequencing both their DNA and the circulating virus," Kate said. "We need to try to see where the stop codons were inserted, or if something was rearranged when they incorporated the changes. We must have turned off a repair gene, and so increased cell death, or somehow upregulated a tumor suppressor gene that is causing them to age rapidly. There are so many genes that could have been affected." She shook her head. She was at the computer again, poring over data as soon as it came off of the instruments. "I'm going to try to identify the stop codons we added within the rhesus DNA and look near those first. Hopefully, one will be affecting a known gene and make it obvious where we went wrong. But it's going to take time, even if we do get lucky."

Beth had busied herself with whatever she could, but as the hours had passed, she had watched as both Reese and Rhonda began to show decreased white blood cell counts and mild anemia. They began to sleep more and were less active when awake. Their fur continued to turn more white and they showed more evidence of muscle wasting. Reese even lost one of his canines. All of the changes pointed to one thing: rapid aging. And as the findings mounted, Kate and Beth began to monitor Luc more and more closely. Beth prayed the changes were only because they were primates and not human, but the knots in the pit of her stomach told her differently.

"I was thinking the same thing. We need to identify it before we lose Reese and Rhonda so we can test it. Otherwise, we will be shooting in the dark until we can replicate the whole experiment." Beth was already anxious about staying in the lab during daylight hours with the Master on the hunt, and now thinking of being here long enough to replicate the process up to this point so they would have another monkey to test was beyond stressful. She kept trying to refocus on her work. Kate and Luc needed her to be fully engaged, but she felt like she was on the verge of an anxiety attack. She didn't think her already rapid heartbeat could go faster, but it did.

Beth had been waiting impatiently for Luc's most recent viral counts and nearly ripped them from the printer when it started to spit them out. She closed her eyes, took a quick centering breath, and opened them.

Her heart sank.

His viral count was rising. Any hope that he might fight it off and not make the change was gone. The virus was replicating. They had to work faster and pray that his DNA was different enough not to be affected in the same way Reese and Rhonda were.

Beth looked up from the paper to see both Kate and Luc watching her. She supposed they could tell from her face it wasn't good news. "Your titer is up, Luc. The virus is replicating."

Luc had been feeding some of the lab animals and continued cutting pieces of apple and banana into bite-size chunks. "We knew that would probably be the case. Nothing has changed. Until I know how the virus is going to affect me, I'm going to focus on what I can do right now."

Beth pursed her lips and nodded. His words were calm and logical. Beth knew he was blocking his emotions from her right now to keep her from worrying, as he had before. But not sharing them was almost worse as she imagined the turmoil beneath.

"Maybe we should go ahead and inoculate Reed," Beth said, looking back to Kate. They had one remaining rhesus they had been saving for the end when they hoped to give him just the new VR, GRv1 virus to see if they could produce all of the positive effects in an uninfected host who had not been previously infected with the original Vampyre virus.

"I agree," Kate said. "Once we fix this, and don't have time constraints, we can circle back around. If we give him the original Vampyre virus now, we can give him the version one virus in eighteen to twenty-four hours, maybe less, and test with the next version of the virus another twenty-four after that. Hopefully, we will have version two complete by then."

"How long until we start to get the initial sequencing data?" Beth asked.

Kate gave Beth a somber look. "About eight hours."

Beth turned her gaze fully on Reed, knowing that if she looked at Luc, she couldn't hide the fear in her eyes. She did her best to keep her thoughts shielded but knew Luc would pick up on her emotions. She hadn't learned to completely hide them from him yet. She walked toward the refrigerator, retrieved a vial of the original Vampyre virus along with a syringe, and drew up a full dose.

She had been so angry with herself when Luc had been injected, then elated when the monkeys survived and had the desired effects. But when the aging changes had begun in Reese and Rhonda, it all had been replaced by fear. The roller coaster of emotions over such a short time left her feeling raw. And the watching and waiting in between testing rounds, leaving her with her thoughts, was the worst kind of torture.

Beth gathered Reed into her arms and injected him with the original Vampyre virus before returning him to his reinforced cage. Kate had begun making up more of the faulty VR virus to use for Reed if need be and for further study. Maybe they could learn as much from the failure as they would the success.

CHAPTER 39

PETER

"WHAT HAVE YOU FOUND?" Peter asked. He stretched back in his desk chair and placed his socked feet on his desk. It was finally Alex Freeman, the hacker who had been helping sift through the tissue bank files in the New Orleans area.

"I believe I've found them. I cross-referenced the list of docs you gave me with the databases of the tissue banks. It took a while given the size of the databases, but finally, two names have hit. Got a pen?"

Peter leaned forward and gathered a pen and legal pad from his top desk drawer.

"Go."

"Dr. Kathryn Giffard and Dr. Dwight Royle. Looks like only Dr. Giffard accessed the samples. The tissues in Dr. Royle's name are still there. Also, he's left the city. I'm gathering information on where he went and will send it to you as soon as I have it."

Peter was certain the Master wouldn't care if they had accessed the tissues or not. If the scientist was dead, he wouldn't have access and neither would anyone else.

"There was no other information about who may have deposited the tissue there. It only listed the law firm as the sender."

"I expected as much. Did you find anything under Dr. Ramsey's name?"

"No, nothing." Peter hadn't expected Beth to be that careless, but she was new to all of this and you never knew what mistakes she might make.

"After you track down Royle, focus on Rome next."

"That's going to take some time. The systems overseas are a lot different from our own and the records will be in Italian."

Excuses, Peter thought, *always excuses.* Or perhaps he was trying to give reasons for increasing his fees. The Master would look poorly on that.

"Shall I tell my employer you are unable to fulfill your agreed-upon duties in a timely manner?"

"No, certainly not," Alex stammered. "I was just saying it may take me a few more days than the US hacks, that's all."

Peter smirked, hearing the fear in the man's voice. *That should nip his objections in the bud.*

"I'll be expecting your call." Peter began to hang up but heard Alex yelling for him to wait. "What?" Peter barked.

"This may be nothing, but I've also been researching anything related to the trust that held Mr. Verde's Kansas City home. There was mention in one of the older documents of a Luke Green as a beneficiary and funds were transferred to a bank in New Orleans. Property records in New Orleans show a house there in the Quarter, on 934 Barracks Street, purchased under that name with the deed later transferred to a Hank Green."

"Is that all?" Peter asked, scribbling the address onto the legal pad.

"Yes." The word was barely completed before Peter hung up. He considered the name and address Alex had given him. *Verde*, he was pretty sure that meant green in Spanish. A quick check on the computer told him it meant green in Italian too. The Master would surely send him in after Handler confirmed the information on Dr. Giffard. While he could send in Handler, something he had done in Chicago had spooked Dr. Henri and they still hadn't tracked him down. Mr. Verde wasn't stupid, and Peter didn't want to take any chances of Handler spooking him too if he and Beth were there. Peter decided to keep this bit of information to himself to look into when he made the trip. If he tracked them down himself, it would earn him a bit more favor in the Master's eyes, perhaps the last he needed for the Master to turn him.

He picked up his phone and called Handler. At least calling him, he couldn't smell him. Just the thought of that made Peter grimace.

"Handler," Peter heard from the other end of the line.

"We have the names of the next two scientists in New Orleans. Ready?"

He heard Handler rummaging for a pen. "Ready."

"Dr. Kathryn Giffard, Kathryn with a 'k' and a 'y,' Giffard, G-i-f-f-a-r-d. Dr. Dwight Royle, R-o-y-l-e. Giffard is still in the city but Royle has left. Take the next flight out and get all the information we need to make contact with Giffard and anything that remains there on Royle. Keep watch for any information on Dr. Ramsey and Mr. Verde as well. New Orleans is the only remaining US city on the list, so chances are, if they're still in the country, they may be close by to keep tabs on Giffard."

Peter imagined, not for the first time, what Dr. Ramsey looked like as a vampire. She was alluring before, and he imagined her features had been accentuated by the change. He knew the Master would want her dead if he caught her, but perhaps, if Peter was changed, he could find a use for her acceptable to the Master, perhaps as his personal slave. Surely the Master would find pleasure in that. He had never been into sharing, but for Beth, he would consider it.

"Got it. I'll check this out, but I don't work outside the US. You know that, right?"

"You can discuss that with the Master if he requires your services any further when this job is completed." Peter knew the Master had him by the balls. His gambling debts kept him vulnerable. If he needed money badly enough, he would go where the Master sent him, US or not. But he also knew Handler's refusal to finish the job in Chicago had not set well with the Master, and Handler refusing to take another job would likely mean the end of him.

Peter hoped the next one smelled better.

"Text me when you arrive."

Peter hung up the phone and stood, stretching before pulling on his suit jacket and shoes. The Master preferred to receive information in person, so he would be making a trip to his compound. Peter knew the Master preferred to look people in the face and suspected he could read their thoughts to some degree, something he couldn't do over the phone. It also allowed him to "deal" with problems immediately.

Peter would be sure to share Handler's objections with him.

CHAPTER 40

LUC

IT HAD BEEN ALMOST forty-eight hours since Luc had been injected. He watched as Kate and Beth continued to work at sequencing the monkeys' DNA and creating more of the faulty virus he had been injected with. The monkeys were continuing to age, becoming more feeble by the hour.

Luc knew the dose he had received was small and that Kate thought this might mean he would be slower to change. But his titers were up. It was affecting him now and he knew it. For the last hour, he had begun to feel feverish and achy, feelings he had not experienced since he had been turned three hundred years before.

He vaguely remembered being sick as a human, but it had been so long he couldn't remember it with any detail. The virus was making him sluggish, and his head began to swim. He needed to lie down but couldn't rise from his seat. A wave of exhaustion rocked him as he tried and he started to fall from his chair. Beth was immediately at his side.

"Luc, are you okay?" she said with a shaking voice, her eyes wide. He could hear her heart racing and feel her fear.

"I'm just a little woozy."

"And you're burning up."

"The virus is kicking in," Kate said, already at his side and placing the tympanic thermometer in his ear. "104."

Beth and Kate nearly carried him to a cot they had added near Kate's desk to grab a rest now and then while working through the daylight hours.

Beth was gone and back again in seconds with a small basin of cool water and a rag. She began wiping his forehead and neck. The cool water felt like ice. He began to shake with chills. He was so exhausted even those could not keep him from closing his eyes.

"I love you." It was all he could say before beginning to drift off. As he did, he heard Beth's voice from far away.

"I know."

Chapter 41

PETER

"Enter," the Master said.

Peter opened the door and strode to face the Master across his desk. The Master sat with a sword on his lap. It was a sword that Peter had seen a hundred times before. It typically hung on a rack on the wall next to the Master's desk. It was a longsword and shone with a brilliant silver blade. The hilt was also silver, but the grip was wrapped in what looked like old but well cared for leather. The pommel was a smoothed corner triangle and engraved with intricate swirls. The center of the blade contained the same swirled pattern ending about an inch from a sharply pointed tip. The Master polished it with gentle strokes, his eyes squinted at the corners, lost in thought.

"We located both scientists in New Orleans. The geneticist, Dr. Dwight Royle, doesn't appear to have accessed the tissue specimens. He resigned from his position there and moved to a new lab in North Carolina. He does not appear to be involved. The virologist, Dr. Kathryn Giffard, did access the stored samples. I've sent Handler to New Orleans to investigate and should hear from him in twenty-four to forty-eight hours depending on his flight," Peter said.

The Master placed the sword and rag on the desk, pushing aside an open file containing an 8 x 10 photo of Handler hunched over what looked like a poker table, cards in hand, cigarette hanging from the corner of his mouth.

"Good. As soon as he locates her and identifies the best access point, send a team to kill her. Then focus on further investigating Dr. Royle before moving overseas. I want no loose ends."

Peter nodded. He had assumed as much.

"Handler says he only works in the US," Peter said. "I think he wants to make it clear he has no intention of going to Italy or Australia to further the investigations there."

"I have more than enough evidence of his previous activities to convince him otherwise." The Master motioned to the file on his desk. "No matter, anyway. He is approaching the end of his usefulness."

"Do you keep a file like that on all your... associates?" Peter asked. He knew he was being bold, but the Master had raised him as his own. Surely he deserved a little insight.

"I do. *All* of them," the Master commented, leveling a gaze at Peter that made his skin crawl.

"I suppose that is an excellent business strategy," Peter answered, trying to look nonplussed.

The Master rose, closed the file, and walked to a row of file cabinets on the far wall.

"I assume there is no word of Dr. Ramsey or Mr. Verde?"

"No, nothing as yet. You will know the moment I hear anything." Peter glanced back at the file on Handler and couldn't help but think about Beth's words to him when she'd been captured. She told him the Master was using him and would dispose of him the moment he was no longer useful. He knew that was true of Handler and many before him, but surely the Master wouldn't treat him as poorly. He had promised to change him when he had proven himself ready, and he had served him loyally. Still, Peter's eyes wandered to the file cabinet.

He couldn't help wondering what might be in his file. He had done some questionable things out of fealty to the Master. Would he have kept a record of those to use as ammunition against him?

"Master, you have raised me as your own. And I serve you with the loyalty of a son. I have and will continue to work tirelessly to achieve your goals," Peter said, staring at the Master's back.

"But?" the Master said, turning to face him.

"I believe I could serve you better if you changed me. With the gift of your strength, I could hunt down Mr. Verde and your other enemies myself and rid you of them." Peter watched as the Master returned to his desk and picked up the longsword, turning it slowly in his hands.

"This gift, as you call it, comes with a heavy burden." The Master's eyes were once again tight, lost in thought.

"I believe I am ready."

"I know you do. But I will decide when the time is right. And as for Luciano, when you locate him, I will take care of him myself. There will be no more mistakes."

Peter winced at the word *mistakes*. He knew the Master meant his failure to burn Mr. Verde alive at his first attempt. But hadn't it been the Master who had lost him the second time? His need to exact revenge by watching Mr. Verde kill Beth had backfired. That mistake was on him. Peter had given him Mr. Verde as he had been asked.

Again Beth's words echoed in his head. Was the Master truly intending to turn him, or merely stringing him along until he, too, had outlived his usefulness?

Chapter 42

BETH

EVERY MOMENT SEEMED TO last a day. Over the past four hours, Beth had left Luc's side only long enough to examine the rhesus monkeys and record findings. Kate worked at vampire speed to continue to sequence both the faulty version one virus as well as Reese's DNA.

Luc's temp had remained near 104 for four hours, and most of that time he had been unconscious. Beth had tried her best to remain objective. She took Reese's temp and began to write it on the clipboard beside his cage only to see she had just recorded his temp minutes before and forgotten. She walked to the sink and splashed water on her face before returning to Luc's side. Except for an hour here and there, she and Kate had been up and working for at least forty-eight hours. Physically, she felt fine. Mentally, she could tell it was taking a toll. But she had no time for rest now.

As she looked at Luc, she noticed there were beads of perspiration on his forehead. Odd, because vampires didn't sweat. She checked his temp once again and found it was 101. His fever was breaking. She bowed her head near him and sent prayers of thanks for his life but also that the rapid aging that was plaguing the rhesus wouldn't affect him.

While her head was still bowed, she heard Luc say, "Don't give me last rites just yet."

Beth's head snapped up to look him in the eyes. He still looked weak, but he was alive and with her.

As much as she tried to hold them back, tears welled in her eyes, one escaping and falling down her cheek. She leaned forward, pulling him into a bear hug that would have squashed a normal human. He was with her, she still had a chance to spend her life with him. Her arms began to tremble as some of the stress and worry began to leave her.

"Hey, it's okay. I'm okay."

She closed her eyes and felt Luc's hand, warm on her cold skin, gently stroke her cheek.

Kate was immediately at his side as well. "Decide to stop sleeping on the job?" While a smile was spread across her lips, her eyes still showed her concern.

"That was a rough one," Luc answered as he began to sit up.

"Take it slow, Luc. Your fever has lessened, but that doesn't mean you're through the change yet," Beth said.

He threw his legs over the side of the cot and sat up, wobbling just a bit as though his head was still swimming, but then righted himself. He stretched his arms and reached up to his face to wipe his forehead before looking at his hand.

"I'm sweating?"

"Yes, I noticed that too," Beth answered.

He rose slowly to his feet and stretched again. "I actually feel pretty good... very well, in fact." He looked at Beth and then did a lap around the lab at vampire speed, causing a pile of papers on Kate's desk to fly into the air before returning just as quickly to face Beth. He said, "That feels the same."

Can you still hear me? he asked.

Yes! Beth responded telepathically. *You?*

Loud and clear.

"Maybe it didn't work. Maybe it made me sick but my body fought it off."

"Feel up to some additional testing?" Beth asked.

"Let's do it."

Beth grabbed the UV light and Kate armed herself with the video camera.

"Ready," Kate said.

Beth turned on the light and slowly brought it close to Luc's hand. "Ready?" she asked Luc.

He nodded.

Beth brought the light over the back of Luc's hand and quickly pulled it away. Nothing. She again trained the light on Luc's hand, leaving it slightly longer.

"Leave it there, Beth. I can take it even if it does start to burn."

Beth once again brought the light to shine on Luc's hand and held it there. He lifted his hand in the beam of light and turned it from back to palm and back again. "Nothing. I don't feel anything except the warmth of the light. This is incredible!" An enormous grin plastered itself across his face.

Despite her worries, Beth couldn't help but return it.

Luc rose to his feet and ran to the mayo stand Beth and Kate kept at the ready, covered to keep it sterile but filled with surgical instruments they might need if some kind of intervention or examination was required. He picked up a scalpel and returned to face Kate's camera. He held his palm up to the camera and sliced it deeply with the blade, wincing slightly. The wound bled heartily, but the bleeding quickly slowed, then stopped. Luc wiped away the clotting blood with a paper towel to show what remained of the wound beneath. It looked like a superficial scratch rather than the deep wound it was just seconds ago. After a minute, it was completely healed, not even a scar or discoloration remaining.

Hearing and vision testing showed his vampire senses remained intact as well. By the time these were complete, his stomach audibly growled. Luc's eyes opened wide and looked comically at Beth, grabbing his abdomen. Perhaps it was the nervous tension bubbling up, but Beth couldn't hold in her laughter.

"Your stomach is growling. I think you're hungry," Beth said through peals of laughter.

Luc, now realizing she was right, also began to laugh.

"It's been three hundred years, I had forgotten how that felt. Vampire thirst is so different." Luc went to the fridge and pulled out a unit of O-positive, opening the tubing at the top and swiftly taking a large gulp. He immediately shuddered, looking as though he might gag, and ran to the sink to spit it out. "That tastes absolutely horrible."

"Reese and Rhonda would agree with you," Beth said, taking the unit from Luc and tasting it herself. "Unfortunately, it still tastes delicious to me."

"How about a banana?" Kate offered, holding one in her hand. She tossed it to Luc who peeled it, smelled it, and very cautiously bit off the tip. He rolled it around in his mouth, brows creased in concentration before swallowing. A goofy grin spread across his face as he quickly downed the rest.

"That was amazing. What other human food do we have here?"

"There are more fruits and vegetables in the fridge that we've been feeding the monkeys. There are probably a few cans of soda left over from before I turned and most likely some ice cream in the freezer. I barely went a day without it before I was changed," Kate offered.

Luc proceeded to try each fruit and vegetable, devouring them like he hadn't eaten in years, which, of course, he hadn't. He was intrigued by the soda and the way it bubbled in his mouth, but it took a few swallows before he was sure he liked it.

Last was the ice cream, a pint of Ben and Jerry's Phish Food. Luc took a large spoonful and crammed it in his mouth, chewing at first. Then he stopped and closed his eyes, letting out a little whimper of joy before swallowing and taking an even larger second bite. With his mouth still full, he said, "This is amazing."

"I know," Kate said with a deep sigh, her bottom lip crooked.

"How is it all settling? Do you feel sick?" Beth asked, watching him cram in even more ice cream.

"No, actually, I'm starving. If this is the last of the human food, I'm going to need to get something more."

"You need to stay close so we can monitor you, not to mention avoid being seen. It's daylight. Why don't we order in."

"Daylight? Are you sure? I can't feel it."

"I'm certain," Beth replied.

"I have to see it," Luc said as he sprinted for the door. Beth met him before he could go out and stood in his way.

"Take it easy, Luc. We don't know if the sun's rays are different from the artificial light or how much you can tolerate." She could understand his excitement, but they were in uncharted territory. They needed to take every step carefully and deliberately. They didn't need another mishap like the accidental injection.

"Okay, I will take it easy. But I have to see it. It's been so many lifetimes."

With a look of concern on her face, Beth sighed and stepped aside. "I'll order you some pizza with extra protein toppings. If your energy requirements are anything like Reese and Rhonda's, you're going to need the extra calories."

Luc turned to go and abruptly stopped, looking back at Beth. He turned fully to face her and pulled her into his arms. Kate, across the room, blushed and turned her back to them to give them privacy.

"I know this hasn't gone as either of us had planned, but I'm thankful to be free of the bloodlust so I can hold you close to me and tell you this." He looked directly into her eyes, unblinking, and said, "I love you, Elizabeth Ramsey, with all of my heart... the rest of me too. There is nothing more in this life that I want than to spend whatever time I have left with you by my side."

Tears streamed down Beth's face, but she had no words. It was true. While he had been tempted by her blood, he really did love her just for who she was. Even more, he was choosing her to spend his life with. Her. Not Cora or Lilly or whatever she called herself now or anyone else. Her.

She pulled him close and kissed him deeply until her fangs began to push against her upper lip and she broke it off. Luc touched his forehead to hers, still holding her, and stroked her cheek with his hand. He kissed her gently on the forehead, looked into her eyes as though he could see her soul, and stepped out the door.

While Kate remained with her back to Beth, and she appreciated that, she could feel the excitement beaming from her like a lighthouse in the night. She smiled to herself knowing her friend shared in her happiness, even if it was tenuous.

"Okay, you're not fooling anyone. You can turn around now," Beth said, needing just a moment of levity to ease the weight of the problems that still faced them.

Kate turned, a smile beaming from her tear-streaked face as she wiped at it. Giggling like a schoolgirl and bouncing up and down, she said, "Can I come to the wedding?"

Chapter 43

LUC

LUC STOPPED BENEATH THE awning just outside the entrance to the lab. He blinked quickly, squinting tightly. The light was blinding as he waited for his eyes, so long accustomed to the dark, to adjust. He moved to the edge of the shaded area and put his hand out into the direct sunlight, pulling it back quickly. Nothing. This time he held his entire hand and forearm directly in the sun's rays, and after a full minute of nothing, he stepped fully into the sunlight. He held his arms out to his sides, slightly raised, closed his eyes, and tilted his head back to feel the rays fully on his face.

It was heavenly.

He had long since forgotten the feel of the sun on his skin and the warmth and comfort that came with it. He opened his eyes, still squinting from the brightness of the light.

His gaze slowly wandered over the landscape around him. Vampire vision made the night vivid, but the colors of the world in daylight were dazzling. The sky was the loveliest shade of blue that Luc could ever remember seeing, and the fluffy white clouds dotted the sky here and there glowed from behind with the sun's light. There were at least thirty shades of green in the foliage around him, and his remaining acute vampire vision made them even more brilliant. The sunlight danced across everything it touched, glinting and sparkling from the shiny green leaves that waved in the gentle breeze. Luc inhaled deeply, letting the warmth fill his lungs. Along with the breath came the scent of earth, cut grass and evergreens.

He had occasionally heard the daytime birds sing as he fell asleep for the day when he was a vampire, but that was nothing compared to hearing them in full chorus as he stood outside with them. A dove made its gentle coo from a tree nearby, and Luc trained his eyes on it. It was so many beautiful shades of gray, silver and soft blue. A robin fluttered to the ground in front of him, searching the earth and scratching for food, its orange breast thrust forward as it strutted. And as he stood, still as a statue, a monarch butterfly, in all its colorful splendor, drifted not two feet in front of him. A broad smile spread across his face.

Tears threatened, but not from sadness. Beth and Kate had done it. After three hundred years in darkness, here he stood in the sun, waiting for a pizza, whatever that would taste like. Even if this cure failed, even if he died, this would be worth it. Well, almost anyway. Nothing was worth losing Beth.

He pushed the thoughts aside for just a moment. He wanted to enjoy this time, especially since he may not get it again. Luc didn't know what God had planned for his life. He had given up on it so long ago, believing himself a monster. Perhaps Beth had given him back more than just his freedom from blood and night, but his soul as well.

A mockingbird sang its happy tune, reveling in the new day and telling Luc that all was and would be well. And he hoped it was true. In the meantime, he was able to walk in the sun. He could use this to their advantage and patrol near the lab during daylight hours while Kate and Beth were inside working. It gave him a sense of purpose, a way to be helpful when he felt like he could contribute little to their work. The Master was still coming, and this may help keep them safer.

He made a quick circle around the building, making sure to keep his speed to acceptable human levels. He sensed nothing out of place.

He knew Beth would worry if he was outside alone for too long this first time, and he had caused her enough anxiety already.

He took one last deep breath, reveling in the warmth of the sun, and went back inside.

CHAPTER 44

PETER

PETER WAS TYING UP loose ends in Kansas City before leaving for New Orleans. As directed by the Master, he would lead a team to deal with the problem of the New Orleans scientist himself. He had collated what information he had found about the scientists they had encountered so far as well as a list of possibilities for the overseas researchers pending the hacker's tissue bank investigation. All the information was in a manilla folder he now carried with him toward the Master's office.

Biceps was outside the Master's study door.

"I have a file to leave for the Master."

"He's still sleeping, it's daytime."

"I know. I'll leave it on his desk for him and pick up the information he left there for me."

Accepting Peter as the Master's second-in-command, Biceps nodded. Peter passed through the study door, closing it quietly behind him.

He walked to the Master's desk and placed the file there for him. He picked up Handler's file, still on the desktop where it had been the day before. He could use it to say he was reviewing instructions from the Master if someone else came by. He flipped through it, seeing notes on Handler's gambling debts and the names of his bookies, investigations he had performed, and newspaper articles about the kidnapping and murder of the lawyers Beth had hired. If Handler ever decided he wanted out, he was screwed.

He walked to the file cabinet the Master had waved toward in their previous discussion. The cabinets were labeled alphabetically, and Peter pulled out the drawer containing the *J*s and began to riffle through.

There it was, just as he had suspected. "James, Peter M.D."

He removed the file and flipped through the pages. It contained information and images of Peter since their first meeting. A few pages contained information on his deceased father and deserting mother. Had the Master collected this information before or after he killed Peter's father? The more recent information made note of nearly every task Peter had performed for the Master that could possibly be construed as illegal. There were copies of the altered autopsy reports, his break-in at Beth's dentist's office, a police report from the fire at Mr. Verde's home, and the name of the hacker he used for various nefarious jobs. It also contained a list of his frequent contacts, including his partners with their addresses and every bank account and credit card number he had.

Anger made his hands shake as he returned the file to the cabinet. Taking the file would do him no good. He was certain the Master could easily get his hands on the information again, and it would alert him to the fact that Peter had been there. Peter knew his scent would be in the office, and he had an explanation for that. But a missing file, he couldn't cover that up. He returned the file to the cabinet, replaced Handler's file on the desk, and left, walking past Biceps without so much as a look.

He was completely engrossed in his own thoughts, fuming. The

Master had raised him and put him through school. He had believed they had a bond, but clearly that wasn't the case. He should have known the Master would form no emotional ties with him. He never had with anyone else. Why did Peter think he was different? And he was in far too deep now to think of just leaving. Until recently, when it appeared the Master may be stringing him along, he had never wanted to leave.

This was going to require some thought. He needed to settle himself. Rash decisions weren't helpful.

He tried to relax the tension in his shoulders, moving his neck from side to side, the joints popping.

Should he be keeping a file of his own? It would be hard to record events the Master had initiated without implicating himself. He needed to consider what had really changed. The Master had clearly been keeping the file since the time of their first meeting. He was collecting leverage in case he needed it. That had always been the Master's method of operation. But perhaps it was more habit than ill intent, a backup if Peter got out of line, which of course he wouldn't... at least until he had been turned. While seeing the file for himself was jarring, perhaps he was overreacting. He needed to keep his head clear and his eyes open.

He would still follow the Master for now, just not blindly.

CHAPTER 45

LUC

Luc FINISHED HIS SIXTH hourly patrol outside the lab, making sure nothing was amiss, pausing several yards from the entrance. Thankfully, there had been no sign of the Master or any evidence of strangers lurking about. Not only did the frequent checks make him feel a little safer, he also enjoyed the brief trips out into the sunlight.

As the light faded on his first day back in the sun, he watched in awe as it set in the west, the brilliant oranges, pinks and yellows having evaded him for three centuries. Soon he would share this with Beth as well. He wanted to walk with her along the river or perhaps a beach and see the reflection of the sunset in the water, and to get up at dawn to watch the sunrise hand in hand. He had never seen her in the light, but imagined her blue eyes would reflect the sunlight as brilliantly as the sky.

As the sun slipped below the horizon, Luc closed his eyes and prayed they would both have that chance and a long life together.

"I don't think Reese is going to make it long enough for us to try the new virus," Beth said as Luc entered the lab. "Maybe we should try reinfecting him with the original virus. The faulty virus has completed its job and his titers have fallen. Maybe if we give him enough of the original virus, it could reinfect the cells and overcome the negative effects. At least as a vampire he would survive until we could finish the next version of the VR virus."

"I don't know if it will work, but I don't think it could hurt," Kate agreed.

Luc felt sorry for the monkey and hoped it would work for the little guy. Reese and Rhonda were aging rapidly and looked weak and miserable. But he knew there was no other way to test that wouldn't cost more lives and also that, at least in Kate's lab, the animals were cared for with dignity and kindness.

"I'll prepare an injection. How is the data looking?" Beth asked.

"I've been looking at the genes on either side of the stop codons we added. One of the codons appears to be inserted in the lamin A or LMNA gene."

"Lamin A... lamin A, isn't that associated with progeria?" Beth asked.

"What's progeria?" Luc asked.

"It's a genetic disorder where the lamin A gene is mutated or damaged. It causes the cells to die more quickly and results in rapid aging. It kicks in shortly after birth. Those who suffer from it rarely live past their late teens." Beth turned back toward Kate. "Perhaps that's it. Maybe we modified the transcription of the gene in a way that's causing rapid aging. The monkeys have a significantly increased metabolism. It could be causing their cells to turn over even more rapidly since they can't maintain the cells properly without the lamin A. Maybe, perhaps... I hate not knowing for sure." She held her hands up near her head, fists clenched.

"Me too, but at least we have something to try. It's the only good candidate I've identified so far. A geneticist would be so helpful about now."

"A geneticist and time are both luxuries we don't have," Beth answered. Luc saw her glance at him then quickly avert her eyes. Even though he was doing well so far, Luc knew how worried she was that he would soon begin to age as well.

"Let's try to repackage the previous viral RNA but add a sequence that will specifically avoid the lamin A gene by placing the stop codon outside of it. There might be more we need to do, but since this looks to be a likely culprit, there's no reason to wait," Beth said.

"I agree. I'll start now."

Beth drew up a dose of her own blood containing the original Vampyre virus and injected Reese. She stroked the little monkey's now silver-white head. "Hang in there, little buddy," she said before gently returning him to his cage.

Luc watched and thought that Reese moved like an old man with small ginger steps. He curled up in his small cushioned bed and quickly closed his eyes to sleep. Luc himself felt nothing out of the ordinary so far, but watching Reese as his strength waned, his movements stiff and cautious with pain, made him hope he wouldn't have to endure the same. Being a vampire, he had thought about dying, sure, but the side effects of growing old were something he never considered.

"Okay, time to have another look at you, Luc," Beth said.

"How closely would you like to look?" Luc joked, trying to keep the mood light as he covered the distance between them to stand in front of her.

The broad smile across her face quickly faded as she looked at him.

"What?" he said.

"You have gray at your temples," Beth said, her voice low and her eyes blinking rapidly, holding back tears.

Luc's heart sank. He had hoped that the rapid aging would be confined to the monkeys because of the differences in their DNA, but it seemed he would not be that lucky.

"Does it make me look more distinguished?" he said, trying to distract from their concerns. But Kate had already joined Beth at his side and stared intently at him, looking for any other visible changes.

"You would be handsome gray, white or bald," Beth said quietly and raised her hand to his cheek.

"It's going to be okay, Beth. You and Kate will figure this out." He raised his hand to gently cover hers, which was cool to his touch.

"You're right, we will. Because I won't stop trying until we do," Beth said.

"That goes double for me," Kate chimed in. "Back to work." She sprinted back to her table, knocking a clipboard off a benchtop with her elbow as she hurried by. It fell clattering to the floor. She hurriedly picked it up and placed it back on the table. "I'm okay."

Beth and Luc couldn't help a small sad smile between them.

CHAPTER 46

KATE

LUCIANO HAS BEGUN TO show skin changes, along with significantly more gray hair, but no hair loss as yet. He is beginning to lose some of his skin elasticity with changes in skin coloration. His increased appetite is still holding and rapid movements do not seem taxing based on his vitals. He appears to be forming a cataract in his left eye, which has begun to mildly impair his vision. He describes it as hazy but still reads 20/20 in the opposite eye. It will be at least four more hours before we will have the first doses of the Vampyre Retrovirus, GR version 2. It does not appear Reese will survive reinfection with the original Vampyre virus, but there is insufficient time to ascertain the reason for this failure. Immune system failure, direct damage from the Vampyre virus itself, or rejection of the virus are possibilities for later study.

As the hours passed, Reese's vitals began to worsen. He became nearly impossible to rouse, and his frail body appeared to either not be able to handle the reinfection in his weakened state or the VR virus, GRv1 had made his system resistant to the original Vampyre virus. Or perhaps the Vampyre virus was just killing him now, weak or not. Kate was beyond frustrated. With each hour that ticked by she knew they were closer to being discovered and killed. And with each of those same hours, the changes in Luciano became more pronounced.

As Kate waited for the VR, GRv2 to synthesize, she took over recording the hourly examinations of Luciano. She could tell each new change upset Beth, though she wasn't talking about it. That perhaps bothered her even more. Beth had spoken so openly to her before. Their friendship seemed to be something they both had come to value. She couldn't help but feel shut out. She wanted to be there for Beth but wasn't sure what to say to help her open up. She continued with her notes.

Rhonda is also failing but more slowly than Reese, so we have opted not to try reinfection with the original Vampyre virus in hopes we can inject her with VR, GRv2 before she dies. The third rhesus, Reed, has successfully been infected with the Vampyre virus and was then injected with VR, GRv1. While it will be a lot for his system, time does not allow for anything but dosing in quick succession. Luciano's health is worsening, so we have opted not to wait in order that we may have Reed in better health for injection of version 2 before Luciano becomes too ill.

She saved her notes to an external hard drive. She had been working diligently to move everything over to it and deleting the files from the lab computers. The sequencing files took up a lot of memory, so those were now housed on a separate external drive with its own backup. The few remaining rats and mice that had been infected with the VR virus were euthanized. Kate hated doing it, but if they had to run, they couldn't leave them behind for someone to be bitten and they certainly wouldn't leave them alone to die. She had written a draft email to one of the other scientists in her building, asking them to take care of the remaining animals. There was no explanation, but she knew from their previous encounters they would honor her request.

She was still struggling with what to do with Reese, Rhonda and Reed if they survived. She knew she should euthanize them if they had time before running, but she just wasn't sure she had it in her heart to do it. She had become more attached to them on this journey than she should have.

Kate stood and checked the refrigerator and freezer once more. She had disposed of any samples not vital to their work and clustered those that remained together so they could be quickly collected as they left, small coolers at the ready. Kate shuddered at the thought of what could happen if the samples, which held the means to make someone strong and nearly immortal, fell into the wrong hands.

She tried to stay focused, but her thoughts wandered. Beth knew she was doing her best and had even suggested she rest a few hours ago, though Kate refused. While Kate had initially assumed they would share only a working relationship, it had grown into that of a mentor and mentee after she turned. But they were beyond even that now. She counted them both as friends. If they lost Luciano, she would feel the pain right along with Beth. The research still meant a lot to her, and she would continue regardless, but it was no longer for the sake of answers alone. Now, she needed to complete it to save the life of a friend.

Luciano and Beth sat in the corner of the lab, hands held together in front of them, looking intently into one another's eyes. They were no doubt having a conversation that they wanted to remain between the two of them. The loss of Kate's parents a few years before had been sudden, an accident, and she hadn't been able to say goodbye. She had imagined many times what she would have said to them if she'd had the chance. She let Luciano and Beth have their privacy and rose to make another check on Reese.

Kate began to check his vitals when she realized she could no longer hear his heartbeat. He was gone. And the stress of all of it was too much.

The tears came, pouring down her cheeks. She fought to hold them back, but it was like damming a river with pebbles. She turned her back to Beth and Luciano and tried her best to cry silently but should have known better. Even distracted by Luciano's health, both Beth and Luciano would feel the waves of sadness and despair as they rolled off her. Both were quickly at her side.

Beth and Luciano each wrapped an arm around Kate and each other and lowered their heads. Kate felt how close they had all become over the short time they had spent together. Their friendship was real and strong and something she hadn't felt before. It seemed the same for Beth. And she wanted nothing more than to save her friend's life and Beth's chance at happiness with him.

CHAPTER 47

BETH

BY THE TIME THE vaccine was ready, the sun had set and Luc was fully gray with significant muscle wasting. His appetite was decreasing and his movements had become painful. He told Beth and Kate that his joints ached and he felt like an old man. He was no longer able to move at vampire speed, the effort clearly taxing. Just watching him move made her struggle to hold back tears. He was changing by the hour, and it was all Beth could do not to panic. The self-doubt and what-ifs were beginning to pile up.

Perhaps she *should* have approached a geneticist. But if she had, their life would now be in danger too. Even if she were able to find one now, there wasn't enough time to convince them to help and for them to be useful. She was beside herself with worry and had no idea what they would do now if the Master or his men came for them. Luc was too weak to run with them until he was treated. It could be a death sentence for him. She wasn't trained to defend herself, let alone the three of them.

It was time to admit to herself that she couldn't do this without more help. As much as she had resisted asking for it and involving others, it was time to put her feelings and pride aside and reach out. She pulled out her phone, typed an email, and pressed send.

The computer on the viral vector platform beeped that it was ready.

Beth was immediately beside it with Kate. There was enough for three human-sized doses. They had decided to up the dose in hopes of creating a more rapid change in Rhonda and Reed along with an extra dose for Luc if it worked.

"Let's get this into the monkeys," Kate said.

Rhonda was barely moving but still conscious. So far, Reed showed no signs of aging, but they both knew it was a matter of time.

After both monkeys were inoculated, Luc and Beth sat down to wait while Kate returned to the instruments, making adjustments for another run.

Beth held Luc's hand as he began to doze off on their makeshift cot. Her nerves made her want to pace, but she didn't want to leave his side until he slept. He needed the rest. It made each minute even more agonizing. But after a few moments, his eyes remained closed and she heard his heart slow into the steady rhythm of sleep.

Beth rose and walked around the lab a couple of times to stretch her legs and calm her nerves before joining Kate in preparing the machine and reagents for a second vaccine-producing run.

They had been working for a couple of hours when Luc jerked fully upright, as though someone had yelled to wake him. He looked at Beth, confusion on his face.

"Jon's here," he said.

Beth jumped up, quickly turned to Kate, and said, "Don't ask."

Kate looked at her curiously. "Ask what?"

Beth was already at Luc's side, helping him to his feet.

Luc rose slowly and walked toward the lab door, Beth running ahead to the outer door to let Jon in. Luc met them just inside the lab door. An intimidating figure stood before him, at least a foot taller than Beth, lanky but muscled with short, messy blonde hair and a broad smile.

"Jon, come in," Luc said.

"Holy shit, you weren't kidding. He looks like crap," Jon said, lumbering forward.

"Kate, this is a good friend of mine, Jon Wilks," Luc said, taking Jon's hand in a vigorous shake and pulling him in to pat him on the back, which Jon returned.

Kate's head snapped toward Beth, and she mouthed behind her hand, *Like Jon Wilkes Booth?*

Beth shot her a warning glance.

"Beth, apparently you two have met?" Luc asked, stepping back from Jon and looking at her with raised eyebrows.

Beth extended her hand to welcome Jon. He shook it firmly with a crooked grin. Beth liked him already. "Not exactly. Jon, thank you for coming."

"Luciano told me you were gorgeous. He wasn't kidding," Jon said. Beth instantly felt heat in her cheeks. Jon turned to Luc and said, "Well done, my friend."

Luc beamed at Beth and then turned back to Jon.

"I asked Jon here to help with security," Beth admitted, smiling timidly at Luc and hoping he wouldn't be angry. "You told me he was a Marine, and from your story, I figured he was more than capable of watching out for the Master and his men. Thank you for coming so quickly."

"I was in Atlanta, it was an easy run. I couldn't miss out on a chance to check in on this guy and meet his girl," Jon said, another grin on his face.

Luc gave Beth a sideways glance and then, reaching for her hand, his face somber, said, "You're right, he is more than capable and I can't help protect you any longer. Until you fix me, it's good to know there is someone here who can."

Beth squeezed his hand and smiled, thankful she had made the choice.

"I'm a liability here," Luc said to Jon. "If the Master comes, Kate and Beth would be in danger trying to defend me. I don't want that." He turned to address Beth. "I should go to the house."

"I've been concerned about Luc being here given his current state of health," Beth said, turning to look at Jon. "We have his shotgun house in the Quarter. Assuming the Master is tracking through the scientists in each city, he will be headed here but shouldn't have knowledge of the house. I've considered moving him to keep him safe, but I'm conflicted. I hate to leave the lab in case we need access to things here to help him."

Jon looked between Luc and Beth and then tilted his head, crossing his arms. "Well then, it's a good thing you called me."

Beth was so grateful for his help. She didn't know all the history between the two, but clearly Luc trusted him. She found comfort in that. It also meant Luc had another friend at his side to support him through this.

Kate chimed in, "Yes it is, and until the virus has time to take hold in the monkeys, I can focus on synthesizing more of the version two virus."

"Jon, you and I need to discuss our plan if things go sideways and we get separated. You remember where my Colorado house is, don't you?" Luc asked.

"Of course. I could never forget that last visit, that fight was epic," Jon replied.

As Luc caught Jon up on what they knew so far and his patrols of the area, Kate caught Beth's eyes. She looked to Jon then back at Beth and wiggled her eyebrows, a stupid grin on her lips.

Beth couldn't help but smile back at the hopeless romantic. Having Jon with them had lifted Luc's spirits and in turn theirs.

Kate gave Beth a wink and headed for the instruments.

CHAPTER 48

BETH

"Beth, Jon needs us outside. Now," Luc said, already struggling to get to his feet.

"Okay," Beth said, confused but helping him up. She glanced back at Kate and shrugged, moving as quickly as Luc could hobble out of the lab, through the outside doors, to the back of the building.

They turned the last corner around the building to see Jon with his hand around the throat of a dark figure, pinning him to a tree with his toes barely brushing the ground beneath them. As they drew closer, Beth could see he was a large man, overweight, with rumpled clothing and a grubby fedora. The mixture of smells rolling off of him was strong. Beth stopped inhaling to keep it from filling her nostrils.

"I caught him snooping around the building. It wasn't hard, he's a stinky little bastard," Jon said.

That's it, the exact same mix I smelled in Chicago at Dr. Riley's and Dr. Henri's homes. Luc evidently thought the same to Jon, as he nodded in response.

"Who are you and what do you want?" Luc growled.

The man held his hands up in front of him and rasped out, "I'm a detective, Handler's the name. The Master hired me to find the scientists you're workin' with and the two of you. He wants you all dead, but I'm no killer. I've had enough of his shit."

"When is he coming?" Luc demanded.

"I don't know, but soon. He sent me ahead to find out what Dr. Giffard knows. Dr. James called for a report this mornin'." Handler coughed, choking from Jon's hold. "I wanted to find you or delay them, but if they suspect I'm delayin' anything, I'm a dead man. Prob'ly already am for refusing to kill for the Master. I've done a lot of things I ain't proud of, but I have never taken a life, and I don't intend to either. You all should get the hell out of New Orleans before they get here." He paused and looked to Luc. "You don't look so good."

"How much do they know?" Beth asked.

"That Dr. Giffard picked up the tissue samples you left for her, that Dr. Royle never picked 'em up and skipped town. They know the location of both of their labs and their home residences. And they are beginning the same search in Rome and Victoria."

"Have you told him where we are?" Luc demanded, fisting his clenched hands even tighter.

"No," Handler choked out, "I haven't told him you're here. I wanted to warn you."

Beth wondered what would cause him to risk warning them. Perhaps this was a trick. "Why would you want to warn us?"

Handler looked to Jon, fear in his eyes, and then back at Beth. "I watched him kill the lawyers you hired by rippin' off pieces of their flesh. It was disgusting. Then he wanted me to kill those two scientists in Chicago. I refused, so I'm already on his shit list. But he'll do anything to get to the two of you and anyone who is helping you. I don't know what you're doing, but if it opposes the Master, I say more power to ya."

"We appreciate the heads-up," Beth said, looking to Luc. He nodded to Jon to release the man.

Handler's feet hit the ground, and he fell to his knees coughing and rubbing his throat before pulling himself up and reaching for a cigarette still lodged behind his ear. He withdrew a book of matches from his jacket pocket and tried to light one with trembling hands. Finally succeeding, he looked at each of them, as if waiting for another of them to grab him, before turning to leave, hurriedly reapplying his hat to his head and straightening his hopelessly wrinkled jacket.

"Thank you," Beth called after him. He nodded over his shoulder and hastened on his way. She turned to face Luc. "I guess our time is up."

"It's time to go, Kate," Beth said as she, Luc and Jon returned to the lab.

"What? We can't leave right now. The monkeys are just completing the change. We have to wait and see if the new dose worked."

"Kate, we just ran into a detective hired by the Master to locate you. He says he's had enough of the Master and is giving us a warning, but I don't know if we can trust that. The Master's men may already be on their way. We're out of time." Beth held Luc's arm and their eyes met before she returned her attention to Kate again. "We need to use the final dose to inject Luc."

Beth hated the idea of injecting him before they knew the outcome for the monkeys. But she knew the end result if they didn't. The lab was no longer safe. If something else went wrong, there was nowhere to go to get the help he would need fast enough to keep him alive. Giving him the v2 virus and hunkering down in a place they had to hope the Master didn't know about was their safest bet.

"But we still have the same problem. If something goes wrong with this new virus, I won't have access to what I need to fix it," Kate argued. "And what about Rhonda and Reed?"

"We'll wait out the change at the shotgun house and figure out what to do about the monkeys. Jon can help us keep tabs on the lab once we're settled. If there's something we need, if the lab looks clear, we can still get to it. When Luc is through the change and strong, we can leave from the shotgun house and head for Colorado tomorrow night."

Kate shook her head. But her shoulders slumped, and she let out a sigh before saying softly, "Okay, let's go."

Jon appeared at her side, carrying her satchel and bag. "You take these and I'll grab Luc." He quickly scooped Luc into his arms and looked at him with a crooked grin. "Are you ready, dear?"

Luc looked at each of them in turn, glaring with more pink to his cheeks than Beth had seen in them for hours. "We shall never speak of this moment again."

Beth paused with Kate just outside the lab and watched as she glanced over her shoulder at the building. She knew how Kate felt. Running away from the job she loved wasn't easy. And Beth thought of her own career back home. She hoped in time, if all their plans fell into place, they could both return to what they loved.

As she turned to follow Jon, Beth's eyes caught a glint of headlights reflecting off a black SUV with a large dent in the front fender, parked near the end of the block. The flash nearly blinded her with her sensitive night vision. She blinked as her eyes recovered and ran after Kate.

The run to the shotgun house took a bit longer than usual. Jon went carefully, trying to jostle Luc and his tender joints as little as possible. As soon as they reached the door, Luc demanded to be put down with, "You will not carry me across the threshold."

Chuckling, Jon set him down. Luc opened the door for them, Beth holding him around the waist as he entered, barely able to stand on his own. She began walking him toward the bedroom so he could lie down.

Kate set her bag in the chair and paused, looking at her satchel before clenching her fists. "Shit, shit, shit!" She turned to look at Beth. "I forget the samples in the fridge and freezer. I have to go back."

"Kate, we have everything we need. Beth has the vial of new virus to give to me and the two of you carry the original virus," Luc said, his voice sounding weaker by the moment. "There is no need to go back."

"No," Kate said, shaking her head and spitting out her answer as fast as the words would come, already at the door. "The samples have the VR, GRv1 virus as well. If we haven't gotten it right, that may still hold the answer as to why. Plus, when my colleagues realize I'm gone, someone will go into the lab. We can't risk the virus falling into the wrong hands or someone else becoming infected trying to see what I was working on. I'll be in and out in seconds." And before Beth could protest, she was gone.

Jon looked at Luc and Beth. "I'll go with her, don't worry." And then he was gone.

CHAPTER 49

PETER

PETER AND A HALF dozen of the Master's drudges waited in a black SUV in the back of the research center parking lot. They had arrived just in time to see Dr. Giffard leaving with a tall and lean-muscled man, who was carrying an old man, and Beth. Peter didn't recognize either of the men, but when he moved so quickly with Dr. Giffard and Beth that they disappeared from sight, he knew all three were vampires. He hadn't been expecting Dr. Giffard to have been turned, let alone another vampire apart from possibly Beth or Mr. Verde. He hadn't been able to get a photo of the tall one before the group had disappeared. That man wasn't in the records the Master kept of known vampires.

Three vampires were far more of a problem than one scientist.

Handler had been able to identify the location of the scientist's labs and residences, but he hadn't been able to enter Dr. Giffard's lab. She had been staying there around the clock, apparently working on the vampire virus. This was Peter's chance to get inside and see what they had, but he had to hurry. There was no telling how quickly Dr. Giffard or her group would return. And as humans, Peter and his men were no match for three vampires at night hand to hand.

"Let's go. In and out in five," he told the team as they filed out of the SUV, pulling down black hoods as they went.

Peter had the device Alex had used to break into the dentist's office to steal Beth's dental records a few short months ago and used it now to quickly bypass the front door lock followed by the door to the lab. He entered to monkeys shrieking loudly and rattling some rather impressively heavy-duty cages. They moved about inside them too quickly for Peter's eyes to focus on them. *Vampire monkeys? You have got to be kidding.*

He quickly glanced over the clipboards at the sides of each cage, but they contained only vitals and intake. Although their food consumption was impressive and odd as it didn't include blood.

"Take the computer," he said to one of the men. They could link it to the hacker when they returned to the SUV and see what Dr. Giffard had been up to.

Peter walked to the freezer and refrigerators and nosed through the contents. There were numerous bottles of reagents and a single vial each of what was labeled VR, GRv1 and VR, GRv2. Of particular interest was a small vial that appeared to contain blood labeled "original Vampyre virus." The spelling was curious and he wasn't sure what it meant, but *original* surely meant the stock virus from Mr. Verde's blood. This was what the Master was so keen to protect and could be Peter's ticket to getting what he wanted, whether the Master wanted to give it to him or not. Similarly labeled frozen vials were in the freezer.

While facing the refrigerator so the Master's henchmen couldn't see what he was doing, he slipped a frozen vial into his jacket pocket.

"Place the charges and let's go," Peter said. "Add charges to the monkey cages too. We need to be certain they don't survive."

The lab had no outside windows, only a single door as an exit. "Perfect," he muttered under his breath as he strode outside to return to the vehicle. The Master's men were close behind him. Now they just had to sit and wait for Dr. Giffard to return.

Chapter 50

Beth

"As soon as this thaws, we're going to get you back on the mend." The syringe of v2 had been in the freezer when she grabbed it to leave the lab and was still partially frozen. She tilted the syringe back and forth, moving the thawed liquid around in the vessel to get it to melt more quickly.

As soon as it felt close to room temperature to her touch and there were no visible frozen chunks, Beth removed the needle cap, depressed the plunger just enough to remove the air, and moved to Luc's arm.

"Sounds good to me," Luc said, attempting a smile before dozing again.

Like the rest of him, Luc's vessels were shrunken and shriveled. While his veins were usually clearly visible on his arms, she had to close her eyes and feel for them now. She located one in his right antecubital space and wasted no time inserting the needle, drawing back a small amount of blood into the syringe to be sure she was in the vein, and injecting the entire contents. She didn't have any alcohol swabs to clean the area but wouldn't have wasted time on it if she did. If this worked, his body would eliminate any other infection he might get from a dirty needle stick.

"There. That's it. Now we wait for you to heal," Beth said aloud, hoping against all hope that her words were true.

He didn't stir. There was nothing else she could do but sit by and hold his hand. She intended to remain at his side through this and, she realized, whatever else came at them in the future. If she had minutes or millennia with him, she wanted to be right here at his side. The Master would try what he would, but she'd fight alongside Luc to whatever end might come her way.

It had been just under an hour since they left the lab, but it seemed twice that. She was beginning to get more than a little worried about Kate and Jon, and the changes in Luc had rapidly progressed. Beth had tried to talk to him. She wanted so much to tell him how she felt but couldn't think of a way to do it that didn't sound like giving up on him. He had the v2 vaccine now, he just needed time for it to kick in. And, of course, for this version to be right.

Luc must have felt the same, because he too had avoided the subject when awake. But he was going in and out of consciousness now. And from time to time, he would forget what he had been speaking about. Beth couldn't stand the thought of losing him without saying the words aloud.

"Luc, I know you're tired. It's okay if you sleep. While you're resting, dream about how much I love you, about how we're going to spend the rest of our long lives together in the sunlight when you're better. That's all I really want and need in this life. I just need you, nothing else I have ever had or will have could mean more to me." Tears welled in her eyes and spilled one by one down her cheeks.

Luc raised a wobbly and wrinkled hand to her cheek and wiped them away with his thumb. He spoke in a raspy whisper, struggling to get the words out. "I'm not giving up either, Beth. Conscious or not, I will fight to my last heartbeat to have that future with you. The last few months with you have given me more joy than any before them. I am a blessed man far beyond what I could ever have imagined. I love you, Beth."

"I love you too," she said and kissed his palm, placing her hand over his against her cheek. It slowly slipped down as he fell back asleep, and she laid it gently at his side. She lay her head on his shoulder and let the tears fall. All her strength and bravery were gone. She was just a woman scared she might lose the only man she had ever loved.

CHAPTER 51

PETER

THEY WAITED FOR ALMOST fifteen minutes before one of the men said, "Two of them are back, next to the front door lock."

Peter watched as Dr. Giffard scanned her badge. The tall male vampire was still with her and followed her inside. *I may not have Beth or Mr. Verde yet, but at least I can complete the Master's orders by taking out the scientist.* Now that he had her, he didn't want to wait long and risk her escaping.

"Give it two minutes to see if anyone else shows up and then blow it," Peter barked.

And two minutes later the entire building erupted with an ear-splitting explosion followed by fire pouring out of all the broken windows and the front door. They watched for several more minutes. Seeing no one exit, they started the SUV and drove away.

CHAPTER 52

BETH

ANOTHER HOUR PASSED, AND Beth was growing more frightened by the second. She paced at lightning speed to the front door of the shotgun house and back to Luc's bedside. Kate and Jon should have been here by now. She pulled her phone from her back pocket and called Kate again. Like last time, after three rings, it switched to voicemail.

She's just hurrying and can't answer, Beth. Try again. She dialed a second time and waited. This time when it went to voicemail, she left a message. "Kate, it's Beth, are you okay? I haven't heard from you and it's been longer than I expected. Please call me back as soon as you get this."

She's just running behind a bit, that's all. She'll be knocking on your door any minute now.

But after another five minutes with no call and no knock, Beth knew something had to be wrong. She ran to Luc's bedside and grabbed his phone. She flipped through to find Jon's number and called him.

Again, no answer.

Beth chewed her lip and sat on the edge of the bed next to Luc. What if they were in trouble? What if the Master or his men had found them and they needed her help? Could she even be any help against the Master and his team? Three would surely be better than two.

Dawn was less than two hours away. Whatever she was going to do, she had to do now or spend a whole day inside waiting. What if they didn't have that long? Luc would want her to be safe, but how could she leave her friends out there alone?

But what if they were wrong and the Master had discovered Luc's shotgun house and arrived while she was out? There would be no one to protect Luc while he completed the change. Or what if she were captured? If the vaccine failed, he could die here alone. She couldn't leave him here either to die alone or be vulnerable.

She closed her eyes and sighed deeply. After dragging Jon into this mess, here she was about to involve another. There was only one person she could call that she knew would come. She searched for the number on her phone and pressed call.

"West Hotel, this is Charlie speaking."

"Charlie, this in an emergency. I'm Beth Ramsey and I need to get a message to Lilly."

"She's just down the hall. Let me get her."

"No, there's no time. Just tell her Luciano is at home and very sick. She needs to come now."

Chapter 53

Beth

Beth ran to the living room desk and scratched out a note for Kate as fast as she could in case they were delayed but still coming.

Kate,

Worried you and Jon are in trouble. Went to the lab to check on you. If you beat me back, please stay with Luc.

Love,

Beth

As she folded the note and tented it on the desk, there was pounding at the door strong enough to rattle the hinges. Beth had no more than turned the lock when the door flew open and Lilly rushed by her in a blur, running through the house at vampire speed until she found Luc lying in bed.

Beth joined her at his bedside. Lilly turned on her, slamming her hands into her chest and knocking her to the wall. Lilly was immediately in front of her, a look of pure hatred on her face.

"What the hell did you do to him? It was something from your damned lab experiments, wasn't it? It's no secret. I've followed the three of you there many a time."

Beth had expected her fury and kept her cool.

"I didn't harm him, but it is still my fault," Beth admitted.

"He looks like he's one hundred. What the hell is happening?" Lilly growled at her, fangs down. Beth didn't realize anger would bring them out as well, but she put the thought and her own anger aside. She needed Lilly's help.

"You can hate me all you like and take it out on me later. I've given him a vaccine to reverse this, we just have to wait for his body to process it. But I believe our friends are in trouble. I have to get to the lab to help them if I'm able to, and I can't leave him alone like this. If the Master's discovered where we are, there would be no one to protect him. I knew you would."

"Shit!" She turned to look at Luc, flattening her hair with her hands before returning her stare to Beth, more fear in her eyes than anger now. "If someone comes to harm him, they'll have to get through me first."

Beth took a step toward Luc only to be blocked by Lilly.

"Quit being an ass and step aside," Beth snarled, her fangs also beginning to extend.

She didn't know if it was because her anger or Lilly's desire for her to leave quickly, but Lilly stepped aside.

Beth went to the bed, kneeling, and held Luc's hand as she leaned over to kiss him on the forehead. "I love you. Be right back." The last part was probably more reassuring herself than Luc, and she hoped it wasn't a lie.

She centered herself with a deep breath. *This won't end like this, it can't. I will be right back.*

At top speed, Beth made it to within a mile of the lab in just a few minutes. Smelling smoke which wafted through the air to sting her eyes, she could see the research building aflame, belching large clouds of smoke through every opening. Bile rose in her throat and she thought she might be sick. Had Jon and Kate still been in the building? She was too late. Her and Luc's friends were gone. It was the only reason she could think of that they wouldn't have come back.

Beth fell to her knees and sobbed. In the short time they had worked together, Kate had been a close friend, almost like a sister she'd never had. She had confided in her, laughed with her, and even cried with her. The loss of Kate alone was a brutal blow.

But knowing that if the new virus failed she could also lose Luc, the only other person on the planet besides her father whom she had ever loved, was just too much. She would once again be alone. She felt like her heart had been torn from her chest. Her mind swam with pain, fear and anguish. The dreams she had of a life with Luc filled her head, and the tears came faster. Would she have any of them? With Kate and the lab gone, if the virus didn't work, these last few weeks that they'd spent working together were all she would have of either of them. How stupid she was to have squandered even a moment.

As she sat, waves of grief pounding against her, the emotions slowly began to change from despair to anger.

The Master had done this.

A guttural scream welled up inside her until she could hold it back no longer. She leaned back, glaring up at the stars, and bellowed into the night. To anyone who heard it, it was both a sound of utter despair and terrifying rage.

The Master wanted to take everything from her including her life. He was winning, and she couldn't let that happen.

She pushed the grief aside and used the anger to fuel her. She had to focus on any hope she and Luc had now, and that meant getting back to him and keeping him safe. Still on her knees, she bowed her head and said a silent goodbye to Kate and Jon.

Then she stood and ran.

CHAPTER 54

BETH

HAVING BEEN GONE LONGER than she would've liked, Beth couldn't help but wonder what kind of shape she would find Luc in. She chanted to herself as she ran, keeping time with her steps, *He's still alive, he's still alive...* It kept the fear at bay and helped her focus on going faster.

Dawn was approaching, and Beth could feel the lightening sky begin to prickle her skin. She rounded the final corner before the shotgun house, her eyes scanning the street in front of her, and froze in the shadows.

Parked at the opposite end of the block was a black SUV with a dented front fender.

What are the chances that there could be two of those near Luc and me in the same night? Beth knew it was slim to none. The Master's men were here. Somehow, they had found the little shotgun house, and Luc was inside. She glanced at the sky, now more blue than black. There was so little time.

Beth ran at top speed to the door, nearly ripping it off its hinges to get inside.

As she came through the door, Lilly had her by the throat, fury boiling in her eyes and her fangs exposed. She held Beth at arm's length. "You," she nearly spat, dropping her to her feet.

"The Master's men are here, we need to leave. Now!" she hissed at Lilly as she ran to the bedroom to scoop up Luc. She burst through the back door to the courtyard, through the gate, and into the street with Lilly at her side.

"Follow me," Lilly ordered, taking the lead. The two covered the ground over the few blocks to Lilly's hotel in seconds.

They ran through the entrance, the door slamming into the wall behind them, and up the stairs to the top floor faster than human eyes could follow them. As they reached the top of the stairs, Lilly stopped to unlock a door with a card, tendrils of steam still rising from their skin.

The door opened into a large open room with one wall entirely made of windows. Lilly touched a panel on the wall and thick shades began to roll down over each, blocking out enough light that Beth could focus on the room around her. The walls were exposed brick with thick wooden beams over the high ceiling. A large and intricately woven rug over the cement flooring defined the living room with its cream-colored leather furniture. The kitchen was to the left, cabinets the same cream with stark black granite countertops. Lilly turned on the lights, mostly dim recessed lighting, as the shades closed.

"Let me put Luciano in bed," Lilly said, reaching for him.

"I can handle that, thanks," Beth said, accepting her glare in return. "Lead the way."

The bedroom was down a short hallway beside the kitchen with a similar color scheme to the rest of the house. An enormous bed took up the majority of the far wall with two oversized stuffed chairs to the left beneath another wall of shaded windows.

The bedframe was dark wood, nearly black, with four tall posters capped by wooden arches that stretched from one to the other.

Cream-colored material was draped over the arches, forming a canopy. There were at least a dozen matching cream-colored pillows in various fabrics scattered over the head of the bed. Beth pushed those aside to gently lay Luc down, then sat next to him.

In her hurry to get him away from the shotgun house, she hadn't even paused to look at him. She didn't think it would have been possible for him to look older, but he did. His muscles had wasted so much his limbs looked like only bones. His hair had thinned and hung in sparse wavy locks against his pale, sunken cheeks. The clothes he had been wearing hung loosely on him now. His breath was shallow and erratic and his heart occasionally skipped a beat. When it did, Beth held her breath, waiting for the next.

"This feels so much like our first meeting, me at your bedside talking to you and wondering if you can hear me," Beth said.

Lilly glared at her from the doorway, hands fisted at her sides. "How long is it going to take before he starts to look better instead of worse?" she demanded, annoyingly tapping the pointed toe of her stilettos.

Beth tried to remain calm. Lilly had, after all, come to their aid... well, Luc's aid... when they needed her and was now sheltering them, at her own risk, in her hotel. She owed her whatever decency she could muster. "I'm not certain how long it might take, but I believe we will know by nightfall."

The sun had risen. Beth could feel its weight and was sure Lilly could too. This meant she and Lilly would enjoy one another's company trapped in Lilly's penthouse until it was once again dark outside.

It was going to be a very long day.

Lilly crossed her arms with a childish *humph* and tossed herself down in a chair. Beth tried her best to ignore her as Lilly stared at her from across the room. She needed to think.

The Master knew they were here, and it was only a matter of time before he tracked them down. When Luc recovered, they had to get out of New Orleans as fast as they could.

She considered carrying Luc if he didn't wake at dusk. With her vampire strength, she had easily lifted his body weight, and he seemed to have made the trip unscathed. But in his weakened state, she was afraid to try to move him again. He was so fragile she feared one wrong step or stumble on her part might break his brittle bones and puncture something vital. No, even after dusk she wouldn't risk it again unless she knew they had been found, at least until he began to show a little improvement.

Beth would be sad to leave New Orleans behind. The beauty of the garden district, the history and music of the French Quarter, and the Royal Street shopping had made quite an impression on her. She and Luc had walked through its streets hand in hand, sharing secrets, hopes and dreams with one another. New Orleans would always hold special memories for her, and she hoped that one day soon, when Luc was healed and all of this was behind them, they would be able to return. Maybe they could even enjoy a human dinner together and beignets from Cafe du Monde at dawn. Thinking of the future she hoped they would have together helped her stay calm when everything felt sideways.

Lilly interrupted her thoughts with, "I thought you weren't coming back."

Her voice wasn't as accusatory as Beth would have expected. When she looked up at her, Lilly's forehead was creased, her lips pursed. And Beth realized she had believed she may have had to stand by and watch Luc die. Beth understood the feeling of helplessness all too well. Lilly clearly cared about Luc, even if she had acted like a bitch toward Beth.

"They blew up the lab—the Master's men. It was on fire when I arrived." She steadied herself, not wanting to show weakness in front of Lilly. "Our friends are dead."

Lilly paused for a moment, her face contemplative, then softening ever so slightly. "So what exactly is this supposed to do to him? And how did he get like this in the first place?"

Beth considered what she should tell Lilly. It was just her and Luc again now. Lilly wouldn't know about the other scientists to send the Master in their direction, so telling her wouldn't put them at risk. But she wasn't sure which camp Lilly was in, those who wanted to be human again or those who would kill anyone who even whispered the words.

"Well?" Lilly demanded, uncrossing her arms and leaning forward in her chair.

"Do you like being a vampire?"

"What the hell kind of question is that? I am what I am and I make the most of it. I have forever to do all the things I always wanted to do and time has allowed me to amass the fortune I only dreamed of. The blood and darkness I could do without, but..." Beth could see the wheels turning as Lilly considered her question. "Is that what this is about? Luciano never wanted to be a vampire, he hated himself for the lives he had taken, especially..." She paused, as if considering what she should share.

"His wife. Yes, I know. But that's on the Master, not him." Beth wasn't surprised Luc had shared the story of his wife with Lilly. He was working past the guilt, but it still colored the man he was.

"Were you trying to make him human again and fucked it up?" Lilly's eyes were as wide as quarters, her lips parted. She pulled no punches, as usual, saying exactly what she thought.

Beth hesitated. *If Lilly knows how much Luc wanted to be human, she has to understand.*

"Yes, that's why the Master is after us. I've been studying the original Vampyre virus and trying to come up with a way to rid Luc and the rest of us of it." She left out that she also wanted to study the regenerative properties to see if they could be harnessed to help other humans. She didn't know how Lilly would feel about that. She might misconstrue her priorities and think she was using Luc for her own gain.

"You're serious." Lilly considered this for a moment, and the rage slowly began to creep back into her face. She leaned forward arms at her side, ready to stand. Beth feared she had been wrong to tell her. "And you used Luciano like a lab rat to test it?"

She went exactly where Beth thought she would. Beth was glad she hadn't shared the rest of her research.

"No. I would never do that. He was never supposed to be injected until we were absolutely certain it was safe. There was an accident in the lab and he was exposed." Beth knew Lilly would not handle the details of that exposure well either, blaming her. Even if she didn't share that with Lilly, she felt the guilt from the knowledge just the same.

Lilly exhaled with another *humph*. She started to pace around the room and then came to a stop next to Beth. "So can you really do it? If he's cured by whatever you gave him, will he be... *human*?" She nearly whispered the last word.

"Nearly so. But if it works, he will retain his strength, speed and regenerative abilities."

Lilly returned to the chair and sat heavily. "So he will be able to walk in the sun again. And he won't need blood to survive?"

"Correct to both." Beth knew it was a lot to take in and she waited while Lilly processed the information.

"So, assuming it works, when will you be able to give it to other vampires who want it?"

Beth lowered her head and exhaled.

"I don't know. Everything but my notes and the dose I gave to Luc was lost, burned in the fire in the lab, or left behind at the shotgun house." Beth realized Kate's satchel, which she assumed contained all of Kate's research, was still at the shotgun house. She kicked herself for not thinking of it, but there just hadn't been time. "I don't know when I might have access to another lab to make it, and I'm not certain I can do it alone." And she wasn't. She had worked alongside Kate, but this was no easy process. If anything went awry, she may not know how to fix it.

Lilly was silent for several seconds before speaking. "If he doesn't wake up, it will still be your fault," Lilly said flatly. "I won't wait for the Master to find you. I will kill you myself."

So they were back to square one. Beth knew Lilly meant what she said. And to Beth, it wouldn't matter. If Luc died, she couldn't imagine going forward without him. The grief would be so intense that she would welcome Lilly's wrath. But they both cared about Luc. She had helped them and they were stuck together. She should at least try to get along.

"Lilly, I know you care about Luc. And he obviously cares enough about you to have stopped by the hotel and reconnect. The two of you had something once—"

"Damn straight, we did," Lilly interrupted.

"We both love him." Beth ignored Lilly's exaggerated eye roll. "He's a grown man and can choose who he wishes to spend his life with. I'm not going to fight you for him."

Lilly narrowed her eyes at Beth. "Well, you do what you want. All the better for me, but I won't say the same. In this world, you have to fight for what you want. Nothing is given to you. If someone does pretend to give you something for free, you can bet your ass there are strings attached. I made a mistake once and lost Luc. It won't happen next time."

Beth swallowed the urge to fire back. She knew all about working hard to get ahead, but she supposed from what little she knew of Lilly's early life she could understand why she felt the way she did. She'd built her life from nothing. And as much as Beth hoped Lilly wouldn't have her "next time," she didn't want to pick a fight by saying so.

Around 10 a.m. Lilly nodded off in her chair, finally leaving Beth in peace at Luc's side. She could hear the rhythm of Lilly's heart, slower than normal and regular. She was tired too, but fought sleep to be with Luc until she could see improvement. To pass the time, Beth decided to talk with Luc about where they might go next. It felt like they were back in her house in Kansas City, her sharing her thoughts, him unresponsive.

"I know that if anything went wrong or we became separated, and this certainly counts as wrong in my opinion, we were to meet up at your Colorado house. So I suppose we should head there as soon as you're up for traveling. But with Kate gone..." Beth held back the tears that once again threatened to fall. She would have to recount the whole evening when Luc awakened. While she had only just met Jon, Luc would have lost two good friends. Beth shook her head to clear it. She would deal with that when the time came.

If Luc survived this, they would in some ways be back where they started. He would be human with a few significant additions and she would be still fully vampire. They had changed roles but hadn't moved too far forward.

Beth leaned over and brushed a lock of gray hair from Luc's face. He felt hot, not just warm like after the v1 virus, but feverish. She watched him closely and saw goosebumps rise on his arms with a slight shudder.

It was beginning. The infection with the new v2 virus was taking hold.

Beth was torn between being thankful it was finally happening and fear over whether or not he would survive it. It had to happen or there was no chance to save him. Watching him go through the first infection was horrible, but in his weakened state, this was worse.

Beth quietly ran to the kitchen so as not to wake Lilly and returned with a damp rag. She gently wiped Luc's face and neck, hoping it would help with the fever, then curled up beside him. She knew her body temperature would feel cool to him and perhaps provide him some relief, but she also wanted to be as close as she could to him. She didn't know if he knew she was there, but she wanted to be present in case he did.

She listened to his heart as she lay against him, still irregular and weak. Alone with her thoughts, unable to help him, was the worst kind of torture.

When they got through this, what if she couldn't recreate Kate's research? While Beth joked that Kate was a genius, she wasn't far from the truth. Kate had a brilliant mind, making leaps that others may not. It would be asking a lot to have another scientist step in and pick up where Kate left off if Beth couldn't. Making more of the new virus could be impossible, or at the least, take years to reproduce. If they had to continue their lives together as human and vampire, it would then be his life at risk.

Beth considered injecting herself with Luc's blood after he

recovered, but there were a lot of unknowns. He had been infected with the VR, GRv1 virus first. Had that made any significant changes to his DNA that would cause the new virus not to incorporate into her DNA properly? There was no way to know without further testing. And Beth knew that if she tried it, Luc wouldn't be able to help her should it go wrong. Worse, he would blame himself.

For every possible answer, there were a hundred more questions. Right now, she just wanted to know Luc would survive to be able to consider them.

Chapter 55

Peter

Peter caught the first available flight out of New Orleans to Kansas City with a brief layover in Houston. He was back in the city by 3 p.m. He had placed his special vial, frozen, along with a freezer pack in his carry-on bag, wrapped in a box marked as medical supplies. He flashed his medical badge before going through security and walked through, no questions asked. He drove directly to the morgue.

"Good afternoon, Phil," Peter said, greeting one of the day shift pathologists.

"Hey, what are you doing here? I thought you had the day off."

"Yeah, I do, but I wanted to go over some paperwork on one of my cases before it goes to trial next week." It was an outright lie, but it slid off of Peter's tongue without difficulty. He was used to adding in a few details when the situation called for it. No harm done.

"Well, you're dedicated. I'm sure it could wait until you get back."

"I'll obsess over it until I check some facts, so I figured I may as well just come in and take care of it so I can relax," Peter said, sitting in his desk chair, back perfectly straight, both feet planted flat on the floor beneath it. He placed his Italian leather messenger bag on the floor beside his feet.

"Okay. Have at it and enjoy the rest of your time off."

"Thank you," Peter said and waved his partner away. He and the other remaining day shift pathologist had cases going in the next room, so Peter was soon alone at his desk. He could hear Dr. Ellison begin to dictate his case along with the intermittent sound of the Stryker saw, so he knew both pathologists were busy with cases.

He leaned over and opened his bag, pulling out the small box containing the frozen blood sample. He stood and walked to the back of the room and opened the door to the storage area. The group maintained a freezer at -80 degrees Celsius for storing frozen patient samples for future study as needed. It was rarely accessed, and he was fairly certain it had never been cleaned. There were samples dating back at least ten years in there.

Peter placed a fake label over the one already on the vial and wrote *John Doe 5150* on it. He dated it with today's month and day but five years previous. He added "blood sample, left inguinal" and added Dr. Adams' initials. He then grabbed a biohazard bag, opened the box, and dropped the vial inside, labeling it with the same information. Though the Master had Dr. Adams killed to give Peter a job, he had been working five years prior, so the name wouldn't raise suspicions like his own would.

He placed the sample in a second biohazard bag, pulled out one of the wire basket freezer storage drawers, and placed the sample in the far back before closing the door, returning to his desk, and grabbing his bag to leave.

Peter walked to his car and couldn't help indulging the warring thoughts inside his head. If he waited, the Master may never turn him. And after seeing the files at the Master's home, particularly the one the Master kept on him, he had a strong suspicion he would disappear if he outlived his usefulness. If he injected himself, he could die going through the change. He knew it happened. The Master had told him so, if he were still to be believed, warning Peter that it was a dangerous process. If he lived through the change, he would be confined to the night. At work, he could make an argument that he was still as useful, if not more, working the graveyard shift. His partners had struggled to fill this position since Beth... left, and he knew the night shift partner would jump at a chance to trade for his day shift position.

Dealing with the Master, though, would be difficult indeed. The Master would know immediately upon seeing him that he had turned. There was no doubt about that. And Peter knew there would be hell to pay because he had taken the matter into his own hands instead of waiting patiently like a good servant, which was what the Master expected. If the Master saw him as a threat, which he certainly could be if he gained the Master's physical attributes, he wouldn't hesitate to kill him. Of that, Peter was certain. He had watched as the Master killed or ordered the deaths of any would-be rivals over the years.

Am I willing to risk it? Or am I at just as great a risk waiting on something that will never come?

Thankfully, the decision did not have to be made today. He had time to sort out the details and make a path for himself. Perhaps starting over somewhere else would be better, but Peter had no illusions about the Master's wrath or his reach. Perhaps if he could make an argument for its usefulness and show that he was an ally and loyal, the Master would allow him to continue here.

Beth's words again echoed in his mind. As much as he hated to admit it, and never would to her face, he was beginning to believe she had been right all along. He needed to face the facts. He was only alive for as long as he was useful. Any other angle didn't work. And if he was going to make any significant changes, he had to do it in a way that would stay below the Master's radar.

For years he had followed orders without hesitation, never questioning. He knew of so many things the Master had done, murders, rapes, blackmail... the list was endless, but could he prove even one of those? No. Because every trail that could lead to the Master had been carefully linked in the Master's files to someone else. If he wanted out of this completely, he needed to take down the Master. But that was a nearly impossible task, especially on his own. Those loyal to the Master were unlikely to turn on him, and those who opposed him were too fearful to rise up.

For now, he was on his own.

CHAPTER 56

BETH

BETH FELT A KISS on her forehead, and in her fitful dream it was an angel attempting to console her after losing Luc. Her tears in the dream matched those she had shed in the field near Kate's lab when she thought all had been lost. Her heart was broken, and she was inconsolable.

There was a second kiss and this time the angel spoke. "Beth, it's okay. It's Luc. Everything is okay."

Beth shot up in bed, eyes wide, her cheeks stained with the tears she'd been crying in her dream. She couldn't believe what she was seeing. It was Luc, looking positively gorgeous just as he had before the v1 virus, only better. His coloring was deeper, more olive than before, and true to his Italian heritage. The wrinkles were gone, and his hair was once again wavy, dark brown and full, just like his lips.

She pulled him to herself, wrapping both arms around him as tight as she could, willing him even closer. He returned her embrace and rolled her onto her back on the bed, then pushed up on his arms and kissed her deeply. She returned the kiss and then suddenly stopped, wriggling free and sitting up again.

"Wait. Am I still dreaming? Is this real?" She pinched herself hard on the arm. "Ouch!" She looked confused and said, "What if I'm pinching myself in my dream?"

Luc laughed and raised a warm hand to stroke her cheek. "You're not dreaming. I really am okay."

Tears welled up again as she stared into his eyes. There was too much emotion to speak. The waves hit her one after another like the ocean beating against a rocky cliff. She took Luc into her arms again and nuzzled her face into his neck, letting the tears fall.

Luc held her, stroking her back and her hair and repeating softly, "It's over Beth, everything is okay."

Beth let it all out, tears for Kate, tears for Jon, tears of fear over Luc dying and tears of joy that he was once again well.

"Ahem," Lilly cleared her throat from the chair beside the bed.

Beth and Luc both jumped and sat up, Beth wiping at her eyes with her t-shirt. In her joy at seeing Luc alive and well, she had forgotten Lilly was with them and that they were in her hotel.

"Lilly? Why are we here?" Luc asked, looking from Lilly to Beth and back again.

"I brought you here to protect your ass," she said, arms crossed, eyes narrowed as she glared at Beth.

"I called her, Luc, when I had to leave you to look for Kate and Jon. You wouldn't wake up and I couldn't leave you alone at the shotgun house. She came immediately, but the Master's men were outside so we left and Lilly brought us here." Lilly had come when Beth had called and, regardless of her feelings toward Lilly, she deserved for Luc to know she had been there for him when he needed her.

"Of course I did," Lilly said, a smug grin on her face.

"She knows about the injection and what it's intended to do," Beth added, not yet ready to talk about Kate and Jon and wanting to fill Luc in on what Lilly knew.

Beth could feel a small wave of anxiety from Luc, but he nodded toward her and turned his gaze to Lilly. "Thank you, my friend. I owe you one." Beth could see a grimace flash across Lilly's face at the word "friend," but it was gone just as quickly.

"So did it work?" Lilly asked. Standing, rounding the bed away from Beth, she sat closely against Luc. She leaned in and smelled him, taking a breath in deeply. To Beth, it was like a predator taking a deep sniff of raw meat from a fresh kill. She wondered if Lilly would try to taste him next. "You look and smell different, not entirely human, but not vampire."

"You look fantastic, but how are you feeling?" Beth asked Luc.

"Great, actually. Warm, but comfortably so. I can still see and smell as I did before. It seems I do need to breathe on occasion but not as frequently as a human. I believe my heart rate has slowed a bit from when I was a vampire, and I am positively starving, but not for blood. I would give my right arm for coffee and pizza." Beth couldn't help but chuckle at that one.

"I've never tasted pizza," Lilly said, "but I am with you on the coffee, or at least what I remember of coffee."

"I would say those are all good signs," Beth said. *Can you still hear me?*

Loud and clear.

"We can test the rest later. But first I need food." Luc looked around and patted his pockets looking for his cell.

"I smashed the chips and tossed the phones," Beth said. "We don't know how much the Master knows, and they're not safe. We have a lot to talk about."

"Okay. I need to go out and grab something to eat then. I won't be long," Luc answered.

"But it's still daylight, can't you feel it? You'll be roasted," Lilly said, rising from the bed and stepping protectively toward the bedroom door, blocking it.

"I can't feel it, now that you mention it, but it doesn't matter now," Luc said, getting a confused frown from Lilly.

"I know v1 let you walk in the daylight, but we haven't tested v2, Luc. You need to be sure," Beth said.

"You walked in the daylight?" Lilly said shaking her head. "I don't believe it."

"Good point," Luc agreed with Beth and immediately went to one of the bedroom windows. He looked back at Beth and Lilly, who could clearly see his intent. Beth moved off of the bed and stood next to Lilly to be sure she could avoid the light.

Luc inched back the black-out shade, being sure he didn't send light toward them, and held his hand in front of the small sliver of light that cut through the darkened room like a fiery sword. Beth heard Lilly suck in a breath. But as they both watched, Luc exposed his entire arm to the light, rotating his hand back and forth in the beam. He looked at Beth and grinned that boyish smile she loved so much. The urge to kiss those full lips again was overwhelming.

"Holy shit!" Lilly said, her eyes comically wide.

Luc held the shade out from the window to bathe himself in the light while still blocking the sun from the two of them. He closed his eyes, clearly enjoying the moment.

"If I hadn't seen this with my own eyes, I wouldn't have believed it. Will it last? Is it permanent, I mean?" Lilly's looked intently at Beth.

"It's all new," Beth said, "but the changes should be permanent."

Lilly kept shaking her head as if she couldn't quite accept what her eyes were telling her.

Patting his pockets again, Luc dug out a pocket knife and swiftly ran the blade across his palm. As Beth and Lilly anxiously watched, the bleeding stopped. After several seconds, Luc held up his palm with no evidence of the cut save for a small pink line.

"No wonder the Master wants you dead," Lilly said, causing Beth to suck in a breath of air.

"He doesn't know about this, Lilly. And for all of our sakes, he can't find out, not yet," Luc said.

"You have to make more," Lilly said, once again looking intently at Beth. "Most of the vampires I know would want this, all the perks without the drawbacks." She thought for a moment. "It's dangerous, you know. Humans would kill for this *cure* too."

Beth knew she was right. Since her talk with the Master the night he forced her to hand over her research, she had considered the same. This virus could make an army nearly invincible. And in the wrong hands, someone could make a fortune peddling it to the highest bidder. Beth had no interest in either.

"It could heal many from human ailments. It shouldn't be withheld from the world to line someone's pockets," Beth said.

"Little Miss Sunshine with her head in the clouds. You haven't lived long enough to know how the world works," Lilly sneered.

"We may not have the means to make more," Luc said, looking concerned. Beth could feel his unease with the conversation through her link with him.

"So she has said," Lilly answered, and Beth got the distinct feeling she thought otherwise.

"You know, I just remembered that there is a lovely new service Beth introduced me to called *food delivery*. I think I'll order home instead of going out," Luc said.

Beth was relieved, not wanting to spend a single moment alone with

Lilly.

"Order *in*," Beth corrected, Luc turning a questioning gaze her way. "We say order *in*."

"Lilly, can I borrow your phone?" Luc asked.

Lilly handed it to him with another of her overly sweet smiles. "You can have whatever you like," she said.

Beth couldn't help but roll her eyes at the response and the pose that went with it. She swallowed the bile that threatened in her throat. *This woman is unbelievable.*

"Thank you, but just a phone will do," Luc said, clearly sending his message and turning toward Beth. "What was the name of the pizza you ordered for me?"

"Supreme," Beth answered, more than a little pleased with Luc's response to Lilly's insinuation.

Luc nodded and put the phone to his ear, having already looked up the pizza parlor's number and dialed. As he left the room, he leaned over and kissed Beth, and, covering the phone mic, he said, "I love you, Beth." Beth could no more help the victorious grin on her lips than she could stop the heat that spread through her body at the words.

Lilly looked as though she had eaten something rotten and glared at Beth. From the other room, Beth could hear Luc say, "Yes, I would like to order in a large supreme pizza. Wait. You better make that two and two coffees as well." Beth still grinned despite Lilly's glare.

Beth could feel the sun setting, and her strength began to return even if her mind was still catching up. She rose and walked to the living room, hoping Lilly would not follow. Beth needed to speak with Luc about last night as well as their plans to leave but didn't want to share any of it with Lilly. She knew enough already, and while Luc seemed to trust her, Beth wasn't comfortable leaving tracks for anyone to follow.

"Have you eaten?" Luc asked Beth as she entered the room. He hung up the phone and placed it on an end table.

"No, I'll get something when I can. We should talk after you get your pizza." *And after Lilly leaves.*

Luc nodded ever so slightly as Lilly sauntered in, now dressed in a snug black dress with spaghetti straps and a very low draped neckline, more of a *waist*line since it nearly reached it, and her signature stilettos in black patent leather.

She walked to Luc, closer than necessary, and said, "So what's the plan from here? Where are you two going to go to find another lab? And how long will it take for you to make more of the cure when you do?"

"*If* we do. It's a big if. We don't know," Beth answered. Luc didn't know that the lab here had been destroyed, only that it was too dangerous to stay. Beth felt her heart grab knowing she would have to tell Luc his friends were dead. "Like I told you, we don't have another lab, and they aren't easy to come by."

Lilly looked to Luc as if for confirmation that Beth wasn't lying.

"It's true. We have to gather Kate and regroup." Luc paused and then said, turning to Beth, "You mentioned looking for Kate and Jon, where are they?"

The stress of it all was too much and again Beth fought back tears. Luc sensed as well as saw her anguish and took her in his arms, holding her head to his chest and gently kissing the top of her head.

"Beth, what haven't you told me?" Luc asked.

"Kate and Jon didn't make it." Beth's stomach tightened and she breathed in sharply, holding back the sob that threatened.

"What happened?" Luc asked. Lilly looked on, arms again crossed with an expression Beth could best describe as boredom. She felt anger heating her cheeks.

"You became unconscious not long after we last spoke." The emotions of that moment came rushing back. She remembered how it felt to try to express her feelings, believing she may never have the chance to say the words again. Despite her best efforts, a few tears escaped and began to fall silently down her cheeks. She hated showing weakness in front of Lilly, but the pain was too much.

"Oh, please. He's fine," Lilly said.

Luc turned to her and glared, a scathing stare that would have had Beth moving in the opposite direction had it been leveled at her. Lilly got the message and held up her hands in surrender.

"Not that I don't appreciate what you have done, but I am clearly no longer in danger, and the sun has set. Perhaps we should let you get back to your work. I'm sure the hotel staff has missed you." *If that doesn't work, I will kiss you until she leaves.*

I couldn't love you more right now.

"Fine. I can take a hint. I'm going. But I will expect to hear from you when you make more progress. You owe me." The last phrase was clearly aimed at Beth. Even though Lilly had come for Luc when she called, not her, she was right. She owed her.

Beth nodded once and then Lilly was gone, the door slamming behind her.

Beth closed her eyes and centered herself. "Thank God," she said. The smirk on Luc's face told her he knew exactly what she meant. Beth's answering smile was short-lived as she returned to her story.

"Kate and Jon didn't come back from the lab, and neither answered their cells. I waited for as long as I could but started to worry they needed help. I couldn't just sit there if they were in danger." Beth sniffed back the tears and wiped at her nose. Luc was gone and back again in a blink with tissues from the bathroom.

"I didn't want to leave you. I was so afraid you would be... that you wouldn't be alive when I got back. I ran to the lab only to find it on fire. Flames and smoke were coming out of every opening. And I knew..." Beth's voice caught as she struggled against another sob. Her shoulders slumped. "They had to be dead. What other reason could possibly have kept them away when you were so sick?"

Beth could see the pain in Luc's face and knew it reflected her own, his lips tightly pursed, his gaze downward.

She and Kate were two of a kind. In her, Beth had found a friend she'd never realized she had longed for, someone to confide in, a friend who saw her quirks and loved her anyway. She had held everyone else except Luc at arm's length, but she had let Kate in. Kate held a place in her heart that she was sure would never quite heal from the loss.

Luc held her again, smoothing her hair. Her forehead rested against his chest, now almost hot to her touch. And a fleeting thought about how his skin had felt cool to her before she was changed passed through her mind. That was how she would feel to him now. But if it bothered him, he didn't let on.

"Beth, I'm so sorry. I know you loved Kate."

"I did, very much. She was the closest friend I've ever had. And I'm sorry about Jon too."

"I wish you had been able to get to know him better. He was quite the character. You would have enjoyed hearing his crazy stories. The man loved to fight."

Beth could see a scattering of emotions cross Luc's face and felt a vague wash of them through their bond. She imagined Luc was remembering his time with Jon as she had remembered hers with Kate. When there was time, she wanted to hear those stories to better know the man Luc clearly trusted with his life and hers.

After a moment, Luc sighed and said, "We need to get away from New Orleans. We'll go to Colorado like we planned tonight and consider where we go next. We should be safe there for now. We could both use a little time to rest. But first... pizza."

Beth knew he was distracting her from more thoughts of Jon and Kate. But they had to move on, so she allowed it. There would be time for grieving their loss and celebrating their lives later. "So do you have a view from your house in Colorado?"

EPILOGUE

BETH

BETH HAD BEEN EAGER to reach Luc's house in Colorado. They had run at top speed for nearly eight hours. They roughly followed the path of US-287, passing through Dallas, Amarillo and finally Colorado Springs, making numerous stops along the way to satisfy Luc's voracious new appetite and to collect blood for Beth.

The air in Colorado was much cooler, and Luc, having not felt the cold for such a long time, started complaining of goose bumps when they crossed the Colorado border. They stopped off at a twenty-four-hour Wal-Mart and bought Luc a warm winter coat and gloves. They both bought boots since the snow had begun to fall. At the base of the mountain still several miles from Luc's house, Beth stopped and started making snowballs.

Luc, having circled back after realizing she was no longer behind him, watched her with a crooked grin. "Now just what do you plan on doing with those?"

Having already made a large pile of snowballs, Beth screamed, "Snowball fight!" She got one good one off while Luc was still off guard. It hit him squarely in the chest, disintegrating and leaving a large white circle on the front of his new jacket.

"Oh, now you've done it!" Luc scooped up loose handfuls of snow and began pelting Beth with snowballs as quickly as he could make them.

Beth let out a scream followed by laughter and returned fire. But Luc, now fully into the game, dodged gracefully. Beth leaned over to reload when a snowball exploded on her shoulder, peppering her face and hair with soft white powder. She launched herself across the field toward him, tackling him into the snow and rolling. She stopped on her back, arms and legs spread wide to make a snow angel.

Luc sat up and watched, a goofy grin on his lips before he, too, launched himself backward into the snow to make his own angel.

"Look at those stars," Beth said, amazed at how far she could see without light pollution. It was truly a breathtaking view.

Luc rolled to lie beside her and pulled her half onto his chest.

After a few minutes, Beth sighed. "We had better get moving, the sky is growing lighter and I can feel dawn approaching."

"It's for the best. I don't think I can feel my toes any longer."

Beth laughed and looked at Luc, his nose glowing red from the cold. She realized that she hadn't felt hot or cold since she'd turned. The cold she didn't miss since she had never been a fan of cool temperatures, but the warmth she definitely did.

So far Luc had shown no ill effects from the v2 virus, although it had been less than twenty-four hours since he'd been injected. If it held, it meant there was hope for her and all the vampires out there who would like to be cured of the affliction. They wouldn't exactly be normal humans with the current virus, but at least the major downsides to this life would be removed. They were a far cry from being able to sort out the genes and their effects well enough to provide any help to normal humans, but in the right hands, they might be able to get there.

She turned to Luc and, looking up at him through her lashes, gave him a broad smile. "Let's get you warmed up."

Luc's house was amazing. It was more of a cabin, nestled amongst tall Rocky Mountain junipers and Ponderosa pines. Were it not for the driveway, a person on the road wouldn't know that it even existed. It was built of logs with an A-frame roof so as not to be weighed down by the frequent snows. The front door contained only a small window, and the windows in the front of the house were covered by heavy drapes, so Beth couldn't see inside until Luc opened the front door. She smiled as he entered 1692, the year he was born, into the keypad. Beth heard the lock rotate before Luc turned the handle.

"After you, my lady."

Beth snickered at the formality and gave him a peck on the cheek as she walked past him into the cabin. Luc flipped on a light by the entry which illuminated a real deer-antler chandelier. The walls inside were also all wood logs with large matching beams that spanned the length of the room, which consisted of a living room in the front and a kitchen in the back. It was decorated in a rustic vibe with buffalo plaid couches and a huge reclining black leather chair. Both faced a stone fireplace with a gorgeous raw wood mantle.

Luc hurried to the fireplace and grabbed some kindling from a carrier next to it. He had a small fire going in no time and was beginning to pile on larger logs. "That feels like heaven," he said, pulling off his gloves and holding his hands before the fire, turning them back and forth to warm both sides.

"It's so beautiful here, Luc. Why did you ever leave it for Kansas City?" Beth realized there was so much about his life she didn't know yet. So many stories about what had made him who he was today that she wanted to hear. And thanks to Kate, she would have that chance.

Luc must have felt the changes in her emotions because he was immediately at her side, wrapping his arms around her.

"I was just thinking about Kate. I already miss her so much. Thanks to her, we have a chance at a life together."

"You helped with that too, you know. Kate wouldn't have been able to pull any of this off without your help. She said herself that she was approaching her wits' end before she became infected and you showed up to help. You were just as much a part of healing me as she was."

Beth thought Luc was being overly gracious, but she had helped Kate and learned a ton in the process. Now they just needed a chance to reproduce and investigate the current version of the VR virus, but who would be up to the task? She and Luc hadn't been following the overseas scientists closely since they had begun to monitor Kate. She supposed that was the next logical step, but an overseas trip was not going to be easy for her, traveling as a vampire and only at night. Planes were unreliable. If they had a delay or, God forbid, were stuck on a tarmac until daybreak, she could be toast, literally.

Beth hadn't shared her thoughts with Luc, but he knew her well. "Let's just relax and enjoy a few days here together before we start on the next adventure, okay?"

Beth beamed back at him. "You've got it."

HANDLER

Handler awoke, groggy, his vision blurred and a thin silver line of spittle hanging from the corner of his mouth. Blinking to clear his vision, he could make out a cement floor in front of him splattered with what looked like rust-colored paint. *Where the fuck am I?*

As the confusion began to clear, he realized he was sitting upright in a wooden chair. It creaked as he raised his eyes, his head bobbing up and down until he regained control of his neck. He struggled to raise a hand to wipe at his mouth. But after a few attempts, the tug at his wrist hit home. He was tied to the chair, hands behind his back and ankles to the chair legs.

Nausea began to creep in, fear making his heart hammer in his chest. He scanned the room in front of him, the familiarity causing him to close his eyes again to shut it out. It wasn't paint on the floor, but splattered blood. This was the same room where he had watched the Master tear the lawyers apart.

His eyes snapped open to the voice behind him.

"By your heart rate, I can tell you are finally awake. I'm sure you recognize this place." It was the Master, walking from behind him and into view, dressed once again in white linen, hands clasped behind his back. He began to circle Handler like the predator he was, teasing his prey before killing him.

Handler's heart fell. There was no coming back from this one. He could beg for his life like the lawyers had. He could promise to kill for the Master, to never fail him again. But the truth was, none of it mattered. Today, tomorrow, or a year from now he would be in a similar place waiting for the same death. He had sealed his fate the day he accepted the first job from the Master. He'd lived the past several weeks since he had refused to kill knowing this was coming. The fear while waiting, always watching over his shoulder, had been nearly incapacitating. The fact that this day had finally come was almost a relief... almost.

The terror threatened to shake a scream from him, but he was determined to hold it in as long as he could. His shoulders began to tremble despite his efforts. Handler had never been a religious man, didn't even know how to pray. *If there is anyone up there who cares, I'm sorry for the all bad shit I've done.*

"Shall we begin?" the Master asked, stopping in front of Handler, mouth open to reveal his fangs. An eerily calm smirk surrounded them. "It's late, and I haven't eaten."

Handler tried to close his eyes, but the terror inside him wouldn't allow him to move. His only response was the warm trickle of urine that darkened his pants and dripped to the floor beneath him.

BETH

They had been at the cabin for a little over a week, and to Beth's relief, Luc showed no evidence of aging or other side effects from the v2 virus. Her thoughts turned toward Kate as they often had since they'd left New Orleans. Even though she would never be able to tell her, Beth knew Kate had saved both their lives; Luc's directly with the v2 virus, and Beth's by his survival. Not a day had passed when Beth didn't miss her.

Beth ventured into Breckenridge just after sunset to find a library or coffee shop where she could use a computer anonymously. The Brewhaus was on Main Street and offered what she needed. Downtown Breckenridge was so quaint with its brightly colored buildings, no two next to one another the same shade. Kate would have loved it. The Brewhaus was a light ice blue with big picture windows in the front. The snow crunched underneath their feet as Beth and Luc made their way to the door.

Beth could already smell the bitter stench of coffee and wrinkled her nose, but Luc looked blissful, led by his nose all the way in.

"Want anything?" Luc offered.

"Just get me a hot tea. At least I can enjoy the smell of that." Luc hurried off to the counter, giddy as a child.

Beth walked to the rear of the business where they had computers on a back wall. She sat down and pulled up the internet in an incognito window to check her accounts. Her Gmail account under the name Cynthia Harris had unopened mail. She clicked on the first from her virtual mailbox service. The email said, "See attachments," as it always did. The service scanned all the mail that was sent to her at that address. It made it impossible for someone to track.

Beth clicked on the first PDF and froze. The screen was a scan of a single sheet of white paper completely blank except for a phone number: (555) 649-8220. *Who could it be? Could Kate or Jon have survived?* Her heart ached with the thought and sped. Or could it be the Master, toying with them and trying to get a response? Beth chewed her lip.

Sensing something was amiss, Luc hurried to her with a giant coffee in one hand and her small tea in the other. He sat in the chair next to her and handed her the cup, eyebrows raised in question.

"Take a look," Beth said. Luc turned to read the screen in front of her. "Who do you think it is? Is it too much to hope that it could be Kate or Jon and they somehow survived the fire? Or is it the Master calling to gloat?"

"Only one way to find out," Luc said.

Beth pulled out her burner phone and punched in the numbers. They both leaned in to listen, the cell phone at their ears between them.

The person on the other end answered on the second ring. "Hello." Beth didn't recognize the voice, so it wasn't Peter or the Master.

"I received your message with your number. Who is this?" Beth replied.

"This is Dr. Liam Henri. I could use some more samples."

Can You Help?

Thank You For Reading My Book!

Did you know? Reader reviews are very important to an indie author's success? They validate our work and help others find our stories. If you enjoyed Vampyre Hypothesis, please leave a review filled with stars.

Thanks so much!
Tammy Battaglia

Don't forget your free gift! Click here or scan the QR code below to tell me where to send it.

Acknowledgements

Special thanks to my family and friends for the support and encouragement to keep moving forward, especially my good friend Jon who inspired my character (embracing the idea with a hearty, "Hell, yes!") and is one of the few humans I know who could probably hold his own with a vampire.

To my beta readers and launch team I send a heartfelt thank you. Not only did you provide invaluable feedback and support, you made this journey enjoyable.

Thank you to all of the SelfPublishing.com team for guiding me along my writing journey, especially my SPS coaches Ramy and Joe for the excellent advice and encouragement to move forward. To my editors, Zac Tighe of Copysmyths (developmental editing—www.copysmyths.com); and to Shavonne, Brit and Kat at Motif Edits (line and proofreading—www.motifedits.com); thank you for the advice and editing I needed to make my book all that I hoped it could be.

And finally, thank you to all of you, my readers, for indulging me. God bless you all.

selfpublishing.com

Now It's Your Turn
Discover the EXACT 3-step blueprint you need to
become a bestselling author in as little as 3 months.

Self-Publishing School helped me, and now I want them to help
you with this Free resource to begin outlining your book!
Even if you're busy, bad at writing, or don't know where to start,
you CAN write a bestseller and build your best life.
With tools and experience across a variety of niches and professions,
Self-Publishing School is the only resource you need to
take your book to the finish line!
DON'T WAIT
Say "YES" to becoming a bestseller:
https://self-publishingschool.com/friend/
Follow the steps on the page to get a FREE resource to get started on
your book and unlock a discount to get started with Self-Publishing
School

ABOUT THE AUTHOR

During the daylight hours, author Tammy Battaglia is a doctor, a pathologist to be specific, who enjoys looking at what makes all living things tick from the inside out. She grew up in Kansas next door to Toto and Dorothy, where she raised three children (all human) with her high school sweetheart. She recently retired from twenty-plus years of mainstream medicine, to explore what her imagination believes it could be.

When night falls and the moon rises, she can't help but imagine and write about the science that would make what others believe to be mythical, well...real. Just because current science can't explain them doesn't mean they can't exist. She encourages readers to indulge her inner mad scientist and look below the surface.

Dr. Battaglia is the author of the Elizabeth Ramsey, MD series, including Vampyre Hypothesis, a **Global Book Awards Bronze Medalist.**

Email: tammy@friendswithmonsters.com

Facebook

Newsletter

Also by Tammy Battaglia

Elizabeth Ramsey, MD Series

Book 3
Vampyre Law
COMING SOON!

www.ingramcontent.com/pod-product-compliance
Lightning Source LLC
Chambersburg PA
CBHW050019120726
47903CB00006B/1827